Wo

Mancini was waiting for Pagan at the bottom of the stairs. Immediately he pulled her into the cavity underneath the stairwell.

'Tell me you didn't enjoy it and I'll know you're lying,' he said.

'If your dick was as big as your ego I might have done.'

At this, his precarious hold on patience snapped. He slammed her up against the grubby wall, his fingers digging into the soft skin of her upper arms.

'Why are you so angry at me?' he asked. 'Don't you realise how I feel about you?'

'So what happened to the last fifteen years? You had all that time and you didn't show your face once. And you ask why I'm angry with you?' she replied.

'Something special happened to us last night and I don't want to lose it. Not now.'

'But I don't want you,' she spat. 'I don't . . .'

His lips crushed the denial on hers. With his tongue deep in her mouth he shoved his hand rudely up her skirt and into her panties.

Wolf at the Door
Savannah Smythe

BLACK LACE

Black Lace books contain sexual fantasies.
In real life, always practise safe sex.

First published in 2002 by
Black Lace
Thames Wharf Studios
Rainville Road
London W6 9HA

Design by Smith & Gilmour, London
Printed and bound by Mackays of Chatham PLC

ISBN 0 352 33693 5

1

Pagan Warner sat wedged between a fat black man sweating in his ill-fitting suit and a dainty female executive sporting sparkling white trainers. The train rocking through the bowels of Manhattan was full to bursting, with torturing bright lights that made her eyes ache. But it was Friday night, and the last day of subway purgatory she would have to endure. No more would she have to stare unwillingly into the armpits of strangers in the subway, trying not to inhale, as her turbulent life was about to change yet again.

That weekend she would be moving into a ridiculously large colonial mansion in leafy Huntingdon County. And in five weeks time she would be marrying the accountant who had advised her to invest her inheritance in the property. She had been won over by the wraparound deck, the opportunity to breathe fresh air whilst she was working, to see cardinal finches and hear cicadas on hot summer nights.

But the weekend had not started well. Greg had cancelled her birthday meal for the third time in two weeks, blaming his new employer. Apparently he was a difficult man but, for the salary he was paying, he was entitled to be. Her tolerance had finally snapped and she pointed out that money was irrelevant if they were never together to enjoy it. He had put the phone down on her.

The first silver threads had started to appear in her dark-red hair, glinting unashamedly under the harsh light of the subway. She wore it in a sleek bob that swung with the motion of the swaying train. Her feline green eyes were warm and inviting, with hints of gold only a lover could see. Although very fit she was still curvy, with long limbs toned and sculpted enough to prove a challenge to any man inclined to put up a struggle. Not that they had done this for a long time.

She heaved a sigh and scowled at the grubby overcoat almost brushing her face. Another opportunity to tempt Greg into bed had been lost. He had never claimed to be a red-hot lover, and she loved him enough not to expect it of him. But since setting the date for the wedding he had insisted on celibacy, to make their first night together more special. It was an antiquated idea but he was an old-fashioned man, which was why she had found him so endearing. But right now her hormones were on the up, wanting a good old-fashioned seeing-to. And it just wasn't going to happen for another five weeks.

The crowd shifted and the view improved immeasurably. The newcomer was standing a few feet down from her, holding on to the support pole as if his life depended on it. She hazarded his age at somewhere around forty-five, maybe slightly older. He looked expensive and uncomfortable, as if he were used to being chauffeur driven. He had glossy black hair brushed aggressively back from a high forehead and his skin was smooth and pale, with no discernible shadow around the jaw. There was no spare flesh to disguise the axe-blade cheekbones or the sensual mouth, with lips slender and perfectly formed. She calculated his height at approximately six and a half feet, which meant he could look down on most of the humanity around him. Greg was also tall but he was blond and rugged, full of charm and bonhomie. This man had the air of a sleek cobra waiting to strike. As the train squealed into another station the crowd heaved, ready to regurgitate onto the platform. Someone knocked the camel cashmere topcoat from his shoulder and he grabbed it irritably, relinquishing his grasp on the pole. The train jerked to a halt and propelled him backwards, causing him to grab the pole again like a lifeline. He cursed loudly, his pale eyes locking onto Pagan's. They were as hollow and cold as ancient caves, the pale blue of an Alaskan sky. Instantly she was transported back to England thirteen years before, on the day she had been seduced for the first time.

She had decided to lose her virginity when she was sixteen. It was a drag, listening to her girlfriends gossip fearfully about the pain, the blood, the overall ghastliness of the whole procedure. She knew differently, thanks to an extensive library of erotica in her father's study, hidden in a drawer in his desk. The problem was finding the right man. And it had to be a man, not a boy. She only had to look at the spotty, gangly youths in the village pub to realise that.

She found him one hot Friday afternoon after school. She was with three friends at the War Memorial in the middle of the village, drinking sweet cider and sharing the cigarettes she had liberated from her father's study earlier that day. A black Mercedes convertible purred to a halt beside them and he had climbed out, very tall, with sleek black hair down to his shoulders. He wore a blue silk shirt that exactly matched the colour of his eyes, as pale as a psychopath's. He wanted to know where to find the Old Manor House, where the Warners lived.

Pagan knew he was the one. He looked about thirty, and when he introduced himself as the Wolf she was the only one who did not giggle. She could almost smell the animal on him. All she had read about chemistry between two people suddenly made sense. Her freshly awakened hormones jangled as she eased herself casually off the concrete step and assessed him coolly, cigarette drooping from her lower lip.

She was thinking fast. Susan Warner, that's a fucking stupid name. Think of something quick. He looks like a god, like the Celts we were studying at school last year. A true pagan...

'I'm Pagan Warner. Who the fuck are you?'

Disbelieving sniggers from her friends, stunned silence from him. She had recently put black stripes in her dark red hair and had it cut in a severe bob, goth style, and now she stared boldly at him from underneath a long spiky fringe and black eye-liner. Her nubile body was just about covered in tight denim hot pants and white vest top, one strap drooping down from her shoulder. Her white bra strap sparkled on her lightly tanned skin and the cups pushed her full young breasts together like fruit on a display shelf. Despite the heat her nipples were hard, jutting through the white jersey. Her legs were very long for a girl her height and honey gold, with little white sock marks around her ankles, and feet in black leather espadrilles, the toenails painted black. She was that most potent of females, a girl ripening into womanhood.

The man explained that he was the son of a business colleague, over from the States, dropping by to give his regards to Arthur Warner, Pagan's father. His accent was cute; a little rough around the edges with arousal. She did not hesitate in climbing in to the car to guide him back to the house.

'There's no one home,' she said as he pulled away from the village.

'Is that right?'

'My father won't be back till late. He's picking up my stepbrother from school.'

'Where's that?'

'Harrow. They always go out for dinner afterwards. It's a father–son thing.' She did not attempt to keep the sneer from her voice. As far as she could remember, she had never had a 'father–daughter thing' or even a 'stepmother–daughter thing'.

The Wolf registered the slight bitterness in her voice but made no comment.

'What about your mother? Is she at home?'

'My mother's dead. My stepmother is at the gym, fucking the instructor.' She grinned mischievously, 'Only joking. It's just up there on the left. Would you like a drink? You look pretty hot.'

He laughed at the unintentional double entrendre. 'That would be good. Thank you.'

The car swept into an exclusive little estate lined with large houses fashioned on pillared Georgian mansions. The largest, most ostentatious of all belonged to Arthur Warner. A red BMW was parked on the drive by the front door.

'Oh, God, she's home. What a crashing bore,' Pagan said irritably. The car stopped half way up the road. She looked at the Wolf, and the Wolf looked at her. In that split second it seemed to her that each of them made the decision that the only thing they wanted was each other.

'Why don't I buy you that drink?' he said. She smiled luminously at him.

'That's a great idea.'

He chose a small pub situated half way between her house and the town where he was staying. The garden overlooked grassy fields that fell away down the gently rolling hillside. Birdsong and the sweet smell of cut grass filled Pagan's senses. She basked in the late afternoon sun, aware of the stares from the small party of dark-suited men on a nearby table. She panicked for a moment, wondering whether any of them knew her father, but then figured it did not matter anyway. Nothing she did mattered to him. She lifted her face to the sun, pushing out her budding breasts so the men could all have a good look. Already she knew how to use the power of her young body on the opposite sex, and it was working, judging by the lack of conversation and their eyes roaming all over her.

'Hey, hot stuff.' The Wolf sat opposite her. 'One thing you should know. Never prick-tease when you're with me.'

She shivered under the hardness of his tone and felt like sulking. She hadn't expected him to be so on her case. He passed her a tall glass clinking with ice cubes, the condensation already making a ring on the wooden bench where it had just been.

'Ever had a spritzer?' he asked, lightening the mood.

She took a small sip from the glass. It was refreshing and easy to drink, bubbles popping fruitily on her tongue.

'It's nice,' she said, taking another drink. Apart from a packet of plain crisps and the cider she had been drinking earlier, her stomach was empty, but it churned with too much illicit excitement to feel any hunger.

'Ice cold tonic water, dry white wine. It's good for the heat.'

'What about that?' She pointed to the squat tumbler he nursed, half filled with amber liquid. No ice.

'This is scotch. Good for anything.' He flashed a sharp white grin at her. 'So, Pagan Warner, do you always get into cars with strange men?'

'No!' She was indignant. 'I trusted you, I guess, when you said you knew my father.'

It was all bullshit but she wasn't about to explain her theories on the chemistry of sexual attraction, which was still very much on her mind. The way he spoke, the way he moved, everything about him screamed danger and sex and all the things she had begun to crave at night, in the darkness of her room. But she had dignity and class, and she wasn't about to cheapen herself by making a crass lunge at him.

'Do you always trust men you find attractive, Pagan?'

She drank deeply, hiding her blush behind her glass. 'You ask a lot of questions,' she muttered.

'Here's another one. Would you like me to take you to bed?'

The softly spoken words sent a shudder down her whole body. She gazed out over the hazy fields. Tiny sheep, tiny tractors, one big life-changing question. The wine had hit her bloodstream almost immediately. The alcohol, the heat and his penetrating blue eyes were affecting her reactions. She felt languorous, ready to lie down and let him do what he wanted. Almost imperceptibly she nodded.

The slight touch on her knee woke her up. She looked startled as his warm fingers caressed her leg under the table.

'Ready to go?'

She took a deep breath, catching the spicy aroma of his aftershave, and followed him in to his car.

As he pulled away he put a cassette in the tape player: Bryan Ferry singing 'Slave to Love'. Her tastes leaned more towards Siouxie and the Banshees, but now she nestled into the hot black leather seat, feeling incredibly sophisticated and grown-up.

'How old are you?' he asked as they drove back to his hotel.

'Sixteen. How old are you?'

'Thirty-two. I don't make a habit of doing this but you're so fucking sexy and you damned well know it, don't you?'

His voice was matter-of-fact, reminding her of her father when he was giving her a hard time. She could not think of anything to say.

'Are you a virgin, Pagan?'

'Don't be daft!' she retorted. But his glance told her she should not lie, even though it meant kissing good-bye to this golden opportunity. Men didn't want virgins, they wanted girls who knew how to give pleasure. It saved them time.

'Well ... yeah,' she conceded. 'I've seen a few boys ... you know, and touched them.' She stalled, aware she was sounding like an idiot. He looked amused.

'Did you enjoy it? Touching cock?'

She blushed at the crude word, but then figured she couldn't think of anything better to call it.

'The blokes they belonged to didn't have much of a clue,' she replied sadly. 'I want to do it properly, the first time. I know it's supposed to hurt but it doesn't in the books. Can you do it like that?'

'That depends if you read the same books I do.'

She shivered at the heat in his eyes, and a rash of goosepimples ran over her thigh. He ran his hand firmly over them, making her jump.

'Relax. The moment you say no, I'll stop.'

His hand was a hot, heavy weight on her thigh. It stayed there until they arrived at the hotel. It was new and chic, geared towards the business crowd. She felt obvious in her tight shorts and was glad when they were behind closed doors.

As soon as they were alone again he moved in to kiss her lips. There would be no messing about, she thought, opening her mouth under his and feeling shyly for his tongue. Some boys were only happy to French kiss a girl on their own terms, but not this man. He growled with pleasure as their tongues entwined.

'You really are a hot little bitch,' he mumbled against

her mouth. In moments he was not kissing a shy teenager but a woman, almost fully fledged, tasting intoxicatingly of fruity wine. Leaning against the door, his hand drifted up her thigh to her waist, his fingers seeking the edge of her T-shirt. She stretched slightly so he could feel the silken skin underneath. His cool dry fingers circled slowly across her stomach, up each rib to her breast. The bra was smooth and gauzy, and her nipples sprang to life under his thumbs. The resulting tingle was answered by her clitoris and sent back up, the frisson of silk under his fingers heightening each stroke. Still kissing her deeply he peeled the small vest top away.

Her breasts were larger than any sixteen year olds' had a right to be, firm and springy to the touch, with fat little nipples as pink as rosebuds. She arched her back and pushed him away, giving him the same feline smile that drove all the local boys crazy.

'You can kiss them if you want.'

He buried his face in their sweet warmth, inhaling her skin's natural fragrance. Then he guided her back towards the biggest bed she had ever seen, covered in a chintzy eiderdown. She stretched out on it, girlishly innocent in her bra and the small shorts. Even with her toes and fingers fully extended she still could not reach right across it. She rolled over to look at him as he pulled the curtains across to cut out the harsh sunlight of the room.

'Are you scared?' he asked as she sprawled on her tummy, kicking at her bottom.

'Not yet,' she answered warily, trying not to feel nervous. She was aware now that he was a stranger and she was miles from home, with no means of getting back.

'It's OK, I'll look after you,' he said, as if he could read her thoughts. She wondered what he would do next. He slipped off his jacket and laid it neatly over an armchair, then stood by the bed.

'You want to do the rest?'

She kneeled up on the bed and approached him. Because of his height she was now at eye level. Shyly she unknotted his tie and removed it, letting it drop to the floor before undoing his top button. His eyes penetrated her as she concentrated on her task, suddenly nervous of looking straight at him. As she undid each small bone button on his blue silk shirt she felt his fingers sliding her bra straps down off her shoulders. She pulled the shirt from his trousers and he shrugged out of it, throwing it carelessly onto the floor. His upper body was well muscled, smattered with dark silky hair concentrated in a small patch on his chest. She ran her fingers through it, wanting to kiss his pearly pink nipples but too shy to do it. He seemed in no hurry, content to let her take her time as he kissed the hollow between her collar bone.

'Take this off,' he whispered softly, tugging at her bra. His eyes glimmered as she reached around, the movement lifting her breasts so they thrust gently against his chest. He kissed her mouth, catching the bra between them as he pressed her half-naked body to his. Her hands caressed his back and he kissed her hard, as a man would kiss an experienced woman, but she took it without fear, aware that his arousal had put her in control.

She pushed him away and stepped back, her hands on the button of her shorts. His breathing was short and fast as he watched her fingers with aching slowness unfasten the button and ease the zip down. She feasted on the greed on his face as he watched her innocent white briefs appear, the same gauze as the bra, flattening a small V of dark springy curls. As she dropped the shorts he walked around the bed to view her backside, temptingly hidden behind the translucent material. Grabbing her hips so hard she stumbled, he pressed his face to the dark shadow between her buttocks, inhaling her animal scent. She was alarmed and too embarrassed to be aroused by the hot breath feathering her nether regions, and she scrambled away from him.

'What is it?' His voice was gravelly with desire.

'I don't ... know.' She was scarlet, annoyed at her own naivety.

He seemed to sense that she had almost reached the limit of her experience and was unsure whether to go further. He took her hand and placed it on the bulge in his pants.

'Have you ever sucked cock, Pagan?'

'I ... No.' She knew she was out of her depth, but it was too late to go back now. Part of her wanted to say no, to grab her clothes and run, especially after feeling the size of the thing against her hand. But she would never forgive herself for passing up the opportunity, so she took a deep breath and opened his zip. He helped her with the button. He knelt on the bed, watching her face as she saw him naked for the first time.

'Oh help,' she gulped, as the erect organ fell against her hand. It was huge, bigger than she had ever imagined, thickly veined and wine red, with heavy balls drooping like ripe plums. She felt like running away but instinct and her pride told her to circle the cock's circumference and rub gently.

'Why don't you taste it?' His voice was husky with expectation.

Tentatively she pressed her lips against his cock, starting as it pulsed under her touch. He groaned as her soft young lips brushed shyly against his straining flesh. He ran his fingers through her hair and fondled the back of her head, encouraging her to continue. The tip of her pink tongue came out and hesitantly ran down the length of his shaft.

His cock felt smooth and alive against her mouth. He tasted as he smelled; musky and clean, seasoned with salt. The great bulbous tip beckoned, a bead of sweet liquid glistening from the teardrop hole, and she was shocked at herself for being so willing to draw it into her mouth. She was alarmed when he collapsed away from her onto the bed. She thought she had done wrong, but he grinned at her from his prone position.

'Be careful. I'll come before I've had a chance to get inside you.'

Panic streaked across her face. 'I can't . . . It won't . . .'

'Yes, it will. I'll show you.' He pushed her back onto the bed. She tried to sit up but he held her down with a firm hand on her chest. 'You're not ready yet. Just relax while I make you nice and wet.'

She covered her eyes with her hands, fighting with mixed emotions. He was moving about, undressing, pulling her panties down and discarding them. She was as tense as a high wire as he lay beside her. He removed her hands and kissed her eyelids, licking them gently. Down to her mouth for more deep plunging kisses before nibbling her throat, one stealthy hand circling her stomach and her thighs, cleverly avoiding the plump cleft between her legs.

She was just beginning to relax when his tongue sweeping around her nipple made her cry out. Tenderly he flickered at the sensitive tip, watching with wonder as it crinkled and grew. He did the same with the other, joyfully listening to her faint mewing sounds of pleasure. The sensations shot straight south, pooling in a well of moisture between her legs. She opened them slightly, arching her back to encourage more attention from his mouth. His tongue quivered and swirled and lavishly licked at each nipple, now dark pink and as hard as a bullet. His breath ran cold over them and his mouth scalded them. Her body jolted with each new sensation, squirming against him until he was tempted just to plunge into her hot sweet depths. He drew back and watched her, back arched and eyes closed with the pleasure of it all.

He licked his forefinger and gently pressed it against the top of her cleft, barely disguised with downy red-tinged hair. As he carefully opened her up with his fingers she spread her legs like a flower needing sunlight. Her tight pussy lips were swollen with arousal; further in she glistened with moisture. He slid his finger up to the first knuckle, revelling in exploring where no other man had been. She made a strangled moan through gritted teeth, lifting her pelvis in an unconscious plea for him to go further. His nostrils flared at her young musky scent. With his finger still in place he pressed his mouth to her tiny clitoris and strummed it gently with his tongue.

The effect on her was electric. She screamed with pleasure, grabbing at the bedhead, a pillow, anything to dig her fingernails into. When he did it again she was calmer but her moan had an abandoned edge to it, as though she had been debased already. With the delicacy of a gourmand he tasted her again, subjecting her clitoris to the same tender but relentless rhythm, until she could sense feelings building that she had never experienced before, sweeping, tightening; feelings that flooded over her, threatening her sanity. She mewed softly, letting them happen, aware that her body was out of her control. From her throat came cries that she had never heard before but she did not fight them. Her orgasm peaked once, twice, three times before she collapsed, quivering amongst the bedclothes, cursing with words she had never spoken out loud before.

As she came down from her mountainous high he

slipped his finger inside her again, feeling for the elastic obstruction of her hymen. He nudged against it gently but she did not cry out. He knew it would hurt but not too much as long as she were too aroused to care. He drank from her again, gently as her clitoris was still very tender, letting her slim hips undulate against him. Her fat pussy lips pouted at him with a sultriness matched by her pretty pink mouth.

He pulled the bed covers down to expose crisp white sheets and shuffled her onto them. She had tensed again, sensing the moment was coming, but he gentled her, stroking her hair and kissing her wondrous nipples until her breath grew short and a flush of love spread again over her neck and throat. He positioned himself above her, being careful not to crush her, and soaked his fingers with his saliva and hers. Thoroughly wet they stroked her pussy, making it slick and receptive, while her breathing quickened and her eyes grew wide.

'Relax,' he whispered. 'Breathe deeply.'

She tried but the blunt tip of his cock was huge and hot and threatening. He eased inside her, trembling with the effort of keeping his body from pressing down on hers.

'OK?' He smiled gently at her, making her relax.

'OK.'

'Good.' He thrust hard into her, making her scream. The pain was shocking, bringing immediate tears to her eyes, but he could not comfort her. He was lost in the supreme tightness of virgin flesh, joyously relishing his triumph. He withdrew, but not all the way, and pushed his cock deep inside her lovely young body again and again.

She felt weak with shock but, as he kept on moving she did not want him to stop. His face had changed, becoming suffused with lust, lips drawn back from his teeth in a prehistoric growl. He plunged into her again, feeling her body responding. Again and there was no mistake. She had got the rhythm perfectly, as if she had been fucking for years. Her fingers dug into his buttocks, pushing him further. She was greedy, wanting ecstasy and expecting him to give it. He took her cue and abandoned himself to the pure joy of hard fucking, his orgasm exploding as her tight muscles squeezed his whole length. He shouted his pleasure, ramming her into the bed, now as if beyond caring that she was new to the overwhelming feelings she was arousing in him. Her high little cries were that of a woman on the brink of control. Almost spent he pounded her until she jolted up against him, her head whipping from side to side in the first cock-driven orgasm of her young life. Despite the fact that this stranger was her first lover, she knew there and then that she would be hard pressed to find anyone who would match his raw, brutal sexual power.

On the subway Pagan started suddenly, aware that the memory had carried her away. Her breathing was shallow and her face felt hot, and she wondered whether it was obvious what had caused the sudden warmth on her cheeks. Then she remembered her subway companion. He had worked his way towards her and was now clutching the rail above her head. His scorching stare told her he had guessed the train of her thoughts. When he stopped in front of her she could not look up at him without hurting her neck, but the alternative was to look straight at his groin. She stood up to move away, but his proximity forced her to be closer to him than she felt comfortable with.

'Excuse me,' she muttered, trying to push past him.

He did not move. As she looked up at him she was reminded even more strongly of the Wolf. What was he doing now? Probably married with three sons and washing his stationwagon on the weekends. The train swayed and the stranger steadied her, catching her hand in his own. Instead of letting go he placed her palm against the prominent bulge in his trousers. The action was hidden by their bodies and the large overcoat, still slung casually around his shoulders. He held on to the luggage rack above her, leaving her to choose whether to move away or keep her hand where it had been put.

She could smell musky Givenchy aftershave and expensive cigars. She should have pulled away and called him a creep and a pervert, but the past few minutes, lost in memories of past passion, had put her reason on hold. With a small smile she squeezed him gently, feeling him pulse in her hand. He gave a little moan of surprise and pleasure and pushed more insistently against her. She increased the pressure, noting with satisfaction the hooded lust in his eyes. Everyone around them looked blank and uncaring, gazing into space as she unzipped his trousers. It was more than he had bargained for, judging by the audible gasp and the flush creeping slowly up towards each sharp cheekbone. As his cock fell into her hand it was her turn to gasp. Unrestrained by any form of underwear, it was rock hard, hot and hefty. As her cool palm wrapped around it his breathing became laboured. Gleefully she thought it would serve him right if he came right here with fifty people watching.

'Bitch,' he gasped weakly.

'Tell me about it,' she said, smiling and jerking him off with maddeningly slow deliberation.

'Go faster!'

The train squealed to a halt.

'Sorry, this is my stop.' She withdrew her hand and neatly slipped away from him. A petite five foot two, she was soon dwarfed in a sea of professional overcoats. He did not see her again until the train began to move.

She walked past the window, giving him a cheeky little wave as she passed. She could see him, vividly aroused and angry as the train pulled away and disappeared into the tunnel.

In the cool night air she came back to her senses and panicked. She really thought she had exorcised the Wolf for good. Over fifteen years had been wasted trying to superimpose his face onto every lover, until Greg Roscoe, the blond superhero, had broken his spell. So what had possessed her now to feel up a total stranger in public because of some ancient sexual encounter? With every step she tried to justify what she had just done. This was New York. People did crazy things every minute of the day. It was almost obligatory. But not for her. Not normal English girls about to marry decent English men.

But he was a stranger, one that hated using the subway, she argued silently. He had probably forgotten her face already. Finally convinced that she would never see him again, she pushed her fears to one side and thought longingly of the pasta left over from last night, sitting in a bowl in the fridge. It had been good, with garlic bread and a young Shiraz. But as she ate it she would try not to think about the succulent duck at Fellini's and the heart-tugging tragedy of *Miss Saigon*, or Greg slaving away for some humourless CEO who stamped his feet like a child if he did not get Greg's undivided attention.

The cold crisp air mingled with the dustier, warmer smell of the subway through the air vents in the sidewalk. She could be blindfolded and still know where she was. After five years Manhattan was in her blood. She picked up her stride down Canal Street and headed towards Chinatown. Mott Street was twisted and narrow, packed with tiny, colourful shops selling Chinese groceries and souvenirs. The area she lived in had become increasingly run down over the years. Marooned in the no mans land between Little Italy and Chinatown, the narrow dark street was quiet compared to the vivid bustling of Mott Street. Iron fire escapes zigzagged the pollution-stained buildings, hiding illegal immigrants sweating their sick guts to make garments for the wealthy. Her own apartment block was lit by a single shop front pulsing with pink neon, advertising The Pleasure Garden.

Pushing past two young men jabbering loudly in Cantonese, she slid through the doorway next to the shop. The manikins in the window were dressed in black PVC bondage gear against a backdrop of hardcore videos and yellowing girly magazines. Relentless bass reverberated from the upper floor as she ran up the two flights of stairs to her door. As always there was the smell of stir-fry and the constantly flickering neon outside shone through the large window into her tiny living space, rendering the need for lighting unnecessary.

Inside the door there was a pile of boxes ready to be filled the following day with the remainder of her meagre belongings. The cheap discount-store furniture would not be going with her. Greg refused to have it in the house. The walls were now bare except for a large patch of damp high in one corner and two large film posters, *Reservoir Dogs* and *King of New York*. It was a dump, but it had suited her.

Whether she would ever feel the same about her new home remained to be seen. It was too ostentatious for her taste but she had fallen in love with the rural location, especially as she would be working from home. Silverskin Software, the ailing company she worked for, were also moving to New Jersey to cut costs, and she had agreed to work fewer hours, which made her very happy.

She went straight to the answer machine, hoping to hear Greg's apologetic voice. There was a message from her best friend Moira, saying she had lost another two pounds in preparation for their weekend away in four weeks' time, and there was a crisp, business-like call from Sylvia Roscoe, Greg's ghastly mother in England. The woman had been trying to contact Greg and had no doubt called Pagan as a last resort. She was organising the wedding with the efficiency of a military operation and, as Pagan had no one to do it for her, she was happy to let Sylvia get on with it. All she had to do was pack her wedding dress and get on a plane in six weeks' time, returning a week later a married woman. There would be no honeymoon for the time being. Greg's new job had put paid to that. But he had promised her two weeks in the sun later on in the year, once he had his feet firmly under the top table.

Greg had not called. She was not surprised, but it did not make her feel any better. In the kitchen she prepared her supper and poured a generous glass of Australian Shiraz. She kicked off her trainers before collapsing onto her bed, which also doubled as a sofa for her guests. She lit a cigarette, thinking that after the weekend she would be banished to the open air to have a smoke. Greg was adamant she wasn't going to do it in the house. She closed her eyes and savoured nicotine until the gentle ping of the oven reminded her she needed to eat.

Her meal was accompanied by a lurid cop show on TV, followed by twenty minutes of aimless mooching through the endless channels before she motivated herself to get into the shower. As she began to soap the day's grime away with rose-scented foam she remembered the ravenous look in the stranger's eyes.

With her eyes closed she could imagine him there in the shower, so tall and with shoulders so wide she would be trapped in the steamy heat, feeling his cock, erect and huge, beating against her belly. His hands would roam over her breasts, sudsy and warm and slippery, teasing out the nipples and holding them under the spray so they would spike with every drop of water that fell upon them. Then he would lift her, effortlessly as she was so much tinier than him, and impale her fully, leaning her against the cool wall so he could use his energy to thrust up into her, whilst her legs wrapped tightly around his waist for added support.

Feeling suddenly very naughty and excited, she poured more shower gel into her hands and rubbed it into her breasts until they became slippery, the nipples tingling with every tug from her soapy fingers. She leaned back against the cool tiles, positioning the shower head so the spray ran in hot rivulets down her stomach, through her springy curls. With soap on her fingers she felt for her clitoris, already swollen and ready for her touch. She moaned softly, squeezing the little nut of flesh very gently then harder as her heart beat faster, stimulated by the heat in the shower, her legs braced to keep her upright. She gritted her teeth as the orgasm flared up from her cunt towards the nipple she was tugging at with increasing fierceness. Her legs weakened but did not give way. She cried out once, twice, as the climax peaked, leaving her breathless but not satisfied. She wanted someone to give her more, much more. Her mind kept going treacherously back to the stranger on the train.

After drying and massaging rose moisturiser all over her body she shrugged on her battered old 501s and a fresh bra, still feeling fidgety. After a short flick through her CD collection she put on Backstreet's 'No Diggitty'. The sultry hip hop beat zeroed in on her restlessness and she began to move.

'Can't get him out of my mind, yeah. Think about the man all the time,' she sang, deliberately changing the lyrics, trying to kid herself that she was not thinking about the Wolf. Her movements became more fluid, breathing life into the syncopated beat. Silhouetted in the window, her half-naked body was as graceful and uninhibited as an African dancer. The neon sign outside picked out the white cotton lace bra too dainty for the size of her breasts, which were full and firm and in perfect proportion to the rest of her generously curved body. Right down to her tiny feet with perfect toes tipped with plum red polish, she knew she radiated raw sexual magnetism. What a shame Greg wasn't there to see it.

Suddenly the music stopped. She was frozen for an infinitesimal moment in a position of total abandonment, rapture shrouding her face, her dark red hair sticking to her forehead in slender spikes. Then her hands, which until then had been above her head, fell abruptly to her sides. It took just a moment to register that someone had entered the room.

'Oh shit,' she said.

2

Richard Arthur Mason was an obscenely wealthy man thanks to his deceased brother's legacy. He had not asked for it. He definitely did not want it. But it was like *Brewsters Millions*, a self-perpetuating mountain of cash he had long ago given up counting. The one-truck removals company run from a lockup on the Lower East Side was now a brash statewide corporation with Richard as chairman, letting his minions run the business for him. He had been a millionaire in his own right since the age of thirty-five, and the one thing he did not need was the Warner family fortune.

He was a striking man, six feet and six inches tall, with a cruel, heavy-lidded beauty accentuated by dark swept-back hair and enviable cheekbones. He always dressed in black and had banned staples and pins from the office, preferring to walk barefoot, even at high-profile meetings. Whenever he was in the office his presence darkened the atmosphere like a pall. He was notoriously difficult, blunt in his opinions and his sarcasm was biting. Every sentence was littered with expletives. He was either loved or hated. There was no safe middle ground with Richard Mason.

Now he drew leisurely on his hand-rolled Cuban cigar and smirked at the prim woman berating him from the other side of his huge ebony desk, fifty storeys above Fifth Avenue. She reminded him of his sister-in-law but with less class. Celia Warner had never told anyone what he had done to her. He presumed she had been too ashamed. He had taken his brother's trophy wife and hung her out to dry. Even now he could grow hard just at the memory of it.

Richard never knew his mother. She had been an avaricious prostitute bought off by his father with a hefty cash payment to avoid scandal. She had left the baby in the care of the Warner housekeeper, saying she was too ill to look after him, and they never saw her again.

Richard was brought up by a series of nannies, under the disdainful eye of Arthur's mother. Arthur was relentlessly unpleasant to him, perceiving the interloper as a threat despite the eighteen-year age gap. But Richard was naturally taciturn and refused to rise to Arthur's teasing, which infuriated him beyond measure. When Richard left home at sixteen to find work in America, the Warner family breathed a large sigh of relief.

For a while he lived an itinerant life, working when his money ran out, until he found temporary peace in Montana, working on a ranch in the foothills of the Rockies. There he learned how to shoot, how to ride a horse bareback and how to handle the big trucks that took the cattle to slaughter. Eventually he took a job as a long-distance trucker and discovered New York.

Twenty years later Arthur had suddenly appeared at Richard's plush Manhattan office. Their father had died two years before and it was clear that Warners was not going to survive under Arthur's leadership. What it needed was a large financial injection and Richard was the one with the requisite spare cash to save it.

Richard took Arthur to The Plaza Athenee for dinner and listened to his tale of woe. For once he flaunted his wealth, giving Arthur the use of Thomas, his chauffeur and insisting that he pay for Arthur's hotel and flight back to England. He knew it was immature but he was amazed at Arthur's audacity in thinking that in one evening, over steamed asparagus and roasted salmon, he could write off a lifetime's worth of insult.

After that the opportunities for sweet revenge kept falling into Richard's lap. He visited England a month later and met Celia Warner for the first time in the somewhat inferior surroundings of Arthur's golf club.

Celia, Arthur's second wife, was fifty going on seventeen, still pretty in a kittenish, overcooked way. But her curly blond hair had turned brassy, damaged by extensive sessions on the sunbed, and she had sharp shiny nails as brittle as her laugh. With calculating interest he had watched her emerge from her scarlet BMW convertible, plumpish thighs firmly clamped together under a white leather mini-skirt, the look completed with white stilettos.

She picked daintily at her food and said little. Nothing was really expected of her. She flushed whenever her eyes met Richard's, and he in turn was fully aware of the effect he was having on her. On several occasions he brushed his legs against hers. Finally he had not moved away and, although she had tried her best to look offended, neither had she.

When he next flew back to England he deliberately arrived at the house a day early. Arthur was staying in London that night for a Freemason's dinner at the Savoy.

Celia had greeted him politely in her best Stuart crystal voice and shown him into the drawing room. He hated the house. It was full of flouncy Belgian blinds and bone china and overstuffed chintz armchairs. She offered him a cup of tea, which he refused, going straight to Arthur's oak drinks cabinet and helping himself to a generous tumbler of Talisker, noting that at least his brother had good taste in liquor, if not in women. It was the middle of the afternoon, a trifle early for alcohol judging by Celia's arch expression. After a delicately disapproving pause she started talking about organising the Chudley Village Harvest Supper. He wasn't interested in her prattle, so he thrust his tongue down her throat.

She could have resisted. She could have broken away from him, told him to get out, or started to scream. She did none of these things. Instead she clung to his broad shoulders and whimpered as he tried to drown her with his kiss.

Within seconds he had broken through the barrier of her tan tights and worked his way under her prim Marks and Spencer knickers. As he knowingly fingered her, Celia tried to push her skirt back down, terrified that they might be seen at any moment through the wide windows. He could not have cared less as he turned her around and pushed her against the back of the sofa. She dared not move for fear of stumbling over the underwear tangling around her ankles. She moaned with shame and excitement as he entered her hard from behind. He screwed her until her calves ached and she had to hold on to the sofa to stop herself tumbling over the top. As she shuddered and squealed he flooded into her, letting out a great triumphant roar. He had not even bothered to remove his coat.

For the remainder of the night she did things for him that she had never even thought of doing for Arthur. He ruthlessly capitalised on the spell he had cast over her, ensuring she would not want her ageing husband after that night. She could hardly cope with his size, but he forced himself into her until her womb ached and her body shook with the kind of orgasms she had only read about in fat blockbusters. She thought he was giving her all of himself, when in fact he was sucking her dry.

As dawn was breaking he reached for her again. This time there was no gentleness, no soft words. Whilst she was still asleep he lubricated her back passage with Vaseline. She squirmed and moaned with pleasure at the wicked slipperiness of his fingers, but the moan became one of protest as he pushed himself fully inside her.

There was no escape. He grasped her neck and pushed her face into the pillow to stifle her cries of pain, and whilst he was still deep inside her he whispered coldly that she was nothing more than a cheap ugly slut, worse than a whore. Whilst still force-feeding her with insults, he came violently inside her, her humiliation just the spur he needed. Afterwards he made her lick him clean and then left without a backward glance.

Six months later she and Arthur fortuitously died, courtesy of an old oak tree, and the controlling share of Warners was passed to Richard, which amused him greatly. He sold up immediately, wiping Warner's off the face of the planet, which gave him immense satisfaction.

'Mr Mason! Have you listened to a word I've said?'

Mrs Bernstein's polished Upper West Side accent could cut glass at twenty paces. Manhattan's charity fundraising high priestess, she had chosen to come in person to persuade Richard to attend one of her highly regarded dinner parties, the tickets for which often topped a thousand dollars a piece. And, as he had done on every single occasion before, he was refusing to play ball.

It wasn't the money that bothered him. He just didn't do the social circuit that kept New York on its feet. He chose instead to ignore the predators who had heard about his wealth and were determined to get a slice of it. As for marriage, he had vowed never to get involved. He preferred to satisfy his sensual side with expensive call girls and his enemies' wives, paying them with diamonds if they threatened to cause trouble. Mostly they accepted with a smile, except for one. After twelve years she was still his easiest screw and his biggest headache.

Mrs Bernstein knew most of this, but the kudos she would gain from his presence (how ever did she manage it?) was worth the time she had invested to use her feminine wiles face to face.

It wasn't working. Even as she was speaking he ordered Eleanor, his personal secretary, to tell Thomas to bring the limo to the door in five minutes. Mrs Bernstein's frosted blond bob shimmied in disapproval and her thin lips tightened to the point of disappearing altogether. He had already unnerved her by appearing from his private bathroom, stripped to the waist after his daily run on the treadmill in the corner of the office and subsequent shower. She had to explain her visit whilst trying not to stare at his lean, tightly muscled body and the curious Celtic tattooed band on his upper arm. Even at forty-seven he looked so predatory, she thought, averting her eyes from his potent masculinity. God only knew what he had been like twenty years earlier. She flushed pink, unused to such bad thoughts, and felt monumental relief when he had buttoned up the white silk shirt and fastened his dark Gucci tie, transforming himself into the immaculate businessman she had expected to find in the first place.

'I've told you before, I'm not interested,' he said smoothly.

'But it's for the children!'

Richard sighed heavily and drew a personal cheque-book from his desk drawer. With his Mont Blanc fountain pen he wrote a cheque for ten thousand dollars and signed it with his usual bold flourish. He handed it to her.

'Take this and get out. I've an appointment on Lexington Avenue with a twenty-five year-old blonde with lips like a vacuum cleaner, and my dick doesn't like to be kept waiting.'

Mrs Bernstein snatched the cheque and stood up. 'You really are the most repellant man I've ever met!'

Richard just grinned at her and thought, how would you like me to lay you across the table and fuck your ass sore, you frigid bitch?

'You won't want me at any of your tedious parties then, will you?' He opened the door and ushered her through. 'Take my advice and cash that cheque in the next half-hour, before I change my mind.'

As he slammed the door on Mrs Bernstein's trim backside Eleanor called again. She sounded hesitant, as well she might when delaying Richard's regular appointment at Mama Toto's.

'Mrs Carlotti's here. She says she wants to say goodbye.'

Richard slumped back in his chair and massaged his temples, collecting his thoughts. So Renate had finally decided to leave Manhattan. She should have done it years ago, but she had insisted on hanging on, futilely waiting for him to tell her he loved her. He had been honest from the start, and she had started out with so much self-confidence, thinking she could change his mind. Over the years he had watched that confidence wither away and it wasn't a pretty sight. She had a built-in self-destruct button but she was still a reasonable fuck, for all her faults.

'OK, send her in. And call Madam Toto. I won't need the girl for another half-hour.'

As soon as he had cradled the phone Renate Carlotti walked into the office and shut the door behind her. She paused so he could admire her long shapely calves in sheer silk stockings. Above them she wore a cream leather trenchcoat, belted tightly around her tiny waist. As she approached the desk her spiked heels made tiny indentations in the plush carpet.

'The plane leaves in two hours but I just had to see you,' she said breathlessly.

'So what did Rocco do to persuade you to leave?'

'There's nothing for me here, is there?' Her voice held a trace of bitterness.

'I told you that years ago. What do you want now? One for the road?'

'I still love you,' she said in a small fragile voice. 'Even though you are a cold-hearted bastard.'

He steepled his fingers and regarded her from behind them. At forty-five she was still a very good-looking woman, tall enough to be a model, with naturally red lips and violet eyes under brows as arched as ravens' wings. He had been screwing her under the nose of her irritating little husband for the best part of a decade. Rocco Carlotti dealt in real estate in California and had lost a great deal of money when Richard outbid him on a substantial piece of land on the West Coast. Carlotti was going to transform it into a lucrative cluster of vacation homes, but Richard had wanted to preserve the wild beauty of the place, building one house that was modest by Californian standards and leaving the rest to nature. Since then Carlotti had harboured a festering grudge, made worse by the suspicion that Richard was also screwing his wife.

But he did not love her, which was what she had always wanted. Instead he had used her, and she had taken his abuse because it was better than nothing.

She stopped punishing the floor and stood in front of him. She unfastened her coat and let it fall open. Her pale breasts were pushed up into succulent mounds by a tightly laced black corset. Her legs were long and slender, her pubis as bare and hairless as a young girl's.

He could smell Youth Dew and moist female arousal. It made his chest tighten with ancient desire.

'Make love to me, Richard.'

'That isn't what I do. Even if I did, I'd be using you.'

'So use me. I don't care.'

He turned away from her scantily clad slender body and stared moodily down into the street. The glass at his feet gave him a full view of the bug-like cabs and cars, all jostling for prime position along Fifth Avenue. His world was silent, except for her soft breathing and the distant chirp of telephones in the outside office.

She moved stealthily towards him and slipped her hand slyly between his thighs, applying gentle pressure underneath his balls. His breathing quickened but he kept his attention on the street, moving slowly against her hand. A slow flush was spreading over her pale skin, up towards her throat as she rubbed against him. With one breath and a wriggle her tiny girl's breasts spilled out of the satin and lace cups. The nipples were long and crisp, like the tips of slender cigars. Automatically he bent down and drew one into his mouth, aware that they could be seen from the offices opposite. People were going about their daily business, but he bet that at least one person would be watching, not believing what was happening before them. It would not be the first time.

'Use me,' she whispered again, guiding his hand between her legs. Her shaven cunt was fleshy and wickedly smooth, arousing feelings of forbidden delight as he cradled it and slipped a finger inside her. Her moisture was sticky on the insides of her thighs. She let her head fall back until her heavy curtain of silky black hair brushed the small of her back. The tip of her tongue appeared between her moist, half-open lips. She wanted him with such blatant desperation he was almost repelled by it, but when her fingers found his zip he turned away from the window and pushed her against the desk, throwing her legs apart so he could stand between them. She unzipped his trousers and felt for his shaft, tumescent and unencumbered by underwear. He growled softly as she gently scratched her long fingernails up and down the entire length. He closed his eyes and enjoyed the sensation, his legs braced to keep his balance. In his head was the woman who had occupied his mind for longer than he could remember. He wanted her with an ache so fierce it kept him awake at night, and that was why his cock was so hard now, recalling her firm breasts, her feline smile, those legs long and strong enough to entrap him within her. His vision clouded as he groped for his chair. He relaxed back into it, twining his hands into Renate's hair and guiding her down to his cock.

'Suck it,' he demanded. Hungrily she pulled him into her mouth, cupping his balls in her hand and squeezing them gently. They were as supple and hairless as fine leather, heavy in her hand. Her tongue trailed wetly up to the swollen head of his cock, hovered for a moment, then wove its way back down again, her lips sucking, nipping gently, over and over. As she pulled the already stretched foreskin back further and sucked at the bulbous glans he could feel the beginnings of an orgasm tickle the base of his balls. His fingers tangled in her slippery hair, choking her as he thrust up into her mouth, distorting her pretty red lips.

'Do you really want it?' he asked roughly, pulling her away so she could answer.

'Yes,' she whispered. Her lipstick was smudged, her hair ruined. He pushed her away and dragged her to a soft leather couch, kicking the coffee table out of the way. There she wriggled onto her back, spreading her legs wide and holding her pussy lips open so he could see her glistening dark tunnel. He did not speak as he hovered over her, positioning himself for the first thrust but holding back to let her frustration grow. Her legs wrapped around his waist, pulling him down until the hot tip of his cock brushed against her molten opening. He let her suck him in, as deep and tight as a velvet glove. In a moment he was drowning in a host of remembered pleasures: wickedly long nails as sharp as her stilettos, her hair a black fan on the cushion, her small breasts bouncing like tennis balls. The first few strokes were measured and slow, until his muscles trembled with the effort of keeping control.

'Oh! You're so huge, I can't take it!' Renate said with a gasp, holding on to his wide shoulders. He clamped his hand over her mouth to silence her moronic platitudes and began to bludgeon her with ever more powerful thrusts. She rose up against him, savouring his crushing weight as their combined panting grunts grew in volume. She readied herself for the first of many explosive orgasms, squeezing his body with her long thighs, pushing up against him until her muscles began to ache in protest. She was uttering hot little cries of joy, her eyes slitted and greedy. He conjured up his woman again, her pussy damp and furry and tight, sucking him in and squeezing his whole length, her dark pink nipples huge and swollen in his mouth. He let go with a roar, shouting her name over and over again with each orgiastic pulse, as Renate's own climax was abruptly shortened by the mention of another woman's name.

Whilst she lay on the couch like a wilted flower, he levered himself to his feet and fumbled in his jacket for cigarettes. He perched on his desk, smoking and watching her dispassionately as she struggled to a sitting position.

'You sonofabitch! I know where that woman of yours is. I could tell her every one of your dirty little secrets.

How would you like that?' She drew on her coat and buttoned it hurriedly.

Richard's expression did not change but his eyes grew icy. 'And when did you last let loyalty get in the way of a free fuck, Renate? You should know better than to threaten me. I'm sure Rocco would love to hear about your gym instructor, your pool cleaner, chauffeur ... anyone else?'

'At least I've been discreet. I hope that bitch buries you, Richard.'

He looked amused. 'It's funny, I've been wishing that for years. As for you being discreet ...' He went over to a wall unit containing a slender Bang & Olufson CD player, flat screen television and video recorder. He pulled a video out of the player and opened a small safe in the wall. After putting the video inside it and turning the lock he grinned at her horrified face. 'I'm sure Rocco would love our home movie. It won't make any difference to me. He wants me dead anyway. You, on the other hand, might be a little less well-off if he finds out you've been begging me to fuck you.' He raised one sleek eyebrow. 'I think that makes us quits, doesn't it?'

'You'll regret everything you've done to me,' Renate said coldly. She was shivering with anger and humiliation.

Eleanor rang. Thomas was outside, waiting with the limo.

'Goodbye, Renate. Just remember to put some clothes on before you get on the plane. Unless you and Rocco are planning to join the Mile High Club.'

With a disgusted sound Renate Carlotti swept out of his office and out of his life. He casually drank the remainder of his coffee. He was not stupid enough to think that he had seen the last of her, but there were more pressing issues to worry about.

He checked his itinerary for that afternoon one last

time. Madam Toto's; a meeting at four with the Wolfen truckers' union boss to discuss increased pay. Later he had dinner arranged with Michael Prosser and Greg Roscoe, Wolfen's latest employee. Richard wanted to keep the evening as short as possible. He had some unfinished business to attend to.

Greg Roscoe felt a deep satisfaction as he inspected his reflection in the bathroom mirror. He ran his tongue over large white teeth, sparkling out of a face permanently tanned from weekly blasts of uva. He straightened the knot in his silk Saks tie, brushed imaginary specks from the wide shoulders of his olive-green Armani jacket and grinned widely. No more was he a lowly audit manager. A month into his new position and already he had very firmly established himself as a senior financial advisor for Wolfen Enterprises, whose ceo had been on the front cover of *Fortune* only a month before. He was already aware of dark mutterings, mainly from the male contingent of the office staff, but he had no intention of letting them get to him. After all, anyone in a position of power was inevitably disliked by a few people with an attitude problem.

His first presentation had gone well and Mason had agreed to Greg conducting a feasibility study on a potential new training centre. There would be some travel involved, which was a far cry from tedious audit work in the bowels of some grim office block uptown.

Satisfied that not one of his fine blond hairs was out of place, he strode back out into the office, humming and snapping his fingers with the sheer joy of smelling success. He passed Wendy and Jo from accounts and he smiled, giving their shapely bodies a frankly admiring glance.

'Hello, ladies. You're both looking lovely today,' he said with unctuous charm.

'Not so bad yourself,' one of them said pertly, turning around to watch him pass by. They watched his tall handsome profile disappear around the corner.

'That man proves there really is a God,' one said.

'Gorgeous Greg,' the other replied wistfully. 'Why is it all the best ones are taken?'

'Break it up, ladies. If any Yank looked at you like he does you'd accuse him of harassment.' The man behind them looked irritable.

'Jealousy gets you nowhere, Peter. He's English, he doesn't know any better.'

'I'd like to teach him,' Peter growled and moved on.

He wasn't alone in disliking the well-bred Englishman. Ever since Greg's arrival he had been generating considerable heat amongst the female office staff, with his mellifluous Oxbridge accent and melting chocolate-brown eyes. Now he was in a cushy job with an over-inflated salary, and in just over a month he would be married to a gorgeous, wealthy redhead.

Sometimes, life was incredibly unfair to the majority.

Greg closed his office door and picked up the phone to call Pagan. His office did not have a window; he would have to wait until he was a director for that privilege. But it was a reasonable size and close enough to where the senior staff were to give him some tacit authority.

When the summons had come half an hour before to dine with the CEO and Richard Mason, Wolfen's head honcho, he did not give his evening with Pagan a second thought. If the big boss wanted to take him out for dinner, he was hardly going to refuse. She would understand, because she always did. Not that she liked it, but she knew better than to say. It was one of the sacrifices one had to make when marrying a successful man.

3

Pagan circled the stranger warily, her heart pounding with a dangerous cocktail of fright and excitement. He was extremely tall, radiating quiet menace. The black Italian mohair suit and the silver Rolex almost too chunky for his slender wrist to support were probably worth more than the entire contents of her apartment.

'How the hell did you get in here?' she demanded.

'Through the door,' he replied simply.

She was about to say that was not what she meant when she realised it was no longer relevant. What was pretty damned relevant was how she was going to get him out.

'Well, now you know where it is, you can leave.'

'I will when I'm ready.'

His accent was low pitched and North American, slightly superior, but in the pregnant pause that followed she noticed his eyes sliding down to her chest like a novice skier out of control, and watched him force them back up to her face again. Having broken into her home, he obviously had no idea what his next step should be. Suddenly he looked little more threatening than a sappy teenager about to ask the prom queen for a date.

Realising she had control, she decided to show him no mercy. Her thumbs were hooked casually in the waistband of snug Levis, exposing a navel deep enough to drink from. And her breasts, gently rising and falling from her exertions, were temptingly displayed in their half-cups like cinnamon buns half dipped in icing sugar.

She shifted her stance, subtly thrusting them out at him.

'So? Who the fuck are you?' The expletive sounded smoky and full of promise.

'Da ... ga ... Franco Giancarlo Mancini,' he stuttered. He coughed to clear his throat and said it again. She grinned widely, showing her slightly crooked but small white teeth.

'Like New York? So good they named it twice?'

'Something like that,' he replied dryly, clearly irritated by his own lack of composure. 'Call me Frank. It's easier.'

Pagan scooped up her Virginia Slims and turned her attention to the CD player. Against an insistent drum beat Bjork's plaintive voice began singing about human behaviour, which seemed appropriate. She turned to meet Mancini's steady gaze, the cigarette between her lips.

'OK, Frank. Get me something to wear,' she said, motioning to the wardrobe in the corner of the room.

His jaw tightened at the imperious command, but after the briefest hesitation he did as he was told. After inspecting the few clothes she had left he threw to her the smallest blouse she possessed.

'Get me something to drink,' he countered shortly. Now he had the advantage, but only for a split second. She caught the garment in one hand and flicked her lighter with the other, holding it to the cigarette, her eyes locked on his.

Smooth move, she thought to herself. If he had fallen to his knees she would not have been surprised. He practically whimpered with joy, his curiously pale, almond-shaped eyes closing briefly. Involuntarily he licked his lips and the reptilian action made her shiver. Her propensity for flirting with danger was aroused further. She slid the blouse over her shoulders.

'Seen enough?' She mocked him, pausing before fastening the tiny satin buttons. They stopped just at the point where her cleavage began, the V-neck edged with the same white satin. Her milky skin could just be seen through the gaps between the slightly overworked buttonholes. It was dangerous to tease him, but she was still too furious with Greg to care. With a slight smile she turned and went into the kitchen whilst Mancini slipped off his jacket and sat on the couch.

Humming softly she reached up to the top shelf for two tumblers, exposing her soft, creamy skin between the jeans and blouse, aware that he was watching her with a scorching stare.

'Scotch good enough for you?' she called over her shoulder, picking up the Laphroaig bottle.

'It's good enough for anything.'

She accidentally spilled precious liquor onto the kitchen worktop, suddenly struck by déjà vu. Distant echoes of conversations past were becoming louder, like an insistent drumbeat. She handed him the tumbler.

'Who are you? What do you want?'

He watched her through an ethereal haze of grey, tapping ash into a black china ashtray fashioned as a cannabis leaf. He smoked slowly, elegantly, taking his time before replying.

'That's a dangerous question, Pagan. But you like playing with fire, don't you?'

'Excuse me? How do you know my name?' Her eyes shifted around the apartment. There was nothing to immediately give it away. Maybe he had been there before, when she was out. What else did he know about her? She backed away from him, suddenly nervous.

'I remember my first fuck. She was a whore in a roadhouse in Idaho. Do you remember yours?'

She was confused. 'What?'

'June 14th, 1980. You were at the War Memorial and

I was planning to visit your father. Until you decided to seduce me, that is.'

The breath left her body. So her instincts had been spot on. And fifteen years on the mantle of maturity and experience had made the Wolf an infinitely potent and dangerous animal. The vivid fantasy she had been indulging in just half an hour before was again flesh and blood, his icy blue eyes smouldering with a heat that seared right through her.

'This isn't happening,' she said unsteadily.

'You're here. I'm here. We're alone. Anything could happen.'

She could not speak. For years he had been the standard by which she had judged every relationship, each sexual encounter. And just when she had pushed him aside long enough to marry someone else, he was back. She could feel that same black magnetism sucking her towards him. She wanted to touch him to see if he was real but dared not. The atmosphere in the apartment was potent with shared sensual memories. All it needed was one spark to ignite something that she knew without doubt would be beyond her control.

'Your timing is crap. I'm getting married soon.' The words rushed out too fast.

'Yeah, to an accountant,' he replied disparagingly. 'Didn't you stop to think when he asked you to marry him just as you were about to inherit a shitload of cash?'

'How did you know about that?'

'I've done my research.'

'Then you'll know he's a sweet man and I love him,' she said firmly.

'Is that so? You love him so much that you jerk off a stranger and prick-tease him into insanity. Shit, I'm glad you don't love me.' He took a deep drag on the cigarette and expelled a lazy plume of smoke at the ceiling. The silence lengthened and became uncomfortable.

'Look, I didn't intend ... I mean, I was angry with Greg and it was stupid of me but I wasn't thinking straight!'

'He let you down again?'

'Yes. No! How the hell do you know?'

'Like I said, I've done my research. I guess he must have a big dick. Why would you put up with him otherwise?'

'If you had done your research properly you'd know, wouldn't you?'

He flashed a heartbreaking white smile. 'I like you, Pagan Warner. I always knew you'd be a pain in the ass.'

'So why find me again?'

'I want to get to know you. You're one hell of a woman.'

'You don't know that.'

'Yes I do. It doesn't take a lot of research to figure that one out.'

He ground the Marlboro to dust with a finality that made her shiver. Almost lazily he caught her wrist and pulled her onto the couch, lying down with her and trapping her with his body.

'Give me tonight,' he whispered, decisively cupping her breast. The caress became a soft squeeze, his breath hot and feathery in her ear. 'Why don't we start where we left off on the train?'

This was moving in for the kill in its most blatant form. Disbelief shocked her into breathlessness, and with galling irony this alone was making her bosom heave against his hand in a totally Victorian fashion.

'For God's sake, stop it!' she hissed, attempting to push him away. He held her tighter.

'Why should I? You don't want me to.' He began to

press gentle yet scalding kisses on the delicate curve under her jaw, all the while stroking her nipple with his thumb.

'You can't just walk in and help yourself! I'm not a bloody supermarket!' But her protests sounded half-hearted, even to her. Having a man hold her and kiss her with such passion felt too good for safety. She tried to push him away again but he was as solid as rock, his body a mass of finely tuned muscle and sinew that could crush her without him even raising his pulse. He manoevred down and sucked at her distended nipple through the jersey blouse and cotton bra, the heat of his mouth almost unbearable as it seeped through to her skin. It felt so good that she melted

'This isn't a good idea,' she whispered as his hand slipped between her thighs, subtly massaging the sensitised nub of her clitoris against the hard denim seam of her jeans. Unconsciously she pressed her thighs together, holding him close.

'It's the best idea I've had for years,' he replied, before locking her in a kiss as deep as any hot penetrative sex she had ever had before.

Not that she had had any for some time. Greg was keeping her for their special night. Good, honest, hard-working Greg. Like a drowning woman she struggled back towards common sense and loyalty. Desperation gave her the strength to push Mancini away. Caught unawares, he tumbled to the floor and she headed for the door.

'Wait! Jesus Christ!' He ducked a well-aimed kick to his jaw and Pagan escaped, scrambling down the stairs and into the street.

Guilty panic gave wings to her bare feet. The store owners hosing down their slice of sidewalk ignored her as she ran by. She kept on until exhaustion and sore feet forced her to stop. Only then did she look around, leaning against a wall while she caught her breath and eased the jabbing pain in her side.

Her situation was not good. The street was rundown and too quiet. Her feet felt sore and gritty, and she had no money for a cab. Litter gathered in the guttering and swirled round her feet in the wind. She could hear faint shuffling in the dark doorways. The sound of sirens and honking horns echoed far away. She looked around for a street number or any landmark to tell her where she was.

Just then she heard the sound of running footsteps. As she slunk into a dark doorway Mancini appeared around the corner. He approached her, his breathing only slightly laboured. In the indistinct light his face was all planes and shadows, accentuating the hollows under his cheekbones and the cruelty of his lips. As he came closer his height was overwhelming, tension sizzling from every inch. She remembered how good his body had felt against hers on the couch, and how idiotic she had been to refuse him.

'You forgot these,' he said, holding up a pair of spiked-heel boots.

After she put them on he moved in on her, backing her against the door. He did not speak. No words seemed necessary. As his lips closed on hers she responded automatically. It was a gentle, sweet, accepting kiss, their tongues involved in a slow rolling dance. Her arms slipped around his waist under his jacket, warming her against the cold night. He was trembling from head to foot, as if holding back some terrible need. As his kiss deepened, threatening to engulf them both, she pushed him gently away.

'Once, for old times' sake,' she said firmly, as much for herself as for him.

'Once,' he repeated. His slight smile suggested that

his interpretation of the word might be slightly different to hers. 'We'll go to my place.'

Silently they walked back to his car, hand in hand. She could have guessed the panther-sleek black Mercedes coupé was his. It was parked in a deserted car lot surrounded by barbed wire, encrusted with the same youths he had earlier employed to look after it. He threw a fat roll of banknotes to the leader of the group and they melted away. The alarm chirped but before he opened the door he pushed her back over the bonnet and kissed her again, a deep, sensual kiss as he rubbed against her, letting her feel his rock solid arousal. It turned her on like a light switch, an answering sticky warmth oozing into her panties. To hell with guilt and complications, she thought distantly, drugged by the assault he was subjecting on her senses. She would deal with them later.

Greg had gone to Pagan's apartment after his gargantuan dinner with Michael Prosser. Richard Mason, chairman and hater of publicity and restaurants, had appeared briefly to pick at roasted sea bass and drink a copious amount of bourbon. He made Greg nervous, with his foul language and air of constant shimmering anger. That evening he had been even worse than usual, and Greg was not alone in being relieved when he left.

But Pagan was not at home, much to Greg's chagrin. Feeling irritated that she had obviously managed to find something better to do than wait for him, he aimlessly wandered for a while before arriving outside a club that he had heard about in the coffee room. No one had been there, but it had a good reputation, if you were into that sort of thing.

Greg was not sure what sort of thing they were

talking about and, as he had nothing better to do, he went in.

The doorman was built like a sofa. He looked at Greg's expensive clothes and growled that it was fifty dollars for outsiders. Greg was just about to leave when a small ebony-haired woman came out, wearing a vivid red rubber corset and lace-up biker boots.

'Hi! I saw you on the security camera. You want to come in?'

'Er...' He wasn't sure that he did. The loud music and dark, seedy hole it was coming from did not appeal to him at all.

'I'm Michelle. If you like you can have a trial session. Absolutely free.' She smiled alluringly up at him. 'I'd be very happy to show you exactly what we do here.'

He could not help but notice her breasts, almost tumbling out of the tight corset, red laces just about holding them in place. They had a smattering of glitter that caught the light as she moved. He found them totally enchanting and felt a familiar tug in his trousers. It was happening more frequently now that the wedding was getting closer, but he had been very good. He had restrained himself. He did not want Pagan discovering that he had been a bad boy just yet. After they were married it would not matter.

But suddenly this girl was making him thirsty for sex in a way that had not happened for a long time. She flipped her long black hair over her shoulder and sparkled at him again, grinning. He nodded and let her lead him down a short flight of stairs to the main bar.

The place was dimly lit with red neon, heaving with the kind of subterranean humanity Greg had only seen on late-night TV shows. A seething atmosphere of latent sexuality permeated the whole room. He tried not to stare at the man with spikes in his nipples and tongue, wearing only a small black leather pouch, or the Chinese girl with a series of leather straps around her thighs and waist, accentuating her bare bottom, and painfully binding her breasts so they pointed aggressively up at the ceiling. Each strap bristled with silver studs, even the tiny black triangle that just covered her pudenda. She caught him looking and whipped a long snake of leather around his waist. As she dragged him towards her Michelle intervened.

'Leave him alone, Kiki, he's mine for now.'

Kiki pouted and reluctantly let him go. 'Later, then, honey.' She tossed her sleek bobbed hair and melted into the crowd.

Greg felt Michelle's small hand on his arm, leading him towards the bar where a gin and tonic was already waiting for him. Michelle ran her hand up Greg's lapel and down his silk tie.

'Nice suit,' she grinned. 'Everyone wants a piece of you already!'

'What do you mean?' Greg shouted back.

She smiled enigmatically. The music changed to Heaven 17 belting out 'Temptation'. She led him out onto the packed dance floor.

Dancing was not his thing. He was too big and awkward, but it did not matter, because on every side bodies pressed against him. He could have sworn that he felt hands on his buttocks and once on his groin, but looking around it seemed that everyone was feeling everyone else. As the tempo slowed Michelle slipped her arms around his waist. She was warm and wriggly and unthreatening.

'Do you want to stay for the show?' she asked.

'What show?'

He was soon to find out. The music stopped and a drum roll sounded. Everyone's attention turned to a stage that Greg had not noticed before. A heavy purple satin curtain swayed and shimmered. The drum roll ended and to a crash of cymbals the curtain was thrown back.

A blond woman was hanging from a leather harness suspended from the ceiling. She was slender with melon-heavy breasts and long muscled legs, but her age was undetermined due to the mask over her face, leaving only her eyes and rosebud lips exposed. She had been spreadeagled to face the audience below, captured by a series of buckles and leather straps that left her unable to move. Her breasts swung down invitingly and her genitalia were totally exposed in front and behind.

Below her stood Kiki, wielding a long leather strap and smiling at the colourful crowd of men, women and anyone in between.

'OK, everyone, you know the score. We need two volunteers. The one who shoots first gets the money –' she held up a fifty dollar bill, to much whooping and clapping '– and the loser goes in the web for you good people to have your way with for five minutes. Then we play again. Are you ready?'

More enthusiastic cheering. Kiki tugged at a rope and the woman was lowered to waist height. Kiki stalked through the crowd, assessing likely candidates, ignoring the more desperate ones. As the tension mounted she picked two men and they came up onto the stage, to more encouraging cheers.

'Oh no, they're not . . .' Greg started to say.

'That's why we're here, sweetie,' a green Mohican-haired man said beside him, as the first man positioned himself in front of the prone woman. People were dancing around them, some watching, some totally ignoring the unfolding scene as if they had seen it all before.

The first man's brown skin glistened under the stage lighting, his white grin flashing as he undid his trousers, displaying a bulging black thong. He cupped his crotch and thrust it at the audience, obviously loving every minute. Even half erect, his cock was an impressive size, encouraging more cheers. He showed it to the woman, brushing it against her lips. Immediately she drew him in and sucked eagerly, until his grin disappeared and was replaced by a look of hard lust. His eyes closed and he began to thrust his hips, holding on to the harness for support, his cock distorting the woman's pretty mouth.

Greg was transfixed by the trapped woman, unable to do anything but take what was happening to her. The thought of being so helpless made his cock thicken so suddenly it became trapped at an uncomfortable angle. Discreetly he rearranged it so it lay flat against his belly, but it still felt huge and obvious. He pulled his jacket closed but it was too dark in the club for anyone to notice anyway.

He did not see the woman walk up behind him, but he spilled his drink when her hand brushed up against the hard ridge in his trousers. It was Michelle again, smiling and squeezing his cock very gently, encouraging more blood to pound into it.

'Just relax,' she whispered, curving her other arm around his waist. It seemed totally natural to curl his arm around her shoulder. They stood comfortably, her fingers playing lightly over every inch of his erection. She did not attempt to get into his trousers, but the indistinctness of her touch only heightened his pleasure.

The second man also made a show of unbuttoning his jeans for anyone who cared to watch, before moving between the woman's spread legs. He also displayed an impressive set of muscles under a white vest. His cock was thick and hefty. He aimed it at the crowd as he jerked off to get hard. To encouraging cries of 'stick it in her!' he reared up behind her and pushed his cock deep inside her. As he began to pump his eyes became slitted and aggressive. Greg was barely aware that his body had begun to pick up the rhythm, moving against Michelle's hand. He bunched his leg muscles to stop himself from toppling over as Michelle increased the pressure, massaging his length in the palm of her hand.

The white man on the stage was locked in a power struggle with the black man, the woman a pawn between them. As she was thoroughly stuffed from both ends Greg could see the blank ecstasy in her eyes. She seemed to be looking straight at him over the massive member pumping between her lips. They tightened around the thick shaft of flesh and sent the man into overdrive. He came suddenly with a long drawn-out howl, withdrawing to spurt over her face. As she greedily gobbled at him the viscous come dribbled from her lips onto the stage. He stood frozen, hips jutting forwards, letting her suck him dry. The man behind had withdrawn. He was next for the harness, and he was saving his erection for what was to come. Greg felt Michelle's hand withdraw but he had become breathless with involvement in the happenings on the stage. He barely felt her take his hand and lead him to a sofa in the darkest corner of the room.

The crowd had dispersed, leaving a hard core of around thirty people. The mood of the crowd had changed. The party atmosphere had gone and in its place was a seething air of lust wanting to be fulfilled. Several couples and threesomes were on the long sofas on the perimeter of the room, making out, talking with hands and roaming tongues. The harness was empty but there was an air of expectation, of finding the next willing victim.

Michelle sat snugly by Greg's side, her hand on his thigh. He drained his gin and tried not to feel nervous.

'You know you're the best-looking man in this place. You fancy a go in the web? Is that why you're here?'

'I heard it was a good place to come,' he said lamely.

Michelle giggled delightfully. 'You're right about that. Why don't you relax? The doors are shut. No one else is coming in tonight. You're quite safe. For now.'

Her words sent a tingle up his spine.

'You want another drink?' she asked.

'Why not?' he said daringly.

She came back with two more gins, ice included. As she sat close to him again he was very aware of her long legs, barely covered by a black leather pelmet skirt, and her nipples grazing the edge of her corset. She toyed with her long black hair as he sipped at his gin. He had lost count of how many he had drunk since arriving at the club, but now he was relaxed enough so that when she put her hand over his crotch he did not go into orbit.

'You have something really special in there,' she said, squeezing gently. 'Can I look?'

The alcohol, her sultry voice and the scent of patchouli oil played havoc with his senses. He leaned back in the chair, letting her caress him. His penis was pressing uncomfortably against his boxers. Michelle hummed in appreciation and unzipped his trousers, letting his cock swell out of the opening, encased in black silk. He gulped his gin, knowing he ought to walk out before he was sucked into something dangerous, but he seemed to be glued to the chair, held there by the gentle touch of Michelle's hand.

Kiki came up and sat beside them. She had a pretty pug face and now her dainty breasts swelled out of a black jersey dress short enough to show the V of her panties. She peeled down the neckline of the dress, letting her nipples pop out, and giggled sweetly at his look of surprise.

'You like to suck?' Her accent was strong and inviting. She took his gin and poured a tiny amount over each nipple. They tightened visibly, crinkling the dark areola around them. Greg licked his lips but did not move. She kneeled up on the sofa and guided his head down. As soon as his lips touched the warm, liquor-soaked nub he did not hold back. Hungrily he sucked, making her laugh to Michelle.

'He like a baby.'

'No. All man,' Michelle replied, placing Kiki's hand against the thrusting lump in his boxers.

Greg looked at the two girls wanting to administer to him every decadent pleasure and his spirits soared. He drained his drink and spread his arms out along the top of the sofa, stretching out his legs to accentuate the swollen organ straining against black silk.

'Well, girls, you'd better have your wicked way with me.'

He allowed Michelle to remove his trousers, shoes and socks, feeling very wanton and daring at being half naked in a room full of people he did not know. But everyone else was doing it, and now he had committed himself he wanted to enjoy every single minute.

Michelle and Kiki's glossy heads shifted down the sofa and nuzzled his cock, heating it through the thin silk with hot little breaths. As he felt their tongues, one on each side, squirm wetly up his thighs towards his balls his shaft swelled even more. He marvelled at its length and girth, his vision temporarily clouded by the wriggling hot tongues circling each testicle. He opened his legs wide as they each took a ball into their mouths, worried it gently and licked it with lavish attention. Then they turned their focus to his shaft, making admiring noises. He had never seen it so hard before, thrusting up at him like a flagpole. He sipped his gin and tonic, undulating his hips and enjoying the slavish attention of the two mouths. He did not want to come just yet. There was so much to take in around him. He saw one woman kneeling on the sofa nearest his being arse-fucked, her satin corset pinching her waist in painfully tight. Her red mouth was open, panting, until another man filled it with his massive phallus, almost choking her. Her lipstick was smeared on his white satin boxer shorts. The man behind her was slapping her backside raw as the man in front pumped harder, making her squeak in protest. Together they abused her until the other man's face suffused with lust and he came violently, choking on his own grunts, his hands almost encircling the woman's tiny waist.

There was one woman he particularly liked the look of, sinking marguueritas at the bar. She looked quite happy to watch the libidinous scenes being played around her. She was tall, older than him, with black hair in a French plait. She seemed to sense him looking at her and she turned and smiled. He grinned insolently back, mentally resolving to seek her out later. All around them were staccato sounds of sex, uninhibited cries and foul-mouthed commands, slapping and grunting, and above it all a sultry saxophone, streaming through speakers hidden around the large room. Greg abandoned himself totally to the hedonistic joy of free fucking, the gin warm in his belly. He tugged Michelle's hair so she would look at him.

'Get on me,' he rasped, and she did, straddling his lap, making a show of pulling her tiny black satin panties to one side and easing his cock into a supremely tight, wet pussy. Only when he was deep inside her did she move, undulating slowly against him, while Kiki climbed on the top of the sofa and tilted Greg's head back so he looked straight up at her shaven cunt. His tongue snaked out and tasted her. She was warm and salty, fragranced with ginger spice. Her high little sounds of joy encouraged him to explore deeper between her snug lips, his tongue picking up the increasing rhythm of Michelle's gyrating. She had opened his shirt and was grazing her nipples against his skin, pinching his own nipples and sucking them into supersensitivity.

'Baby, you're so fine!' Kiki gasped as Greg's tongue probed lasciviously deep up her hole. Michelle leaned forward and fluttered her tongue against Kiki's exposed clitoris until she came with little shrieks, contracting against Greg's tongue and washing his face with her juices. As Kiki collapsed onto the couch beside them Michelle licked Greg's face clean and they kissed with open mouths and flickering pornographic tongues. He was being so bad and his cock throbbed at the joy of it. He spread his legs wide and pumped up into Michelle's willing pussy, watching the stage over her shoulder. Two women were in the harness, being used as a human roulette wheel. They were spun around and where they stopped they had to give head until the men spurted. The floor beneath the women was slick with come as one by one the men shot their load and staggered away. The women looked dull-eyed and sated, their mouths mechanically opening for the next cock.

Their entrapment and helplessness pushed him over the edge. His balls contracted, ready to explode. Michelle fucked him with the virtuosity of a musician giving the performance of her life, her hair falling over her face, her golf-ball breasts cupped in her hands. She was tiny, tight and hot, and his orgasm came with a flood, emptying his balls, pulsing and pulsing so vigorously that their simultaneous cries echoed around the room.

4

The lift was huge and old-fashioned, with a noisy outer mesh door and fat brass buttons. Pagan expected Mancini to leap on her as soon as the door drew closed but he did not. On the way up they stayed at opposite ends, eyeing each other warily like animals in a cage. They had not spoken since getting into the car.

At length the lift jolted to a stop on the fourteenth floor. His door was as anonymous as the rest, and opened with a futuristic keypad that seemed at odds with the faded 1930s splendour of the building.

The ultra-modern theme was continued inside the spacious apartment. The floor was Scandinavian blond wood, softened with a single densely piled cream rug. The walls were cream and minimally dressed with large splashes of modern art. Two huge black leather sofas straddled a chrome and smoked glass coffee-table. A floor-to-ceiling window gave a spectacular view towards the Chrysler Building and, beyond it, the Empire State Building. The vista sparkled like a magic kingdom in the dark.

A single lamp highlighted a wide, low-slung bed made up of chrome bed knobs and vertical bars. It looked almost clinical, right down to the cream sheets but, when she moved closer, their soft inviting sheen told her they were satin.

He had gone into the galley kitchen. It was small but immaculate, fitted out in brushed steel and white marble. The fridge was almost empty but his bar was well stocked, a testament to how much importance he placed on alcohol over food.

'I have an excellent single malt, if you want to try it,' he said, holding up a bottle of Talisker.

'That's weird. My father used to drink that,' she said, peering at the label.

'He obviously had good taste.'

'In some things, yes.'

She collapsed into a black leather La-Z-Boy by the window and stared out at the city lights.

'It's great, isn't it? Until now it's been the best view in the house.' Mancini watched her hungrily, holding out a heavy crystal glass half filled with the precious peaty yellow liquid.

'Why did you call yourself Wolf?' she asked, trying to deflect the heat in his eyes.

'The same reason you called yourself Pagan and not Susan. It was the way I felt inside when I first set eyes on you.' He grinned and she smiled back, shaking her head ruefully at being found out. The Talisker was fiery and pure. With one small sip her body felt warm and dangerously languorous. She relaxed further back into the soft leather chair.

'I wish I had found you again sooner,' he said suddenly.

'Why didn't you?'

'Reasons I'd rather not go into now.'

'And what if I say that just isn't good enough?'

'I'll agree with you, but it won't change anything.'

'But why now? Just before I'm about to get married?'

'So many damned questions. Let me ask you one. Why did you hand-fuck me in the subway? Get into my car? Why are you right here, right now?'

'That's four questions,' she pointed out helpfully, and she did not have a single sensible answer to any of them.

He watched her speculatively for a moment before slipping off his jacket and hanging it neatly over a dining chair. The black silk tie followed and he unfastened the first four buttons on his black shirt. He looked leaner, hungrier, the pale skin of his throat glowing silver in the near dark. He picked up a remote control and pressed a few buttons. Instantly Bryan Ferry's honeyed vocals floated softly from speakers placed around the room. The song was, inevitably, 'Slave to Love'.

Mancini pulled her to her feet and held her close. As they swayed to the music Pagan fought a host of bittersweet memories. The Wolf was back, his face in her hair, their bodies sharing the same warmth. The intensity of feeling was so much that she had to break away.

'Is your name really Franco Giancarlo Mancini?'

'Don't you like it?'

'I don't even know if I like you. This is a nice place.' She gestured around the apartment. 'Whatever you do must be pretty lucrative.'

'I'm involved in a few things around the city.'

She raised an eyebrow. 'Things? Are they legal?'

'You do ask a lot of questions.'

'It's in my nature to be curious, just like you.'

'Yes, we are alike, aren't we?' He seemed to find satisfaction at the thought. 'I'll tell you when the time is right. But if you insist on giving me a label just call me –' he thought for a moment '– Chairman of the Board.'

She laughed. 'That means you don't want to tell me. Fair enough. Unless you're some underworld kingpin I really couldn't give a shit.'

'I pay my taxes along with everyone else. Scouts honour.' He placed his hand over his heart and grinned.

'Al Capone said the same thing.' She sat in the La-Z-Boy again and swirled the alcohol around her glass. 'So, Mr Chairman of the Board, what are you proposing?'

He gulped visibly at the unexpected liquid sultriness

of her words. He took the glass from her and placed it on the coffee-table.

'I propose a feasibility study,' he replied, somewhat shakily.

'On what, exactly?'

'On whether or not I should eat your cunt.'

The abruptness of it made her shiver and go slightly damp, but she kept her voice level. 'I don't think that's a very good idea.'

The dismay on his face was almost comical. 'Why the hell not?'

'Why waste funds and personnel on a study of something that you really believe will succeed? Surely in your position you're able to make an executive decision.' She lifted and extended her leg so her spiky booted foot rested on his stomach. He caught it and guided it down to the pulsating lump in his groin, moving slowly from side to side, pleasuring himself.

'So you don't think I should consult my directors?'

She shook her head. 'This one's down to you, Mr Chairman. The buck stops –' she jabbed her slim heel not too gently into his balls '– right here.'

He gasped silently. She was delectable in her tight jeans and the too-small white blouse, the twin mounds of her breasts swelling gently above the V-shaped neckline.

'An executive decision,' he muttered thickly, sinking down before her, his knees nestling into the thick rug. He picked up one foot, unzipped the boot and eased it away, inhaling the animal smell of leather and polish. The other followed. Then he lifted her feet and examined the soles. They were black with dirt from her barefoot sojourn into the back streets earlier that evening.

'Hmmm. Genuine Manhattan filth,' he said and went into the bathroom.

She reclined the chair fully and gazed out of the window to the magnificent vista. It felt so right to be here. Awkward questions and justifications could wait until the morning.

He came back and began to wash her feet. Mingling with Brian Ferry's honeyed voice she could hear the gentle lap of water being wrung out of a yellow sea sponge, and smell the masculine aroma of cedar wood bath foam. He was gentle, dabbing each foot dry with a soft towel.

'That's better,' he said, kissing her toes. 'Now take off your jeans.'

She stood up and began deftly unbuttoning her 501s.

'Slower,' he said. His authorative tone left her in no doubt what he wanted. She stood up, her fingers lingering on the remaining silver buttons. He gulped visibly as she undid them slowly, teasingly, easing the jeans from her hips and turning so he could admire her rounded buttocks barely covered by white cotton panties, the legs high cut on her hips and narrow at the back, making her legs seem even longer. She stepped neatly out of the jeans and discarded them, then hooked her thumbs into the top of the panties.

'Leave them on.' His cold eyes had become feverish, the pupils dilated but, as she sat down again he began to massage her feet, using strong circular motions with his thumbs. She relaxed under his touch, her eyes almost closing. They flew open again when he licked at her big toes. The warmth of his tongue set all her nerve endings jangling, and when he drew one big toe into his mouth she sharply drew her leg away, telling him to stop. It was too much, too soon, so he stroked her calves instead. They were toned and shapely, shifting under her satin skin as he fondled them. Pressing her legs together, he ran his tongue up the crevice between them to her knees, leaving a cool trail in his wake. After nibbling at her knees he continued the trail up between her thighs, feeling her tremble and her mouth open in a silent gasp.

He ran both forefingers along the edge of each leg of her panties, letting her fluffy curls escape. He blew on them gently and his warm breath made her thighs quiver. Edging closer, he cupped a knee in each hand and gently opened her legs, pulling her down so they opened wider and made her more accessible to him. Kneeling comfortably between them he undid the tiny satin buttons on her blouse, again revealing the half-cup bra filled to overflowing with her divinely full, pliable breasts. His fingers trembled as they played lightly over her flesh. In the soft, flattering light she was caramel and cream, a veritable feast of a woman. He freed one breast from its delicate lace cup and ran his thumb over the raspberry nipple, watching with wonder as it crinkled and grew. A growl sounded in his throat as he bent his head and ran his tongue round it, finally resting his mouth on the dark cone and teasing it into life.

She bit her lip to stop herself crying out. It had been such a long time since she last had a man lavishing so much exquisite attention on her breasts. He gathered them together until the nipples were almost touching and licked them greedily, one after the other, until each sensation merged into one divine, surging channel arrowing straight down between her legs. They widened and she whimpered, sinking lower in the chair. At the unspoken invitation he dipped his head and pressed his face to the plump pad of flesh, breathing in her scent, his hands on her breasts, pinching each nipple until it was long and supersensitive. He had rolled up his shirt sleeves, revealing almost translucent skin and a smattering of silky black hair. His arms were long and prominently veined, his fingers immaculately manicured and as elegant as a pianist playing a delicate concerto. In his subservient position he looked as if he were worshiping her, his hot breath adding to the moisture already threatening to ooze tellingly through her panties.

Their eyes met, her encouragement needing no words. He worked the panties downwards as she lifted her hips so he could be rid of them, then she felt him grasp both ankles and widen her legs, hooking them over the chair arms so she was totally exposed. Her pussy was already glistening, leaving a damp patch on the leather, her labia displayed like the petals of a rose.

'You look delicious,' he murmured, feasting his eyes on the succulently plump cleft before him.

'So eat me,' she answered, widening her thighs further, wondering how she had become so wanton in such a short time. Her breath caught as his tongue thrust deep inside her, exploring and probing the walls of her pussy, working up towards her cervix, so deep she cried out. With a small sucking sound he withdrew and found her clitoris, already distended from the intense stimulation it had already succumbed to that evening. At the first delicate touch all those distant memories came flooding back. As the tip of his tongue circled the swollen nut of flesh before fluttering directly against it like a butterfly, she knew why she had judged her other lovers against him. Some of them had been good, but not one of them seemed to understand her body quite as well as he. His mouth and her pussy were a marriage made in heaven; a constant stream of understanding flowing between them. She buried her hand in his hair and held him in place as he drove her on and upwards until her juices flooded over his face and she was groaning uninhibitedly, straining against him, wringing out every last drop of sensation until it became too much and she had to kick him away. He lay on the floor, panting, wiping his mouth and licking her essence from the back of his hand. She squirmed in the chair, floating back down to earth, her breath still coming in short gasps. He pulled her to her feet as she was still in the final throes of ecstasy and guided her stumbling across the room to the bed.

He pushed her back onto the cool, slippery sheets and removed the remainder of his clothes, starting, she was pleased to note, with his socks. As he stood over her, letting her eyes roam all over his naked body, she remembered the panic she had felt as a gauche teenager, seeing a fully aroused man for the first time. He had gained maybe a stone but carried it well, a solid chunk of a man with broad shoulders and no fat on his hips. His stomach was flat, a thin silky line of hairs running from a deep navel to his pubis, where they fluffed out around the massive stalk of flesh that had given her such a scare once before. Now she shuddered deliciously at the prospect of having him push inside her, fulfilling the fantasy she had had in the shower.

He crawled onto the bed and lay beside her on his side, head propped up on one hand. With his free hand he stroked her from thigh to shoulder in a lazy figure of eight. He seemed to be in no hurry. She lightly fingered the tattoo encircling his left arm. Her name was written in curly black Celtic script, entwined with a simple barbed rose. It looked as if it had been done some time ago.

'I'm flattered,' she said.

Again he saw no need to reply. His body was as long and supine as a cheetah and as pale as cream, except his cock, which was a dull, angry red with his need for her. He was such a strange, silent man, but he radiated a potency that was almost overwhelming. Suddenly she was sixteen again, looking at the Wolf for the first time with tremulous wonderment.

'It won't bite, you know.'

She laughed to cover her embarrassment. He took her hand and guided it down, watching her face. It suffused with colour again as her fingers found delicate flesh. His balls were big and pendulous in a sac as supple as fine leather. She lifted them tentatively, feeling their weight, the tips of her fingers tangling in the dark, springy hair. She moved her hand upwards. His penis seemed curiously fragile despite its hefty magnificence. She started slightly as it leapt under her touch.

'I haven't done this for a very long time.'

'Not even for your accountant?' A thought suddenly occurred to him. 'Jesus, you haven't told him you're a virgin, have you?'

'No.' Her voice was patient. 'If you don't mind I'd rather not talk about him right now.'

'I'm glad to hear that.'

After that there was no more talk. He took her over completely and his skill was consummate. He knew erogenous zones that she did not know existed: in the pits of her arms, the small of her back, between her toes. He found a mole on the inside of her thigh and sucked the flesh around it until it came up red and bruised. He opened her up with his tongue and made her weep at the very pinnacle of ecstasy, time and time again, until she had to beg him to stop. When he finally hovered above her, cruelly teasing out her expectation, she wanted him with a desperation that frightened her.

'Don't make me beg,' she whispered, yearning with her whole body. She gathered her breasts together and proffered them, the nipples huge and hard and edibly pink. Her small, voluptuously curved body was spread out amongst the glossy sheets and he watched as the expression on her face change to greedy delight as he pushed deep inside her. She was fantastically tight but, unlike the first time, she now knew how to use her inner muscles to massage his whole length. Pagan saw him grit his teeth, as if trying to savour the first slow, measured thrusts, but it was no good. The sweet temptation of her cunt seemed too great, her fingernails too spiky on his back, her breathless demands to fuck her too urgent to ignore. He clung on desperately, like a man slipping into an endless chasm, as her frenzy began to surpass his. She matched him thrust for thrust, goading him into giving her more, until her commands became abandoned cries and she was falling with him into that void, that seemingly endless velvet black hole of exquisite pleasure. She came first, pummelling his back with clenched fists, biting his shoulders and uttering stifled, guttural moans that she could not stop. She was a wild woman, wanting to hurt him for daring to wring such emotion out of her. As she continued to assault him he came in huge pulses, sobbing out his joy, and with each throb she punished him more until he was spent, sagging against her, his breath hot and moist in the hollow of her neck.

Afterwards they lay peacefully, Pagan stroking his hair, feeling his seed seep slowly onto the expensive satin. He nuzzled at her ear.

'The chairman or the accountant. If there's a choice to be made, it's yours.'

'Shut up, Mancini.' She pulled him back into her arms. After a while, his breathing became slow and deep. She pulled a sheet over them both and sank her orgasm-racked body lower into the mattress. Greg's reproachful face floated into her vision. She pushed it away and fell asleep.

Sometime during the night he woke up and began to love her again, sucking on the tender tips of her nipples until she murmured and her eyes slowly opened. She smiled and pushed him back amongst the pillows.

'It's my turn now.'

He relaxed and let her tongue bathe his face. She drank the salt from his closed eyelids and covered his throat with neat nibbling kisses. He was totally under her thrall as she continued to move down his body, nibbling on his tiny shell-like nipples, running her tongue around each jutting pelvic bone. His hands itched to guide her to where he desperately wanted her to go, but she anticipated his thoughts and caught his wrists.

'Close your eyes,' she commanded softly. He could feel exactly where she was and his hips lifted, trying to encourage her touch, but still she held back, feeling his hands bunch into fists of frustration. When he was least expecting it she swept her tongue around his balls.

'Jesus.' He swallowed. 'Oh, sweet Jesus,' as she did it again. She sucked at the tender globes, watching greedily as he grew back into stunningly erect life, his back arching with pleasure. Then he was fully inside her warm moist mouth. He grasped at the pillows and buried his face into them as she continued an endless cycle of pulling, squeezing and sucking.

'Stop!' His ragged cry made her look up. His eyes were heavy with desire, his body moving as if through molasses as he sat up.

'On your knees,' he growled.

'Like this?' She rose up onto all fours, thrusting her shapely backside towards him.

'Just like that.' With a hefty slap on her rump he was inside her, so hard and fast the spittle from her half-open mouth beaded the pillow. Turning her head she could see him biting his lip to stop himself coming, as he continued to brutalise her body, crouched before him, hot and tight and soft.

63

She could not remember the last time she was so turned on. The feel of his balls banging rhythmically against her inner thighs heightened her pleasure to stratospheric levels. In seething, guttural tones she commanded him to fuck her, to do it hard, to make it hurt. When he pulled out of her yet again she punched the pillow, cursing at him. His fingers silenced the stream of desperate obscenity.

'Make them wet.'

She did, and the moist warmth of her lips enclosing his fingers seemed almost too much for him to bear.

'This will hurt a lot less if you relax,' he whispered in her ear.

'Frank, what . . .?' she started as he explored her tight anal hole, the wetness of her saliva sending cold shivers up and outwards as her muscles instinctively contracted.

'I don't know about this,' she continued softly as she felt him kneel behind her and the rude, round tip of his cock nudge against her secret passage. She felt too small for him, sure he would damage her in some way if he continued, but he massaged her bottom with tender hands, holding back with monumental effort. He entered her and slid all the way in as she made hot, desperate sounds of pleasure, pain and panic at the total invasion of her body. His fingertips dug into the soft flesh on her hips as her muscles tightened reflexively around him. His groan was deep and heartfelt.

'Oh, Pagan . . . baby . . . I love you . . .'

'Just . . . be gentle, OK? Very, very . . . God, that's good!'

She had never felt anything like it. She was a horny slut in a pornographic movie, a whore in an alleyway. As he moved slowly inside her there were feelings building she had no idea what to do with. His fingers slid round and toyed with her clitoris and at that moment he could have done anything to her. She came screaming until her punished throat could take no more and she was sobbing, hoarse and faint with mixed emotion. He held her close and when they finally fell asleep again they were curled together like cats.

In the morning Mancini awoke to cold sheets and a note on the pillow in the indentation where her head had been. The note said, simply, 'Goodbye'.

5

When Greg woke the next morning his whole body felt as if it had been put through a mangle and his mouth felt as furry as a small animal. The first thing he did was stumble blindly into the kitchen for water and a double dose of codeine for the headache that was sure to come, before collapsing back on the bed to let the spinning of the room continue.

'Never again,' he said with a groan, but the erection he now had just thinking of what he had done the night before belied his words. His appetite had been whetted. Now he was counting the hours before he could go back for more of the same.

Pagan turned up at his door just before midday, together with a bottle of his favourite port and a true prize, Friday's copy of the *Daily Telegraph*.

'A peace-offering,' she said, smiling tentatively. She peered closer at his bloodshot eyes and pasty complexion. 'You look like shit, Greg. What time did they let you go last night?'

'About one. Coffee?'

'Sure. I'll make it. You sit down.'

'Thanks.' He sank down onto the couch with the newspaper and let her get busy in the kitchen.

She was grateful to be useful, to take her mind off what she had been doing for most of the night before. Before six that morning she had sneaked out of Mancini's giant bed and had breakfasted at a mediocre diner near the Flatiron Building, using espresso to rationalise her actions. Her whole body ached as if she had gone

66

fifteen rounds with Mike Tyson, such were the physical demands he had put upon it. Now she did not know how to look Greg in the eyes when that deep, voluptuous ache of punishing lovemaking still throbbed at the base of her stomach. She had inspected her body in the shower that morning for telltale bites. There was one on her inner thigh, but Greg was hardly going to spot that, she thought wryly.

Greg's voice beside her ear made her jump so suddenly she almost dropped one of his prized bone china mugs.

'I called by to see you last night but you weren't there. Where were you?'

'I went clubbing with some friends from work. I didn't get back to the flat until this morning.' At least the last bit was not a lie, she thought guiltily.

He drew her into his arms. 'Making the most of your last weeks of freedom?'

'Something like that.' Pagan gently pushed him away. 'I've packed my stuff. I'm ready to move out whenever you're up to it. Or we can do it tomorrow. It doesn't matter.'

'Let's do it tomorrow. I'm taking you out to lunch to make up for last night.'

They shucked oysters at the Seaport and washed them down with a light fruity Chardonnay. The weather was fine; Brooklyn bathed in hazy sunshine over the river. It seemed the perfect end to her time in Manhattan, apart from the running battle she was having with her conscience.

That evening they went back to her apartment for the last time. They ate pizza and watched *The Matrix* on pay-per-view TV until Greg fell asleep. She stroked his hair for a while, watching his beautiful face in sleep. His lower lip pouted outwards, giving him an innocence that she found so endearing she just had to kiss him.

She licked the puffy flesh tenderly, making him shift and moan and change his position so he was lying along the sofa. She knelt on the floor beside him to avoid being squashed. As he straightened his legs, still three quarters asleep, she noticed the tent in his trousers. Whatever he was dreaming about, it was obviously erotic. She stroked the plump bulge, feeling it shift and swell. Then his hand came up and removed her fingers.

'You wait, you bad girl,' he murmured, watching her through half-closed eyes.

Pagan sighed. 'It was worth a try. What are you thinking about, anyway?'

'Our wedding night. What else?'

She could think of plenty but she shifted off the couch and went to the bathroom so he would not see the frustration on her face.

She was still in the bathroom when the intercom buzzed. Greg reached it before she did, putting on his modulated Oxbridge voice.

'Who is it, please?'

'Who the hell are you? Oh, the accountant. Is Pagan there?'

Greg bristled visibly at the rudeness of the man's tone. 'Who is this?'

'Just tell her to get down here.'

Pagan instantly recognised the tinnily brusque voice. She hoped the panic did not show on her face.

'It's one of my friends' boyfriends,' she said hurriedly, hating herself for lying. 'They argued last night. I'll go down and sort him out.'

Greg looked doubtful. 'Are you sure you should? He sounds a bit ... rough.'

'He's an arsehole but I can handle it. Keep the sofa warm for me.'

Mancini was waiting for her at the bottom of the

stairs. Immediately he pulled her into the cavity underneath the stairwell.

'I guess your local charm school was closed when you decided to join,' she quipped before he could speak.

'Sorry I've spoilt your nice little evening in. It hurts my pride when a woman walks out on me.'

'It happens often, does it?'

'Tell me you didn't enjoy it and I'll know you're lying.'

'If your dick was as big as your ego I might have done.'

His precarious hold on patience snapped. He slammed her against the grubby wall, his fingers digging viciously into the soft skin on her upper arms.

'You're hurting me!'

He relaxed his grip but only slightly. 'Why are you so angry with me? Don't you realise how I feel about you?'

'So what happened to the last fifteen years? You had all that time and you didn't show your face once. And you ask why I'm angry with you?'

'So you do feel something for me,' he replied softly, studying her face intently.

'I love Greg.' She tried to wriggle out of his grip to no avail.

'No. Something special happened to us last night and I don't want to lose it. Not now.'

'But I don't want you! I don't . . .'

His lips crushed the denial on hers. With his tongue still deep in her throat he shoved his hand rudely up her skirt and into her panties.

'God, you're slick,' he murmured, probing knowingly beyond the small scrap of cotton into her very core. She was smooth and slippery and tightly muscled, drawing him in. He plundered her hot depths, corkscrewing, scissoring, stretching her inner walls until her juices flooded into his hand. His mouth found hers, his tongue demanding and brooking no protest. She pushed against him, alarmingly excited beyond reason by the horny fingers invading her body. He broke the kiss and looked down at her, still finger-fucking her relentlessly.

'You don't want me? Shall I stop now and send you back up to golden boy?'

If she had said yes he was probably cruel enough to call her bluff and do it and, right at that moment, she would have done anything to keep him inside her. Yes, it was wrong and totally crazy, with her future husband upstairs waiting for her, but a ravening need was sweeping like wildfire over her entire being and that betraying inner voice was telling her to take the opportunity before it was too late. Boldly she placed her hand over his cock and squeezed, giving him the answer he needed. After that there was no time for grace. He was as hard as iron and she wanted him, fumbling with greedy fingers at his zip, and then felt turgid bare flesh fall into her hand. He clawed at her panties and as they gave way with an elastic snap he cast them aside. He kicked some rubbish out of the way and lifted her, setting her down on his cock. Her legs locked around his waist, her arms roping around his neck and pulling him to her for another penetrating kiss as he impaled her against the wall. No words were spoken; none were needed as their bodies communicated perfectly, each silently screaming its need.

In the distance she heard Greg tentatively calling her name. She froze but Mancini had no intention of letting her go. His breath came as fast as hers though their mouths were still locked, their only vocal communication grunts of lust sparked by anger and fear. She heard her name again, nearer this time. Greg was taking one step at a time, slowly, peering into the gloom lit only by a single bulb.

'Keep going,' Mancini whispered hoarsely, as if she

had any choice. At any moment Greg would see her being screwed blind, Mancini's slim hand clamped firmly over her mouth to stifle her staccato cries of passion. Relentlessly he hammered her against the wall as her fingers dug into his buttocks, grinding him against her. In the dark, stinking recess they rutted like a couple of cats, Pagan abandoning herself to Mancini's unique brand of sleazy fucking, feeling like a whore, ashamed that she did not want to stop. They came together in a stormy sea of heaving breaths and muffled sighs, barely audible to anyone more than a few feet away but to her they were deafening. She tried to regulate her breathing as he buried his face in her neck, sporadically pumping the last reserves of his orgasm into her shellshocked body.

As Greg's footsteps became louder Mancini gave her one final hard kiss and pushed her out into the light. She stumbled towards Greg, who was standing with his back to her in the doorway, looking up and down the street. Her panties had been left in a tattered scrap on the filthy floor, and now semen was beginning to ooze slowly down her leg. She rubbed her legs together, hoping to stem the viscous flow.

'Hi,' she said casually. 'I was just having a cigarette.' She wiped her mouth, hoping that it did not look too bruised.

Greg turned around. 'Oh, there you are! Is everything all right?'

'Fine! He'd been drinking, that's all. He said he was sorry for being rude.' She led him away from the door, allowing Mancini to slip past them like a shadow into the night. For the first time she noticed that Greg had his jacket with him.

'I think I need to be in bed. Too many late nights recently. You don't mind, do you, darling? You know how it is.'

At any other time she would have urged him to stay, but the trickle of semen was now tickling the back of her knee. She tried to wipe it away with her other knee and could not reach it.

'You go,' she said, wobbling on one leg. 'Try and get some strength back for tomorrow.'

'Thanks, darling. I'll call you tomorrow.' He pressed a quick kiss to her cheek and left her, and for the first time she was actually relieved that he had gone. Wearily she dragged her abused body back up the stairs.

As she reached her door someone fast and silent suddenly slammed her against the wall and put a rapacious hand between her legs. His fingers became soaked with semen and her juices; tiny, wet sounds echoing in the quiet corridor. She tried to squirm free but only succeeded in skewering herself further onto his hand.

'Let me go!'

'Give me one good reason why I should.' Mancini's breath was raspy in her ear and smelt of Chivas Regal.

'Because I want to kiss you, you idiot.'

He turned her around and their mouths locked. He half dragged, half walked her into the apartment and kicked the door shut.

6

The next morning she woke up overblown with sex, internally bruised and alone. She had been woken by a delivery from Dean & DeLuca: hot coffee, orange juice and a golden, freshly baked bagel, exquisitely presented in a white box with the message, 'until next time'. As she was eating the bagel, the roses came. A dozen white buds on long stems, with the words 'you bring out the wolf in me', on the accompanying card. The corniness of it made her laugh with embarrassment. It was so unlike him, but then it dawned on her that she hardly knew him at all. All that day she tried to push him out of her mind but his presence was constantly with her, even in New Jersey, where she was supposed to be starting a new life.

Her new home was a white-iced colonial confection in duck-egg blue, with an imposing front door flanked by four formidable white pillars. A deck wrapped around three sides and on the front was a swing seat from which she could see over the tops of the trees into the valley below. The main road was noticeable only for the cheerful yellow school buses that trundled by. There were no other visible boundaries on the hillside. The six other neighbouring houses were just as large or even larger, in the same Colonial style, painted the soft colours of spring. The sign by the main entrance pronounced CRANFIELD CHASE in curly letters hewn into smooth pale wood. She could have done without the blanketing feeling of a bland executive estate, preferring instead to live on Main Street where there was a bit more life, but Greg had won that argument. It was all such a far cry from snatched espressos on hideously uncomfortable stools, from dark bars with filthy floors and deafening conversation, where the smoke stung her eyes and left her voice hoarse until late the following day. After only one day she already missed Manhattan sorely.

But all weekend she was happy nesting; putting pictures up and adding the finishing touches to their bedroom. Greg disliked the plain Shaker furniture she had chosen, including the four-poster bed swathed in muslin and finished with an antique quilt from a local craft shop. She had gone for simple and romantic as a welcome foil to the chintzy English suburban look Greg had chosen for downstairs. She had done it during the week, before he could protest, and had endured a frosty couple of days as a result. But it would be worth it when he finally realised that he was marrying her, not his mother.

It was strange living with and cooking for someone other than herself, even with the help of the three glossy Delia Smith recipe books Sylvia had so thoughtfully sent as a housewarming present. The message had been clear. There was no excuse for not feeding her son properly.

The remainder of the week was unremarkable and Wolf-free, much to her relief. She worked and went to the gym and tried to avoid Carla, the beautiful but rather annoying woman she had recently met there. Carla was always oddly ambivalent, despite seeking out Pagan's company on a regular basis, but now her interest in the wedding plans and Pagan's relationship with Greg was becoming intrusive. Pagan suspected she was lonely but she had no desire to take on someone else's emotional baggage when she had enough of her own.

With Silverskin's office move as well as a training course she was running in Princeton she had been able to neatly avoid any circumstances where Mancini might catch her on her own. In fact there were times when she had barely given him a thought. It was only in the early hours that he came to her and then he would not get out of her head.

On Friday morning she had her final dress fitting in Manhattan. Afterwards she went to eat lunch in Central Park. The weather was getting warmer so she wore a short black denim skirt from Gap and snug-fitting white DKNY T-shirt. She had slipped off her black nubuck loafers and was sitting curled up on one of the iron seats, eating a smoked turkey and alfalfa sprout pitta wrap, and enjoying an impromptu jamming session between a street saxophonist and a classical cello player. A crowd had gathered, buffeted by others pushing past. Inline skaters and ancient poker players joined the throng. The place was heaving with the usual scene of tourists, dropouts and posers but she sat serenely in the midst of it all, her body occasionally picking up the beat as she licked mayonnaise from her fingers.

When she noticed Frank Mancini walking towards her she immediately untangled her legs, pushed her feet back into her shoes and set off at a fast pace. He grabbed her arm, forcing her to stop and look up at him. His closeness and the charcoal grey suit did not make him look any smaller.

'How did you find me?'

'I followed your scent.'

'Oh please!' She tried to go but he held her fast. They stood on the path, rocks in a fast-moving river of people.

'You've been avoiding me,' he said accusingly.

'I've been working.' She turned to go again but he took her arm and starting leading her the other way.

The Mercedes was parked on the other side of the boundary. The alarm chirped and he opened the door.

'This hostility thing is getting just a little wearing,' he said patiently, shoving her onto the back seat and climbing in after her. The darkened windows hid them from view. In the cocoon of black leather he grabbed her and pulled her onto his lap. His kiss was so hard it drew blood.

'You bit me, you idiot!' she exclaimed, dabbing at her bottom lip.

'Sorry.' She let him kiss her again, tenderly this time, licking the blood away with a pointed tongue. 'Did you enjoy your breakfast last week?'

'And the roses. Thank you. But . . .'

'You would have preferred me to deliver them personally?' Her skin was warm and satin as his hand slid under her skirt. She forced it back down.

'Show some class for God's sake!'

He burst out laughing. 'Christ, you sound just like your mother!'

'She wasn't my mother. She . . . How would you know, anyway? You never met her!'

'I . . . no. Forget it. I just meant . . .' He slapped the palm of his hand against his forehead in irritation. 'Stupid motherfucker!'

It suddenly dawned on Pagan.

'Are you saying you have met her? Don't lie because I'll know.'

'Well, once. I . . .' He groped for words. Swiftly she straddled his lap and forced him to look at her, her warm palms on either side of his face. Her skirt had ridden up and the darkened V between her legs pressing against his groin ensured that all defensive excuses would go flying out of the window. 'Oh shit,' he mumbled, his sleepy, almond-shaped eyes drooping with sudden desire. His nostrils flared at the scent of her warm mound, pressing against a painfully trapped erection. He slipped his hands under her skirt and squeezed her thighs.

'The truth, Mancini. Did you do my stepmother?' She undulated slowly, revelling in the effect she was having on him. She didn't care what his answer was but he did not know that yet, and seeing him suffer was incredibly arousing. The smell of his aftershave, the softly creaking leather and the heft of his cock pushing up against her had revitalised a host of greedy memories of the previous Friday night.

'Did you fuck her?' Her voice was hot and tickly against his ear, her breasts thrusting against his chest. His eyes closed and his head rolled back on the seat, a sibilant hiss whispering between his half-open lips. She pushed closer, dry-fucking him to a frenzy. He felt for her buttocks, bare except for the sliver of cotton thong plunging deep into the crevice between. He cupped the malleable globes and squeezed them together, holding her tight against his body.

'Yes,' he admitted hoarsely. 'I screwed her senseless.'

'When?'

'A few years back. I came to find you but you had gone. The opportunity came up so I took it.' His smile was twisted. 'She wasn't my preference and I wasn't hers, but . . .'

Her kiss was feather soft on his lips, silencing him. She did not want to hear any more. He was such a strange, enigmatic man. Some things were perhaps better left unsaid.

'Good for you,' she whispered and felt for his zip, setting him free. She kissed him again, more hungrily this time, feeling him throb strongly against her. He hooked his finger under her panties and pulled them to one side.

'Sit on me,' he commanded. 'Please.'

'As you said the magic word...' She positioned the tip of his cock against her damp well and sank slowly down, feeling his whole body stiffen and then melt with the pleasure of being inside her. As he filled her she tensed. She had forgotten just how large he was. She squeezed him tentatively, her inner muscles barely able to move, and his answering pulse set off a flood of moisture that finally allowed her to relax and engulf him to the hilt. Her hands snaked above her head, her body moving in a sinuous dance.

'Oh yes, definitely a bespoke fuck,' he murmured, grinning lazily at her.

'Thank you. I presume that was a compliment,' she said wryly, squeezing him again. He sighed contentedly and let her ravish him, his long legs trapped against the front seats. She peeled away her top like the skin off a ripe fruit, showing off her breasts, pressed together by a white satin push-up bra. The straps came away from her shoulders and she rubbed her bare breasts over his face, her breath catching as he lapped hungrily at each bullet-hard dusky nipple. She carefully leaned back until she lay against the central console like a banquet before him. She imagined people walking by within feet of them, some glancing at the Mercedes, maybe wondering what was happening inside it. The speed of passing traffic made the car rock, and sirens and horns were a constant accompaniment to their heated breathing. She felt a deep, vicarious thrill at being able to lie half naked, being stuffed with cock in broad daylight with so many people around them. Her luminous skin glowed against the dense black leather as he licked his finger and stroked her clit, exposed from its hooded protection by the mass of his cock thrusting deep into her body. She sighed sharply and pushed against him, undulating her body as effortlessly as an Egyptian dancer. The pressure on her clit became intense, his fingers acting almost instinctively. She bit her lip to stop herself from screaming as the first strong vibrations hit, giving her a shuddering climax that reverberated deep within her body. As her swollen waves of ecstasy crashed against his deeply embedded flesh he uttered a base animal sound and pulled her to a sitting position again, grinding her against him, their silky pubic hair entangling amidst their clothing.

'Fuck me,' he said through gritted teeth. It became a chant as mindless ecstasy took over. 'Fuck me, fuck me,' until his eyes rolled back and he could no longer speak. She rolled his nipples between her fingers under the fine silk shirt as he spurted, pulsing so hard it rocked her to the core. It tilted her over the edge again and she came just as violently, making the car rock as she slammed down onto him, her hands buried in his hair, guttural cries rising from deep within her throat.

'Jesus,' he hissed as they came back down to earth. She held him close, his head resting on her breasts, and rocked him while he recovered. The leather seats creaked softly, reminding her that they were in the middle of a street surrounded by people. Rather belatedly she hoped he was in a parking zone.

As she shifted his seed began to ooze between her legs, aided by gravity. He handed her a handkerchief from his top pocket. She could smell him on her, the musky scent of Givenchy mingled with the sea-fresh aroma of semen.

'I was going to wait until I got you home,' he said mildly, struggling to rearrange his clothing. She buttoned his shirt.

'And what if I didn't want to come?'

'I'm going to make you come.' He smiled at the play on words, cupping the back of her head in his hand and drawing her close for a deep lascivious kiss. 'Let's go.'

'I can't, Frank. I should get back to work.' But she

sounded unconvincing, even to herself. He kissed her face and throat, small imprints designed to weaken her resolve.

'Please,' he whispered against her skin. 'Let me take you home. This may be the last chance we'll have.'

'Why?' The question came out before she could stop it. He stopped kissing her and looked at her instead, his expression serious.

'Does it matter to you? You're getting married, remember?'

She did, all too clearly, but when she was with him it seemed irrelevant. Staring now into those cold pools of ice she wondered whether what she saw in them was anguish, or whether it was her imagination.

'Are you in some kind of trouble?' she asked.

'Up to my neck,' he murmured, kissing her again to stifle any more questions. He nibbled at her neck, eating away at her will power, his hands weaving their magic over her skin, setting her alight with renewed passion. The blood in her veins began to fizz with fresh electricity. Unbelievably his cock was shifting again, gathering together an undeniable force that gave each kiss an added piquancy. She wanted him more than ever, hearing his pleas, feeling how much his body raged for hers yet again. In no time at all she was kissing him back, the passion behind it giving him the answer he needed.

Greg was very happy when he got the call from Pagan, saying she was out for dinner that night with potential clients. That night he went back to the club, where he had been every free night since first discovering it. As he explored Kiki's sweet wine-tasting mouth and Michelle's slippery pussy they were joined by another woman, the one he had noticed on the first evening sinking margueritas at the bar. She was almost as tall as he and as thin as a line of cocaine in a red-sequined sheath dress, her long black hair in a chic French plait. She had sharp red talons for nails and spiky stilettos. From the barely visible lines around her eyes, he could tell she was older than he but expensively maintained. She handed him another drink.

'I'm Renate. Do you mind if I join you?'

'Feel free,' he replied expansively.

'Thank you.' Renate gave each girl a one-hundred dollar bill and told them to go. They melted away immediately and she sat in Kiki's place. 'They say you're a good customer.'

'I give as good as I get,' Greg said, grinning broadly.

'Is that so? How did you find this place?'

'By accident.' Greg hoped she did not want to just talk. The reason he came here was for the sex, not the stimulating conversation. She seemed to sense it, for her hand dropped lightly onto his leg. She scratched her long nails along the inside of his thigh, making his cock quiver with renewed life.

'I hear you're pretty hot for an Englishman,' she said.

'Well, I do have Negro blood in me, somewhere down the line,' he said jovially, feeling sweat begin to prickle the back of his neck.

'Is that so?' She walked her fingers up the rapidly stiffening lump in his trousers. He uttered a gasp at the light pressure. 'I'd like to see if the reality lives up to the hype, but I don't have much time. Why don't we go to the restrooms?'

He stared at her. She seemed a lot more classy than the other girls and a direct proposition was the last thing he expected. But she was beautiful, even though she was obviously older than he. He fancied having a mature woman, one who could only enhance his level of experience. From under feathered lashes he studied the long white line of her throat, the tiny breasts under the skin-tight dress and the tip of her tongue sliding over slick scarlet lips. His cock was now standing at full attention. He could see it outlined under the fine wool trousers, lying along the crease between pelvis and thigh. His grin became sly.

'You're after a quickie then, you bad little fox.' He tapped the end of her narrowly tapered nose.

'A taster', she corrected him, 'of perhaps something to come?'

'To come, eh?' Greg stood up, taking her hand and helping her to her feet.

One wall was covered in mirrors, the other held a line of five sparkling metal urinals. The spotlights set into the ceiling reflected off the black tiles covering the floor and walls. The ten cubicles were larger than usual to accommodate more than one person in comfort. Greg pushed Renate into one of the cubicles and bolted the door. Renate's skin looked pallid under the artificial lighting, her features harder, her lips a slash of red, but it did not stop him wanting them around his cock. She opened his jacket and rubbed herself against him, undulating her hips against his. He placed his hands on her small tight buttocks and squeezed them hard. They felt like firm grapefruit in his hands, her hipbone rubbing hard against his erection. He pushed her onto the toilet seat, where she sat and looked up at his face, florid with arousal. The dirtiness of what they were doing had him fired up, and the small pouch he was wearing was grossly misshapen by his hard-on, the glans escaping from the top. Renate's eyes widened. It was of average length but as thick and meaty as salami, the great dewy hole at its tip dark and open. Greg braced his legs and pushed it forward at her lips.

'Have a taste then,' he said, his voice rough with desire.

Renate began to pull on his prick with her lips, easing it out between them before gobbling it back in, all the while tweaking her long pointed nipples, now hanging out of the red-sequined dress.

Suddenly hard breathing could be heard next door, then a voice.

'You want to give me some?'

'Fifty dollars,' Renate replied, smiling up at Greg before pulling him into her mouth again. Greg did not know whether to be shocked or even more turned on. A crumpled wad of greenbacks was stuffed through a hole in the cubicle wall. Renate snatched it and stowed it away in her dress, still sucking on Greg. Then there was another scuffling sound. Greg looked down and there, sticking through the hole, was another cock, long and heavy and rigid.

'Suck it,' the owner rasped, pushing against the partition with a soft bang. Renate looked up at the second cock, inches from Greg's own, and her tongue snaked out to lick it. The two cocks jumped and pulsed, vying for her attention, with Greg tapping her on the cheek when she gave too much attention to the other man. Then she was concentrating on him again, sucking him deeply whilst jerking the other, occasionally flickering it with her tongue. The unknown man was practically sobbing with pleasure. As Greg watched, the man's cock stiffened and jerked, then unleashed a long stream of semen over Renate's tongue. The partition shook as the other man hammered against it, grunting loudly as Renate washed him clean with voluptuously long licks.

The cock disappeared and Greg sniffed disdainfully.

'What a lightweight,' he murmured.

Renate looked up at him. 'Oh? You can last a lot longer, can you?'

'A lot longer,' he grinned.

'We'll see.' With her mouth still slick with semen she

drew him in, the added lubrication making him slip further down her throat. He steadied himself with his hands on her shoulders, letting the decadence of what they were doing wash over him. Her lipstick was ruined, her French plait wispy and askew. She had her hands firmly on his buttocks, holding him against her. He had been wrong. He wasn't going to last any time at all with her lipstick smearing against his balls, using the entire surface of her tongue to lap at his cock.

The climax jumped from his balls, knocking her backwards, her mouth still attached to his cock like a leech. He came deep in her throat, holding on to the top of the cubicle as she drank him down. His knees felt weak and his heart pounded wildly with every last throb of pleasure as his hips rocked against her. For now he was sated, allowing Renate to run her lips lovingly over his sagging cock, licking his foreskin clean.

'That was precisely two minutes longer,' she said, glancing at his gold Breitling watch.

'I was overcome by your beauty,' Greg replied breathlessly. He slipped the straps of her dress back onto her shoulders, giving her nipples one final tweak before tucking them away.

'Well, I haven't made up my mind yet,' she mused, stroking his cock. 'But I'll be here on Monday if you want me. So long, lover.' She gave him one last sultry smile and a squeeze and left him to go back to Kiki and Michelle.

When she slipped into the waiting limousine five minutes later, her lipstick and hair were perfect again.

'You took your time,' her husband said tersely.

'You want the job done properly, don't you?' She picked up a small poodle and began to fuss its ears.

'That damned dog is getting hairs everywhere. Well? Do you think he'll do what we want?'

'I think we're going to have to reel him in slowly. I'm meeting him again on Monday. Mommy's going to have a nice evening, isn't she, pet?' She cooed at the poodle.

The man's close-set eyes narrowed. 'What the hell for? We don't have time to fuck around.'

'If you want him to co-operate you're going to have to be nice to him. And that goes for me, too. If I'm going to do your dirty work I might as well get some enjoyment out of it.' She smiled secretively into the poodle's curly head.

Her husband looked sharply at her, as she silently mocked him from behind the small dog.

'Do what you like. You have a week and then we're bringing him in.'

The car drove off smoothly into the night.

7

The following evening Pagan inspected her reflection one final time and decided she had rarely looked better. It was amazing what good sex could do for a girl's looks. Her skin seemed softer, her lips more kissable and her eyes glowed with a knowing spark. She was glad for the boost to her self-confidence. She would be meeting Greg's work colleagues for the first time and did not want to let him down.

Her dress was a slim column of dusky rose velvet, with small sleeves that dropped below her shoulders, leaving them bare. The décolletage was trimmed with simple organza roses and the skirt was split high enough to afford a glimpse of thigh and to enable her to walk. The modest pink diamond Greg had given her as an engagement present nestled between her breasts. She was conscious of her deepened cleavage, but the dress would not have looked right without it. As Greg called her from the living room she remembered her velvet clutch bag, embellished with a silk rose, and smoothed her hair.

'You look nice,' Greg said as she came out of the bathroom.

'Thanks.' She sighed inwardly. Her fiancé had an English literature degree from one of the finest universities in the world, and the only word he could think of was 'nice'.

In the cab her thoughts were with Mancini. He had looked almost stricken when she finally left him the night before, but he refused to tell her what the problem was. She had not pressed him, as he was the sort of man who would only tell her when he was ready. Were they having an affair? No, it wouldn't be an affair until after she was married. Fine, so what would she think if Greg tried to use that argument with her?

A tap on her knee saved her from answering the question.

'We're nearly there. Just remember to . . .'

'Not swear, smile a lot and ask about their kids. Yes, I know.' The street pulled at her attention. Fast-moving people, vivid shop fronts, soaring towers of concrete and marble. She wanted to be out on the sidewalk, walking with the rhythm of the city underneath her feet, not stuck in a herd of sequined, bejewelled bodies.

'Look, you knew you were going to have to do this when you agreed to marry me. It's all part of being in a professional relationship.'

He caught her full attention then. 'I'm sorry, Greg, I thought we were in a loving relationship. If I knew I had to be professional as well I would have negotiated more housekeeping money.'

'I don't think you're taking this seriously enough,' he replied stiffly.

'Serious? I thought these occasions were supposed to be fun?'

'I just need you to make a good impression. The chairman is very keen to meet you.'

'Oh? What is he like?'

'Well . . . he's a strange man. Not very natural on the old charm stakes, but you get used to him. The important thing is to . . .'

'Be nice,' Pagan finished for him. 'Don't worry, I'll be so nice he'll want my babies.'

Greg laughed nervously. 'Steady on, old girl.'

'So does he have any other name? Apart from "The Chairman"?'

'Mason. Richard Mason. Or Sir, if you're lower in the pecking order. He doesn't insist on it, but he's one of those men it seems to apply to naturally.'

She was no longer listening to him. No, it could not happen. Her uncle's name was Richard Mason and he was living in New York. She had never met him, but she knew what he had done to Warners and had written him off as a greedy, calculating bastard. How many other millionaires named Mason were living in New York? She could not explain the sudden sense of foreboding or the tightness in her lower stomach.

'Darling? Did you hear me?'

'Hmmm?'

'I said we should have the Knapps for dinner when we get back from England. They seem like a very nice couple. I understand he's a director for Honeywell Bull.'

Their arrival outside Wolfen's offices stalled her response. The early spring air was cool on her skin before they were ushered into the echoing marble hallway, strangely empty except for a single security guard surrounded by television cameras.

Fifty-one floors up in Wolfen's conference hall the party was already lively. Champagne flutes were pressed into their hands almost as soon as they shed their coats. Her cream cashmere looked limp next to the abundance of mink and white sable. As they walked through the throng the pianist playing Gershwin on a grand piano was almost drowned out by high-powered small-talk.

Greg steered her further into the fray with a firm hand on the small of her back as a smallish man worked his way towards them, beaming widely. Somehow she knew that this was not Richard Mason.

Greg introduced him as Michael Prosser, Wolfen's chief executive. Michael held out his hand. Whippet slender and carrying his tuxedo with grace, he had bright bird eyes and a comforting handshake. He reminded her of someone. As Greg introduced them she groped for it. Fred Astaire. She prepared to be very nice.

A vision in hot pink floated towards them: enough diamonds to sink the *Titanic*, coupled with scarlet lipstick and a frosted bouffant. Bette Davies put through a blender and served up on vanilla ice cream. She was introduced as Rachel, Michael's wife. Rachel sparkled at Pagan with a small country's worth of good dental surgery and curled a clawlike hand around her arm to drag her away for more introductions.

Starched waiters proffered silver platters loaded with exquisite delicacies. Oysters in the half shell, dainty parcels of salmon mousse wrapped in smoked salmon and served on circles of rye bread, and caviar nestling on mini blinis. Pagan ate the food but hardly tasted it. By now she was convinced that she was standing in the midst of her uncle's empire and that Greg was a part of it. She had not before made the link between WEC, the holding corporation named on the legal documents she had seen after her father's death, and Wolfen, who employed Greg. Wolfen: the name made her shudder in the heat created by all the bodies engaged in top-flight back slapping. Suddenly she wanted to run and not face the other horrible truth that was beginning to dawn.

But there was no escape. Greg and Michael had found them again.

'When is Richard going to make his speech? My feet are killing me.' Rachel eased her foot out of a spiky-heeled stiletto and waggled her scarlet-painted toes.

'Soon. He's been waylaid again.' Michael craned his neck to see a tall man standing on the other side of the room with his back to them.

'Well, tell him to hurry up. These things are giving me bunions.' Rachel eased her foot back into the punishingly tight space and hobbled away in the direction of the bathrooms. Michael went to retrieve the man from his companions.

Greg smiled professionally as he returned and murmured at Pagan to do the same. Pagan did not hear him. Frank Mancini was walking towards them, a solid and towering presence overshadowing Greg's shining beauty. He held a crystal glass in long, well-manicured fingers, the only man in the room not in a tuxedo but a black three-piece suit. With it he wore a white silk shirt, open at the neck, and solid gold bar cufflinks. No tie. His glossy black hair was dead straight and curved gently to the nape of his neck. The perfect icon of corporate menace.

'Hello, Pagan,' he said.

She looked at him.

'Hello ... Richard.'

Greg was smiling inanely, totally oblivious to how ruthlessly he had been used.

Michael glanced at his watch. 'Five minutes, Richard. It's speech time.'

'I'll be there.'

Michael disappeared, leaving the three of them alone.

'Pagan, this is Dick Mason. Chairman of Wolfen Enterprises,' Greg prompted her.

Pagan was unable to respond immediately. Her mind was too full of memories of the previous night, when she had left him after lovemaking so intense her back still ached.

'Dick?' she said incredulously, fighting a sudden urge to laugh. Taking a deep breath she quelled the rising hysteria and held out her hand.

'Pagan. Such a beautiful name.' He raised her hand to his lips, brushing the cold skin gently. It took all her willpower not to snatch it away. Aware that Greg was watching her closely, she struggled for her standard opening line.

'Greg has told me so much about you,' she said crisply.

Richard handed Greg the empty glass. 'Get me another one of those, Roscoe. I need it before I address the masses.' As Greg went running, Richard moved closer to Pagan's side. 'You look absolutely stunning. Half the men in this room want to fuck you, including me.'

'I don't believe this! What kind of man are you?'

'I told you I was in trouble,' he said mildly.

'You think it's funny?' So many questions, so little time, and never before had she wanted to hit a man so hard.

'No I don't. It's probably the worst thing that's ever happened to me.' He guided her to a spot where there were few people and leaned comfortably against the wall, lighting a Havana. 'If you walk away now, people will know there's something going on.'

She was just about to do just that. Instead she sat down and stared out of the window to the sparkling buildings across the town.

'Are they talking already, then?'

'Probably. Now you're refusing to look at me. If I were watching that scenario it would seem obvious that we were sharing something so intimate it excluded everyone else. That's fine with me, but you might want to continue the devoted fiancée act. For the time being.'

She could see his point. She stood up again and pasted a bland expression on her face. Even so, they seemed to be surrounded by some invisible force field that prevented others from going anywhere near them.

'So, what do I call you? Frank? Richard?' She paused delicately. 'Dick?'

'Richard will do. It's Roscoe who insists on calling me Dick.'

'Seems he's more perceptive than I give him credit for.'

He grinned savagely. 'I love it when you're mean to me.' He moved even closer. 'In fact, the more you insult me, the more it turns me on.'

Miraculously Greg returned with the replenished glass. Richard raised it in a silent toast and left them. A moment later the room was quiet and the presentations for long service began.

Watching him in his real-life role was surreal. She had labelled Frank Mancini a slick, wheeler-dealing type but not like this; not a multi-millionaire presiding over a respected statewide corporation. Yet it wasn't as if he had not given her enough clues. Mentally she kicked herself for not seeing them earlier.

He let Michael have the main word on performance throughout the year and the welcoming of new employees, and it was clear who was more popular. Richard was obviously respected but arrogant enough to be kept at arms length by just about everybody. As he spoke he seemed to be seeking her out. And when their eyes met he paused, as if losing the train of his thoughts. Then he seemed visibly strengthened by her presence. The remainder of his speech was fluid and a good deal warmer than when it had started.

After an age the music struck up again and people filtered onto the dance floor. For a while Pagan sat with Greg, who was deep in conversation about the next month's marketing conference in San Diego with the marketing director. Bored and knowing she should be mingling, she chose instead to watch Michael and Rachel. They were executing a salsa borne of years of practice on ocean cruises, Rachel's pink sequins shimmering in the soft light. Pagan could not see Richard, but as the tempo of the music slowed he tapped her on the shoulder.

'A woman as beautiful as you should be dancing.'

He pulled her to her feet before she had time to think of a good excuse and led her to the dance floor. He had taken his jacket off and the white silk shirt against his translucent skin and jet black hair gave him an exotic magnetism unmatched by any other man in the room.

'Thanks very much! You've had fifteen years to tell me we're related but you choose to let me find out like this!' she whispered fiercely as he pulled her close.

'Why are you so angry? You said yourself that unless I was an underworld kingpin you didn't give a shit.'

'Yes, but that doesn't include sleeping with my own family! All you wanted to do was bed me again before I found out the truth!'

'Partly that, yes. And partly because I wanted to give you the chance to fall in love with me.'

'Thank you. Sorry to say you wasted your time,' she replied acidly.

He held her tight enough so she would have to struggle noticeably to get away from him. Their bodies began to move with a liquid unity that dismissed everyone else in the room. Maybe someone would rescue her, but the chance of anyone cutting in was remote when she was dancing with the chairman of the board. She shuddered at the memory of that first night, a week and a lifetime ago. He pressed his body intimately against hers, making her painfully aware that he was getting harder by the second.

'OK, shut up and listen,' he murmured. 'I found you the first time because I wanted to get back at Arthur for treating me like shit. I was going to rape you, make you pregnant, do anything to cause him grief, but when I met you I couldn't do it, because I stupidly went and fell in love with you, all in one afternoon.

'I tried to forget you. Even when you came to Manhattan I kept away. Then I found out you were marrying the biggest prick in the city and I had to act before it was too late.'

'But why employ Greg?'

'I wanted to keep an eye on him. After all, you're my niece and I have a very well-developed sense of justice when it comes to family.' She felt his hand pressing against the small of her back, dangerously close to her buttocks, and the movement of his hips matched her own. His erection was now an omnipotent presence between them. She tried to digest all he had said but two small facts kept getting in the way. *He's your uncle and you slept with him.*

'Why don't you go into the toilet and jack off before someone mistakes you for a real pervert?' she muttered.

'Keep that up and I'll fuck you right here.'

'Doesn't the fact that we're related mean anything to you?'

'On the contrary, it means everything. All these years I've been trying to cure myself of you. Don't make the same mistake and waste even more time.' He turned her, letting her float away from him before pulling her inexorably back. 'Let me take you somewhere quiet,' he whispered, his fingers drawing small circles on her back. 'You're so beautiful I want to lay you down right here and worship your cunt. Can you feel it, Pagan?'

'Go to hell,' she hissed. Even so, she could not help staring at him. The dark vulnerability echoing behind his cold blue eyes was plain to see. For a crazy split second she wanted to tell him that she understood but she closed her eyes, blocking him out, willing herself to feel disgusted at the deceiving monster he had just become. The length of his cock pushed so hard against her lower belly that it ached voluptuously, echoing that feeling she had after he had first taken her. Why was life so complicated?

The featherlight brushing of lips against hers opened

her eyes again. For a moment she was confused enough to open her mouth under his and feel his tongue sneaking slyly between her lips and slide against her own. Her thumb stroked the tender skin beneath his ear, her other hand on his lower back, unconsciously pressing him closer to her.

As he uttered a deep groan of need she realised that she was in the middle of a dance floor, casually snogging the big boss whilst surrounded by Greg's work colleagues. She drew violently away but was still trapped within the circle of his arms.

'I guess that answers my question,' he said, backing away from her and kissing her hand. He seemed to shimmer with barely restrained emotion as he led her back to Greg.

In the bathroom he lit a cigarette with shaking fingers, willing himself to get a grip. Her velvet kiss had assaulted him with a need so fierce it hurt, but he would not do the obvious thing and jack off into the toilet. That would mean she had defeated him. He caught the crazed sparkle in his eye and laughed self-consciously at himself in the mirror. How many other middle-aged men could get it up faster than a teenage quarterback?

'You old alley cat,' he murmured to his reflection. 'I bet you've got more juice than Gregory Roscoe.'

As he reached the door it opened and Michael Prosser walked in. After a lightning check to see that they were alone, Michael practically dragged Richard back into the bathroom. He seemed about to lose his customary tranquillity.

'What the hell did you think you were playing at out there? I know how you feel about this woman but try to be a bit more discreet about it!'

'Thank you, Michael. You've made your point.' Richard

strode towards the door again but the smaller man stopped him.

'What about Greg? Like it or not, he's a brilliant finance man and if we don't come good on the promises we made in his interview he could sue us for breach of contract! Unlike you I believed in the things I was telling him. What do you think he's going to do when he finds out why he's really here?'

Richard gestured impatiently with the cigarette. 'Wolfen won't even come into it. He'll get a private settlement from me somewhere in the region of ten million dollars. I'll set him up with another position anywhere but the US and I'll buy him a house as big as the Ritz if that is what he needs. In return he will sign a contract agreeing not to contact Pagan or cause any adverse publicity that could damage us. Where's the issue in that?'

'That's the insanest thing I've ever heard, even coming from you!'

Richard glanced at his watch. 'This conversation is useful but right now I need to say goodbye to our employees.' His tone turned to granite. 'Just remember where your loyalties lie, Michael.'

'My loyalties lie with Wolfen. Where are yours?'

A cold, glassy stare told Michael he had hit home. Richard walked out without replying. Michael watched him go. He could see a huge mess rearing up on the horizon, with him standing in its path without a shovel.

Within half an hour the crowd had thinned, leaving only a hardcore of senior executives clustered around three rapidly emptying bottles of vintage ruby port. Greg was in the thick of it, his cheeks ruddy, his laugh as hard as the next man's. Their women made tight-lipped, polite conversation. Only a few of them knew each other and they were the bright, chatty ones, swapping news on the latest Prada shoe collection. The remainder floated on the lonely periphery, waiting for their men.

Pagan had found herself in the first group, dragged there by those glossy-haired, sharp-taloned vultures curious to know how she had managed to seduce Richard so effectively that evening. She had sidestepped the delicately veiled questions and had now been tacitly cast aside as one by one they realised she was not going to feed them any scraps of gossip, however meagre.

As the attendant searched for Pagan's wrap, Greg thanked Richard for the use of the limousine to take them back to New Jersey. Richard kissed her hand and did not let it go.

'By the way, I'm in Jersey on Monday morning, inspecting the depots. I'd like to talk to you about your company's services. I take it you'll be at home? Around eleven?'

'I'll be in meetings all day. Why don't you let my sales director call you instead first thing?' She extracted her hand with some difficulty.

'I'm not interested in sales patter, I want it straight from someone who really knows what they're talking about. I presume that means you?' He arched one sleek eyebrow. Her hands twitched, wanting to hit him. Greg was giving her a pointed look. *Don't let me down*, it said.

'Then I'm sure my morning can be rearranged. Eleven will be fine.' She said it through clenched teeth.

'I look forward to it.' He winked lasciviously as he left.

8

The roses arrived as they were eating lunch the next day; twenty-four of them, the vivid red of arterial blood. There was a note, saying, 'a true pagan is beyond price.' Holding the flowers and the small card Pagan could sense the unsaid words lingering between them.

Greg didn't mention Richard again until that night as they were getting ready for bed.

'So how does it feel when the big boss fancies you?' he asked casually as he buttoned his pyjama bottoms firmly around his trim waist.

'Overrated,' she retorted grumpily. The previous night had been sleepless. Even now she could still feel the imprint of Richard's arousal against her thigh. It was not meant to be, but she had wanted him nonetheless. She dreaded how she would feel the next day when he was actually in the house.

'Oh, come on, he's besotted with you! People couldn't believe it. He's never danced with anyone before and suddenly he's all over you like a bad rash! I know what will be the main subject of conversation tomorrow, anyway. Especially if they find out he's with you, discussing software!'

She was appalled at Greg's avid expression. 'Don't look so bloody pleased about it!'

'It's not going to do us any harm, is it?'

'Oh Greg, please! Next you'll be wanting me to sleep with him to get you a promotion!'

He nuzzled her neck. 'That may not be such a bad idea.'

'It's a lousy idea.' She turned the light out and listened to his steady breathing for a while, trying not to compare his smell and feel with that of Frank, or Richard as he now was. Actually his new identity suited him better than his old one. Or was it the other way around? Either way, she was secretly relieved that Frank wasn't his real name.

She felt for Greg's penis to give it a goodnight squeeze.

'Oh my god! What's this?' she exclaimed softly, when she felt the firm plumpness under the thin cotton.

'Just the thought of you being rogered by the boss.' Greg stretched out and closed his eyes, his long lashes feathering against each rose-tinted cheekbone. He looked almost adolescent with his boyish dimples and full-lipped mouth that could turn sulky as rapidly as it smiled. Now he was looking at her with an uncharacteristic dark, sleepy sensuality.

'You like that idea then?'

'Very much.' He stroked her back as she fondled his balls. His cock quivered under his pyjamas. He did not protest as she unbuttoned him and began to pull the tender foreskin over his shaft, back and forth, very slowly. 'Tell me how it would happen,' he implored.

She sighed. The irony was almost too much but perhaps a shared fantasy would ultimately bring her and Greg closer together. And maybe then she would stop thinking hungrily about the real thing.

'OK, imagine we're standing in his office. I'm wearing a white shirt and black leather miniskirt, with sheer black stockings and high heels.' It was hardly original but it seemed to have the desired effect, by the way he was moaning. 'You've asked him for a raise, but in return he wants to fuck me. He tells me to lift my skirt, which I do, slowly, reluctantly, hating both of you for making me do it. As the skirt reveals my black satin panties he runs his hands over my trembling thighs. He can smell me, like a dog with a bitch.' She paused, realising that the scenario was actually turning her on. She pressed her whole body closer to Greg's and scattered small kisses on his neck.

'Go on,' Greg said raggedly.

'He slides his hand into my panties,' she continued in a lascivious whisper, 'but instead of being dry and unreceptive I'm moist, sticky, because I already know how huge his cock is. I've already sucked it once, in a board meeting the week before where no one could guess that the blank expression on his face was anything other than sheer boredom.'

'Do it on the boardroom table,' he muttered, thrusting harder into her hand. 'I'll watch you.'

'He pushes me over the table. It's so highly polished that I can see the untamed lust on his face. He wrenches my skirt up to my waist and tears away my panties. My stockings rip in his desperation to get at me. I'm slithering around on the table, trying to get away, but he holds me down. I'm swearing at him, telling him to stop, but he doesn't. He forces his cock into me, bang up to the hilt, and starts fucking me, so deep and so hard that I can't help but enjoy it, my pussy juice smearing the table. Then he tells me to suck your cock as well, so you come closer and push your cock into my mouth. Together you fuck me from both ends, two wealthy businessmen, still fully clothed, abusing my lusciously exposed body.' She was losing herself in the image, her clitoris tingling, the sensation of having someone deep inside her almost palpable. Greg was moaning louder, arching against her hand.

'He starts to spank my naked backside, slapping me hard enough to make me protest but I can't. My mouth is too full of your cock. It's so hard, choking me, but I don't care. Having both of you losing yourself in me is the ultimate fantasy. I'm coming as you and Richard compete with each other for the final shoot . . .'

'Oh, God!' Greg jolted suddenly, white heat exploding from his cock. Semen landed between her breasts, great thick gouts of it. His body jerked spasmodically, gradually calming down until he heaved a sigh and closed his eyes, nestling into the pillows without so much as a thank you. Pagan wiped the stickiness from her chest and his stomach with a Kleenex and prodded him. No response.

'You're such a prick, Greg,' she muttered, unheard.

At eleven thirty on Monday morning Richard was waiting outside her front door. She had deliberately returned late from a meeting in the Parsippany office to find him leaning against a long Mercedes the colour of champagne, smoking and taking in the cool late spring air. The car had spiked hubcaps and a British number plate with bold black lettering on a white background, proclaiming 'RAM 101'. Not an ounce of discretion.

As she climbed out of her nippy red Mustang he threw his cigarette butt on the ground and crushed it with his foot. He shrugged the camel overcoat closer around his body.

'It's about time. I'm fucking freezing out here.'

'You could have sat in the car,' she said reasonably.

'And not give the neighbours something to talk about? Nice suit, by the way,' he added, admiring the snug dark-green wool skirt and matching short fitted jacket with brushed brass buttons.

'Nice car,' she countered. 'What happened to the other one?'

'I'm too tall for it, so I gave it to Eleanor. It was her birthday last week.'

'I guess she needs some incentive to work for you.' She remembered Eleanor as a dignified but permanently weary-looking woman at the party. Richard deigned not to answer. He followed her up the wooden stairs into the house. The lining of her skirt rustled alluringly as she walked.

'Shoes off. New carpet,' she said succinctly. He did as he was told, pulling off his socks as well and slinging the heavy coat over the pine banister. Wandering into the living-room he cast a disparaging look at the plump floral sofas and sumptuous jacquard drapes, stopping at a yew corner cabinet filled with porcelain Japanese dancing girls. He raised a sardonic eyebrow at Pagan.

'They're Greg's. He collects them,' she said defensively.

'Glad to see he doesn't let taste get in the way of a good investment.' Richard continued his critical assessment of the room. She followed him into the primrose yellow kitchen, dominated by a long pine table displaying his roses in a white Italian vase. He nodded his approval at the uncluttered New England styling and the two Warren Kimble prints of old-fashioned schoolhouses.

'This is much more you,' he commented.

'I don't want to hear it.' Pagan marched towards the coffee machine and began to fiddle uselessly with it. Greg had moved the filters again. When she turned around, Richard had gone.

She found him upstairs in the master bedroom, sitting on the four-poster bed, her silver silk chemise tumbling through his hands.

'You have a real knack for design,' he said, looking around the light, airy room.

'Out.' She cocked her thumb towards the door. He left the chemise on the bed and followed her as the phone began to ring.

She answered it in her office. It was one of her clients with a software problem. She smoothly took them through it, perching on the desk, swinging one small foot. On the phone her curt manner had gone and she was friendly and reassuring and patient. Richard slunk over to the desk and sat in her chair. She kicked him away when his hand whispered over her nylon-clad knee. He caught her foot and stroked it, edging her legs further apart. She swatted him away like an annoying fly and began to unzip her boots, slowly so the caller would not wonder what she was doing. She was also well aware of what the action was doing to Richard, as he watched her calf appear out of the black leather. She handed the first boot to him and he waited for the other, a tense, expectant expression on his lean, pale face. He took it and zipped them up again, manipulating the soft leather still warm from her skin. She covered the mouthpiece with her hand.

'Make yourself useful and do the coffee.'

The speed with which he moved was gratifying. She smiled to herself as he saluted her at the door before disappearing.

As she put the phone down it rang again. It was Roberto Sanchez, work colleague and former lover. She and Roberto talked for nearly half an hour whilst Richard brought in vanilla-scented coffee and the cinnamon cookies she had baked the day before. He simmered in the background, refusing to remove himself from the light-hearted, flirtatious conversation, watching her relax back in her chair, scratching an imaginary itch on her stomach, affording him a glimpse of milky skin. After she closed the call, promising to see Roberto in a couple of days, she became instantly businesslike again, ignoring his potent stare.

'OK, you're looking for a new booking system for Wolfen, is that right? It's probably best if you give me some idea what your requirements are. We . . .'

'Who was that? Your other lover?'

Pagan ignored him. 'As I was saying, we've designed

software for several blue chip companies in Manhattan, including Merck, Ryder and . . .'

'Have you fucked him on the marital bed yet, Pagan? Two days ago you would have been only too happy to do it with me.'

'Look, if you're not interested in talking shop you'd better leave right now. I'm too busy to waste time in pointless conversations about something that's no longer relevant.' She tried to keep her voice steady.

'It isn't? Then let's talk shop. Tell me exactly what you can do for me. These cookies need more cinnamon by the way. You should never be apologetic about adding spice, especially to your life. But it seems you already know that.'

They stared each other down. Pagan cleared her throat and redundantly shuffled papers.

'What we offer is the opportunity to streamline your current booking system, making it more user friendly and less susceptible to failure. Depending on the complexity of the system, we could have you up and running within three months. We offer full training . . .'

'I like the boots. In fact I'd like to fuck you in them.' He picked one up and caressed the supple black leather before holding it out to her. 'How about right now?'

'OK, that's it. You're leaving.' She moved past him to get to the door. 'Time to go, Uncle Dick.'

He spun her around and thrust her up against the wall, easily holding her there with one arm under her breasts. She dangled uselessly, face to face with his incandescent fury. The speed with which his mood had changed took her breath away.

'Don't *ever* call me that again! If you want to fuck with me, I'll fuck with you. Like this.' He shoved his spare hand up her skirt, clamped it over her satin-clad pubis and squeezed it cruelly. 'And like this.' His mouth came down hard on hers, forcing it open, his tongue burying itself deep into her throat, choking her. She could smell the lust on him, taste it on his hot breath and feel it in the hard thrusting of his tongue. It was all she could do not to respond but she knew that if she did, there would be no stopping him. Endless seconds later he broke the kiss, dropping her and wiping the traces of her lipstick from his mouth. He was breathing hard, his pale skin flushed with anger and arousal. She dared not move as he stormed down the stairs and slammed the door. When she heard the loud spin of wheels on gravel she peeled herself from the wall and went to repair her make-up, feeling very shaken.

When Greg arrived home that night the first thing he asked was how the meeting went. She dismissed it as nothing, although Richard's raw emotion still disturbed her deeply. She tried to tempt Greg instead with duck à l'orange, followed by chocolate mousse, bringing in his port and cheese wearing only a deep burgundy corset top and matching panties that she had bought that afternoon at Victoria's Secret. He laughed, saying it was a nice try but it wasn't going to work.

'Why not? This is driving me nuts, Greg. It's the twenty-first century and we're already living together. Our wedding is a formality, that's all. A good excuse for a party.'

'I doubt if my mother would see it quite like that. You seemed happy enough a few months ago. What's got into you now? It's only four more weeks and you've turned into some kind of nymphomaniac.'

'Some men wouldn't see that as a problem,' she replied dryly.

'Well I do. Doing all this –' he motioned to her sensual underwear '– and begging for sex all the time is just a bit common, isn't it? I thought you were better than that.'

She felt stung but also knew he had a point. She had been trying to reaffirm her intimacy with Greg as a way of exorcising the Wolf but had obviously been heavy-handed in doing it. She went upstairs for a long bath and slunk back down again in a floor-length flannel robe. Greg patted her knee approvingly.

'Cheer up, old girl. It's only a month until the wedding. I'll make us a cup of tea.'

Early next morning he dropped his bombshell.

'I'm moving back to Manhattan during the week,' he said casually as she made the coffee for breakfast.

'What! When?'

'Tonight, actually. Richard suggested it and I have to say I agree with him. Wolfen have a place on 44th Street. It's not big but it's better than a hotel room.'

'But we'll never see each other!' Which was the plan, of course. It was Richard's vindictive act of sabotage to punish her for her jibe the day before.

'Of course we will! I'll be home on Friday nights and I'll drive back on Monday morning, or Sunday night if work is heavy. I'm always on business trips anyway so it's hardly going to make any difference at all.'

'But we bought this house so that you could commute! That was the whole point!'

Greg hid behind the *New York Times* and did not respond.

'Did you hear me?' she demanded.

'I should think everyone in the Chase could hear you,' he said calmly. 'There's no point getting ratty with me. If the boss suggests something what he really means is go and do it. Frankly it doesn't bother me. Four hours commute a day is not my idea of fun. And before you say it, no I didn't realise what a pain it would be before we chose the house.'

'You chose the house,' she corrected him. 'Maybe next

time Richard Mason makes another of his *suggestions*, I *suggest* you consult me before you make a decision. OK?'

His deep-chocolate eyes looked so wounded that she wanted to cry. She gave him a warm hug, which he responded to stiffly.

'I'm sorry,' she said. 'Put it down to pre-wedding nerves.'

'There's nothing to be nervous about, so just calm down.' He kissed her briefly. 'I'll see you at the weekend.'

After he left she scrambled for Richard's business card and the phone. He was unavailable so she left a blistering message on his voicemail.

He called back just before midnight.

'Have you calmed down now?'

'If one more person tells me to calm down I'll chop their bloody balls off! How dare you try to take him away from me like this!'

'It isn't me. He's doing the job quite adequately by himself. If you want some company you know where I am.'

'Go fuck yourself,' she said coldly and slammed the phone down.

9

Richard did not contact Pagan for over a week, presumably to let her stew in her own anger and frustration. If that was the case it was working, although she did not try to seduce Greg over the weekend. His comments still hurt and she did not feel strong enough to cope with another emotional battering.

On Wednesday morning she had an excitable conversation with her boss in Parsippany, who informed her that Pagan and Roberto had been summonsed to Manhattan for a meeting with the chairman of Wolfen Enterprises. Why had she not told him that this was about to happen?

She said honestly that she did not know but secretly wondered whether Richard knew that Silverskin were struggling. What would the business proposal be? Sleep with him and he'd save the company?

'Just do what you can to close that deal,' Clive said breathlessly. 'The one thing we need right now is a heavyweight contract.'

Pagan was angry with Richard for involving them in his games. She had been with Silverskin for over five years and had seen many of its highs and lows. This was a definite low period, with increasing competition from more aggressive software houses. At the moment their existing clients with ongoing maintenance contracts were keeping them above water but they desperately needed more high-profile business.

'Tell me about it,' she sighed. 'But shouldn't one of

the sales guys go with Rob? I'll only be useful after the thing is installed, if it ever gets that far.'

'Sorry, Pagan, he was very specific. You and Rob. You've met major clients before so what's the problem?'

'When does he want us?'

'Tomorrow. Five o'clock sharp.'

The same afternoon Richard found Greg by the water machine and informed him they would be going to his club that night for a drink. There had been no question of refusal.

An hour later they walked out of the office together. Richard's stark monochrome looks contrasted sharply with Greg's honey-gold healthiness. Greg's voice had the subtle richness of mellow coffee compared with Richard's jagged New York twang. As Greg checked his reflection in the lift mirror he noticed the attention they were getting from the two very attractive female occupants. He grinned at the women and fluffed himself up to his full height.

'As I was saying, there's a definite window of opportunity in the motorcycle courier market, not only in the city but all over the tri-state area. Even beyond. Your reputation alone should ensure a solid client base before we even hit the ground with it.'

Richard stalled him with one freshly manicured hand. 'I hear you, but there are two things you may not have grasped yet, Roscoe. One, don't try to suck my dick. And two, I keep this company as tight as a virgin's cunt. Bear that in mind if you want your ass on the Board.'

The women looked offended. Greg grimaced an apology at them.

'Is there a problem?' Richard was watching him with a glacial stare.

'No! Not at all. I hear you.' Greg fell silent, feeling humiliated.

The lift door pinged softly and opened. Richard pushed through first, deaf to the barbed comments from the women. Greg had to practically scamper to keep up with him. Their footsteps rang in the cavernous marble hallway. Outside Thomas was waiting with the limousine door open. Richard rarely socialised with anybody, so Greg was very aware of how privileged he was. It also made him wonder if Richard had a hidden agenda.

'Don't expect anything fancy. It's the Lower East Side,' Richard said as the car began to move.

Greg stared out at the dark, increasingly rundown streets. 'But why here? You could afford somewhere a little more salubrious than this, surely?'

'I started Wolfen around here. This is my backyard. It isn't pretty but it's been good to me. The club is my way of giving something back.'

The long white car pulled up outside an unassuming doorway, underneath an unbossy neon sign proclaiming THE BAR WITH NO NAME. A thug built like a sofa guarded the entrance. He was Benny, Richard's personal minder.

The crowd parted like the Red Sea as Richard walked through, exchanging curt nods with some of the clientele. The barman was busy serving behind a highly polished granite counter and clusters of men hung around two pool tables. Others propped up the bar. There were relatively few women and those looked like hookers, with tight skirts, long nails and low-cut blouses. Like the men they were smoking, drinking hard liquor and looking around with sharp eyes for the next conquest. They all stared at Greg, who felt out of place and uncomfortable. He was glad when they reached the door and he was ushered up red-carpeted stairs towards a room furnished in the kind of unfussy luxury he had been expecting.

A long plum-red leather sofa and glass table ran

along one wall below three black and white photographs of Manhattan in slim silver frames. A tall black ash cabinet held Richard's personal liquor store and an extensive collection of hardcore videos. Benny appeared with a full bottle of Jim Beam and two tumblers. He set them reverently down on the glass table and melted away. Greg settled uneasily on one end of the sofa, again wondering why he was here. In the end he asked.

Richard assessed him as he sat at the other end of the sofa. 'You're the best. Harrow, Oxford, Waterhouse. That's some pedigree. Everyone knows the best accounting people come from the UK. But I didn't ask you here to talk shop.' He pushed a leather humidor across the table towards Greg.

Greg looked at the ten-inch cigars with horror. He didn't have a clue what to do.

'No, thanks. I don't smoke.'

'I won't hold it against you.' Richard went through the ritual at a leisurely pace, sighing as the rich smoke hit his lungs. He kicked off his shoes and propped his bare feet up on the table. Greg could not help noticing his ankles, which were as finely boned and slender as a woman's, and his toes, long and prehensile, the second toe on each foot longer than the big toe. Wasn't there some theory about that?

He tore his attention away from Richard's feet and stared at the wall opposite, which was dominated by a large panel of television screens. There were ten in all, a constantly moving mural of silent black and white shadows, all showing the same pornographic movie. He could not see the couple's faces, but she was as small and shapely as her companion was tall and broad. The camera lovingly focused on her nipples as her man tongue-teased each one, moving slowly down her curvaceous body to her moist, furry mound. Greg gulped and ran a finger around his collar as the man began to perform expert cunnilingus on his partner, his fingers digging deep into her flesh to stop her squirming.

Richard enjoyed Greg's wide-eyed expression for a few moments.

'It beats CNN, doesn't it?' He replenished Greg's glass and handed it to him. 'I bet it gets lonely during the week without that woman of yours. I mean, your dick doesn't just get hard at weekends, right?' He was looking at Greg in a strange way, intense and narrow.

'I'm too busy to think about it,' Greg replied hurriedly.

'Oh, come on, Roscoe. You're a red-blooded male, just like me, I assume? Haven't you ever been tempted to stray?'

Greg gave an embarrassed bray of laughter. 'You've met Pagan. She'd eat me alive.'

'Maybe that's what you want.' Their eyes met. Greg scratched his neck, then his ear, looking back at the screens and flinching away.

'So tell me, is she good in bed?'

Greg laughed nervously, pushing a hand through his hair.

'Don't be shy. Isn't this what men talk about away from their women? Compare notes? That kind of thing?' He refilled Greg's glass again and relaxed back in the chair. 'I have to say I find her intensely stimulating. Does she satisfy you? Does she have any deviant desires?'

'Deviant desires? Good heavens!' Then he remembered how Pagan had actively incited him to fantasise about her and Richard. Since then his head had been filled with any number of erotic possibilities. He shivered, knowing he would never get an opportunity as good as this one again. He chose his next words carefully. 'I think she may be interested in having someone else while I watch, but she hasn't said so in so many words.'

'Really? Would she go for it if you gave her the opportunity?'

Greg ran his fingers nervously through his hair. 'You know women. Say one thing and mean another. I guess it would depend on who the other person was and how much he was prepared to pay me.' He laughed lightly.

'How much would you take?' Richard blew an ethereal smoke ring, sounding casually interested.

Mentally Greg calculated. 'I don't really know. It's a big deal, letting someone else roger your girlfriend. I think the going rate is still a million, isn't it?' He grinned at his own wit, but Richard did not smile.

'Roger? And I thought English was the language of kings.' Richard tapped ash into a crystal bowl and drew on the cigar again.

'Well ... I can't think of anyone who would be interested anyway. It's a fantasy, that's all.'

Richard leaned forward in his chair, watching him with narrowed eyes. 'I would.'

Greg's heart lurched sickeningly. He ran his fingers nervously through his hair again. 'Crikey,' he murmured, 'I don't know what to say.'

'She's a very attractive woman. I could make it worth your while, if you need persuading. Nothing to do with Wolfen, of course, just a private arrangement. Say, five hundred thousand dollars?'

'Five hundred thousand...' Greg gagged on the amount and stared at him in disbelief.

'I believe she's worth a lot more,' Richard continued smoothly, 'but I'm a businessman and not into extravagant gestures. My only caveat would be that if you told anyone about this, I would fire your ass quicker than you can breathe.' He smiled to soften his words but in the shadows the smile was wolfish. 'You might as well say yes. After all, I could drive to New Jersey and fuck her brains out anyway, leaving you out of pocket.'

'Well ...' Greg thought fast. What if Pagan preferred Richard to him? It was something he had not considered until now. After all, he was wealthy, single and devastatingly attractive, even though his manner was sometimes unfortunate. 'She does have certain ... preferences,' he finished delicately.

Richard lifted a sleek eyebrow. 'Is that so?'

'She likes it much rougher than I can face giving, I'm afraid. She's even asked me to knock her around a bit. You know ... so it hurts. But I can't. I'm too soft.'

'Is that so?' Richard poured another bourbon and watched Greg over it. 'But you would want to watch us. Is that right?'

'No negotiation on that, I'm afraid.' Greg was feeling confident now. 'It's what she likes.'

Richard shrugged. 'Fair enough, but I have to say I admire your spunk, Roscoe. What if she refuses me? I won't pay for something I don't get. And if she gets tricky it could mean kissing your raise goodbye for at least two years.'

Greg smiled smugly. 'Pagan worships me. She'll do anything I say. And it isn't as if she isn't getting something out of it, is she?'

'You're right, of course. In that case I'll come for dinner Saturday week.'

Greg gulped visibly. 'Next ... Saturday?' Pagan would kill him. They were flying to England early the following Monday morning. But Richard's expression warned him not to refuse. 'Right! Next Saturday. I'll tell her to get her apron on.'

'Good. You'll have ten days or so, just enough time to organise your offshore account, if you don't have one already.'

Benny appeared in the doorway. It seemed that Greg was being dismissed.

Back at the apartment Greg stood in the shower, brimming with a deep and fearful joy. Five hundred thousand easy dollars. He would not tell Pagan. It would be a lot less complicated if he got her drunk instead. But he would time it carefully. He did not want the meal turning into a shambles. He closed his eyes and imagined the three of them together, but now the picture was real in all its sharply focused glory.

Afterwards he stood in front of the mirror, admiring his lean, tanned body, the great penis rearing up in front of his taut abdomen like that of a fertility god. Turning to look at himself in profile he looked even better, with his buttocks firm and tightly bunched. Packing his phallus inside HOM bikini briefs it looked pretty impressive, almost glowing pink through the straining, translucently white cotton. He cupped it in his hands, feeling its weight and heft. It was like a separate being, a naughty friend. It turned him on so much he wanted to jack off right then, but his balls were tight with seed ready to be slurped by that hot minx Renate, and he did not want to disappoint her. He wondered what expensive trinket she would present him with tonight, on top of the gold Gucci cufflinks and the Vuitton attaché case she had already bought for him, not to mention the vastly expensive meals and endless quantities of Cristal champagne. He decided he liked the role of gigolo, especially as he still had the energy to satisfy the other voracious girls at the club when Renate was not there. Life, it seemed, could not get any better.

10

The next day Pagan and Roberto Sanchez walked into the cavernous entrance to Wolfen's office block at precisely ten minutes to five. Roberto was wearing the dark, chalk-striped Hugo Boss suit he saved for meeting potential clients. His dark wavy hair had been tamed for the occasion. Pagan was dressed just as sharply in a fitted black jacket with wide cream lapels and a tight skirt just long enough to be judged decorous. With the long black boots it was no-bullshit battledress calculated to show her enemy she would not tolerate her time being wasted.

In the lift Roberto pulled her close. 'Time for a quickie? I've had a blinding hard-on all the way here looking at you in those boots.'

She shoved him away, laughing. 'Behave, you're as bad as Richard!'

As soon as the words came out she knew she had slipped up. She might have got away with it but her involuntary wince gave her away.

'You don't mean the guy we're meeting? Clive mentioned you knew him. Are you fucking him?'

'No!' Pagan felt her face grow warm. 'It's complicated. Don't even ask.' But she knew he would.

'You have thirty seconds to explain,' Roberto said warningly.

'OK! Clive doesn't know this but he's an old boyfriend. He resurfaced recently and tried it on and I said yes, strictly for old time's sake. Now he won't leave me alone. And that was before I found out last Saturday that he's Greg's boss and ... that's it,' she finished lamely.

'That's enough, I think,' Roberto said mildly. 'Are we on a shit assignment today?'

'I don't know. Give it your best shot. Apparently he's now worth a fortune.'

'Sounds like you're marrying the wrong guy.'

'You haven't met him. Oh, and Greg doesn't know. Do you think he would have taken this job if he did?'

'It won't do him any harm, will it, if you're shagging the boss?'

'I'm not shagging him! Not now, anyway.'

'So tell me, the first time did he dump you or you dump him?'

'I dumped him, of course.'

Roberto mischievously rubbed his hands. 'This is getting better and better. How many times have you screwed him since?'

A soft ping indicated that they had arrived at the fiftieth floor. Pagan held up three fingers. Roberto waggled his finger admonishingly at her and grinned.

They signed the visitors' book and were almost immediately collected by Eleanor, who greeted Pagan with a friendly smile. She led them down the long quiet corridor to the directors' quarter of the building. The offices were chic and spare, with plush cream carpet and monochrome furniture that had Richard's hallmark all over it. The atmosphere was strangely hushed, all activity hidden by tall screens and large vases of white lilies. On the way she saw Greg sitting at his desk. He was on the phone but managed to give her a cursory wave as she went past.

They were shown straight into Richard's office, which was as spectacular as she had expected. Two sides were sheer glass from floor to ceiling, creating the dizzying feeling that they could easily topple into the street far below. It made her feel slightly nauseous.

The information technology director looked tense, but Pagan knew it was the effect that Richard seemed to have on most people. Richard himself stood by the window, resplendent in a black three-piece suit, smoking a long Cuban cigar. Roberto did a double-take at his bare feet. Pagan nudged him sharply in the ribs.

Richard let his thin, prematurely grey-haired IT director do the introductions whilst he shook Roberto's hand with intentionally bone-crunching force and gallantly kissed Pagan's hand. They were ushered onto an informal arrangement of elephant-grey leather sofas and chairs, surrounding a smoked glass coffee table. On it Eleanor placed a *cafetière* of coffee and four dainty white bone china cups and saucers, together with small slivers of almond biscotti and a teapot of delicately fragranced jasmine tea for Richard.

Richard waited until Roberto and Pagan had sat down on the sofa before placing himself directly opposite Pagan. His legs were so long that his feet could touch hers and from his position she realised he had an uninterrupted view right up her skirt. She clamped her legs together with an audible slap and cringed inwardly. Roberto bit his lip, trying not to laugh.

They began their hastily prepared presentation. For nearly an hour they discussed Wolfen's need to update their system for booking clients and co-ordinating their fleet's whereabouts. It was a large project, one that would not only save Silverskin but give it a profile boost as well. Pagan learned as much as she could take about the haulage industry whilst Richard stroked her boot with his bare toe as casually as scratching his nose. He had been observing her throughout their meeting with heavy-lidded eyes, so intensely that she imagined sitting there naked before him. In turn he was a spellbinding presence, from the razor-sharp creases in his trousers to his axe-blade cheekbones. He periodically smoothed the indiscernible wrinkles from his waistcoat and fiddled with his diamond cufflinks, and she picked up every single movement. She could smell Givenchy Gentleman, the woody aroma of his cigar and her own rich Paloma Picasso perfume, mingling in an exotic cocktail for the senses that, once inhaled, was bound to chemically react with her body's deeply repressed desires. She hardly heard Roberto talking about costs and time-scales.

She shifted on the leather sofa, dismayed at how moist she had become. It was the frankly sensual way Richard was watching her, smoking that damned cigar and blowing the occasional smoke ring exclusively in her direction. If her body continued to let her down she would leave a mark when she stood up; that thought mortified her.

It also made her angry, so after that she was not so careful about keeping her knees together. Every time she moved the small skirt inched higher. As she added to what Roberto was saying she turned her body so that only Richard could see her lace stocking top. When she was sure she had his attention she parted her knees just enough to allow a glimpse of shadowy silk panties. It soon began to have the effect she was hoping for. In the middle of a crucial question to Roberto about the disruptive consequences of installation on their computer network, he totally lost track of what he was saying.

'I'm sorry, Mr Mason, what was that?' Roberto prompted him helpfully as Richard paused, obviously trying to tear his concentration away from Pagan. He pulled himself together with a visible effort and struggled with the remainder of his question. Roberto gave Pagan an enquiring look, which she met innocently. The IT director carried on talking as if Richard's behaviour was an everyday occurrence. After that Richard was careful not to let her lure him into the same trap, which was a shame. She had rather begun to enjoy herself.

As the meeting drew to a close Roberto was dispatched with the IT director for a more detailed look at Wolfen's network, which gave Richard an irritatingly plausible excuse for getting Pagan alone. A quick glance down as she stood up reassured her that she had left no evidence of her arousal, but the finality of the door closing them off to the outside world gave her a more pressing problem.

She moved away from him as he strolled towards her, waiting until she had backed herself right up against the sheer glass window. Sudden vertigo made her close her eyes against the breathtaking drop to the street below.

'It's OK. The glass is four inches thick.' His voice was very close; so close she could smell him, feral and dangerous beneath the sleek professional exterior. She caught her breath as he grabbed her shoulders and forced her around to face the window. As he smeared her against the glass she dared not look down.

He placed one hand proprietarily on her pubis, the other hand working under her jacket to cup her breast. She tried to push him away but he held her tightly. They stayed in that deeply intimate embrace for several heated moments and she wondered how many people could see them from the buildings opposite. She could feel him all the way down, legs pressed against legs, an insistent throbbing just above the swell of her buttocks.

'Haven't you been lying in bed at night, wondering if us being together is really so wrong? All the while knowing that you won't ever find another man who makes you feel like I do. Don't deny yourself, Pagan. Give up the lie.' His voice was as soft as sable, hypnotising in her ear. His fingers applied constant gentle pressure to her clitoris through her clothes. 'All I want is for us to be happy. Why won't you let me into your life?'

'You're already in my life, Richard. What the hell do you call this?' Her voice trembled. He buried his face in her hair and breathed in the fragrance of sweet apple shampoo, holding her closer so she could feel how hard he was. At the same time he gently pinched her nipple between forefinger and thumb and tugged on it. The sensation was heightened by the frisson of satin separating her flesh from his. A betraying tingle shot straight down her body. Her knees wanted to buckle, her body suddenly too heavy for her legs to support.

'If you want this contract you're going to have to be nice to me,' he murmured, giving her breast a gentle squeeze.

'I'm getting so pissed off with your stupid games, Richard. Just tell me what you want.'

'First of all, I want your honesty.'

'What?' She could see his reflection in the glass, overwhelmingly tall with broad shoulders that blocked out the light.

'You heard.' His voice was so soft it was almost a whisper. 'Are you wet?'

'No.'

'Liar.' She felt his hand brush against the hem of her skirt. As it moved further up, a knock at the door rescued her.

Richard cursed under his breath, his irritation palpable. After a long pause he gave her one long slow lick from jaw to eyebrow and strode to the door. Pagan slipped into his bathroom to check her make-up. Outside she heard Roberto saying something about the network being backed up. She flushed the toilet and went back out, mouthing 'thanks' to him behind Richard's back.

Richard's suave veneer was back in place. He was challenging Roberto to identify the meaning of a large artwork displayed over the sofa they had been sitting on. It was made up from a series of vertical lines spread evenly apart. Small horizontal blips punctuated each line at uneven intervals all the way down. At the bottom, in Richard's dramatic black script, were the words, 'Susan and the Wolf – 2000.' Roberto looked blank, obviously not finding any meaning at all.

'I give up,' he said eventually. 'What is it?'

'It's a portrait of two people in love.' A small smile played around Richard's lips.

'Uh, it is?' Roberto stepped back, turned his head this way and that. 'I can't say I follow you.'

Pagan felt fingers slyly working their way up her skirt to snap her suspenders. Roberto's attention was still on the picture as Richard's warm breath feathered her hair. His hand snaked between her legs, making short work of her panties, his finger stroking her well-lubricated pussy lips with lewd affection. She felt rather than heard him react when he realised how damp she was, a heartfelt shudder bolting through his body.

'It's DNA,' she said, more shrilly than she intended.

Richard smoothly retracted his hand as Roberto turned to look at them. 'She's right. The combination of semen and pussy juice have a certain artistic poetry, don't you think?'

Roberto opened his mouth but nothing came out. It was Pagan's turn to rescue him. She picked up her briefcase and thrust out her hand for a farewell handshake.

'It's fascinating but if you want your figures by tomorrow we really ought to start working on them.'

'Of course. I look forward to seeing you again, Pagan Warner.' Richard took her hand in his own, the one he had used just seconds before to touch her so intimately. As he drew her hand to his lips he closed his eyes and inhaled her musky woman scent. 'Such beautiful perfume,' he murmured, before his eyes snapped open and penetrated her so sharply it felt like a physical assault.

As Eleanor escorted them back down the corridor Greg bounded out of his office like an exuberant Labrador. He dragged them in, shutting the door behind them.

'How did it go?' he asked eagerly when Pagan had introduced them.

'We won't know until they've examined the costs and the feasibility,' Roberto said.

'And what did you think of the main man?' Greg looked crafty, as if he already knew.

'Mason? Scary as hell,' Roberto replied shortly, 'but if he gives us this contract he can be the Boston Strangler for all I care.'

'Oh, good.' Greg dismissed him abruptly. 'Darling, did I tell you he's coming for dinner next Saturday? Apparently he wants to get to know us better.'

Roberto's mouth twitched and he looked away. Pagan was irritated with Greg for the blatant display of one-upmanship. It was one of his less attractive foibles.

'Saturday? But we fly out on Monday morning! Why can't we go out for a meal instead?'

'I suggested it but he wants to see the house. I said you wouldn't mind.' He looked reproachful, as if she were being the selfish one.

Mindful that Roberto was studying Greg's gold-framed accountancy certificate with more interest than it deserved, Pagan caved in.

'No, I don't mind,' she said wearily. 'It's what being a corporate wife is all about, isn't it?'

'That's my girl,' Greg said cheerfully. He gave his new

Rolex an ostentatious glance. It was after six o'clock. 'Oops, better run along and get working on that contract.'

'You're kidding, it's time to hit the bar,' Roberto said. 'Why don't you come with us? Have a curry and a few beers?' he added politely.

'No can do, old chap. Have to put in some hours if this young lady wants me back in England in two weeks.' He kissed Pagan briefly on the cheek. 'Have a good evening, darling. Don't do anything I wouldn't do.'

'I'll make sure she does,' Roberto replied, but Greg had already forgotten him. Greg escorted them to the express lift and gave a little wave as the door closed.

'That was Greg,' Roberto said flatly as he pressed the button.

'Yes,' Pagan replied.

'And you're marrying him in two weeks,' he said in the same flat voice.

'Yes.'

'Tell me, has he ever done this?' As the stomach-flipping descent started towards below ground, he pushed her against the side of the lift and dropped to his knees, pushing her skirt up as he did so. She could feel hot breath on her thighs as his tongue worked under the sodden scrap of panties and lapped at the juices in and surrounding her hot, sticky sex. Fired up by her extended foreplay with Richard, she responded with alacrity, holding his head and pushing against his tongue. Her body weakened and she bit her lip, trying to remain standing as he forced her legs further apart and lapped deep inside her cunt, making greedy sounds of pleasure. Her panties strained against her widened legs, threatening to rip as her body cried out for release. As his tongue played lightly over her clitoris she jolted, threatening to topple over. If the lift door had opened they would have no time to recover, but right then she did not care. She felt the first quivering of her inner muscles as she held on to Roberto's thick dark hair, defying him to stop. The strong, regular tonguing of her clit tilted her over the edge and she cried out, thrusting her body against him, holding his head so he could do nothing but pleasure her, her juices sliding down her thighs, mingled with his saliva. Confusing images filled her head, Richard banging her against the wall in a dirty alley, taking her over his desk from behind, slapping her buttocks until they hurt, telling her she was such a bad girl. She peaked with a high moan, so hard that Roberto felt his tongue being sucked back into her depths. It felt like forever, but in fact he had brought her off in the time it took to get from the fiftieth floor to below ground level.

Roberto pulled down Pagan's skirt and wiped his face as the door opened. Two elderly gentlemen looked at them with varying levels of amusement and disapproval as they stumbled past them towards Roberto's new 3-Series BMW. The alarm chirped and they wordlessly climbed in. The seats were cream leather, separated at the front by a console holding his phone and the automatic control.

'The answer is no,' Pagan said a little shakily. 'He's never done that.'

'I bet Mason has though.'

'Can we not talk about him?'

'We don't have to talk about him, but there's a price to pay for not doing so.' Roberto leaned over and slipped his hand inside her jacket. Underneath she wore a simple cream camisole and lace bra in oyster silk. Her breast was heavy and warm, the nipple as hard as a nut. He stroked it with his thumb. 'Somehow I don't think you'll find the price too high.'

'You're such a piece of shit.' But she moved sensuously against his hand.

'At least I'll be satisfied with just once. I'm married, you're almost married and I definitely don't want Mason breathing down my neck. I did see him put his hand up your skirt, by the way.'

Pagan turned scarlet. 'You saw that? Oh, my god!'

'I also saw how much you were enjoying it. What the hell were you doing to him in there? I thought he was going to cream his pants.'

'Women should never give away their secrets,' Pagan said primly.

Roberto pinched her nipple gently, leaning further to kiss her on the lips. In the dark of the car park they seemed cocooned in their own small world, one that smelt of leather and Eternity aftershave.

'I haven't christened this car yet,' he mused.

Pagan giggled. 'Oh, please. That's the lamest excuse for a screw I've ever heard.'

'Who needs an excuse? You're a great girl. I hope Greg Roscoe appreciates what he's getting.'

'I'm going to make damned sure he does.' Their lips melded together for a few heated seconds. Slyly she felt for his nipple under the fine cotton Ralph Lauren shirt. It was already as hard as a tiny bullet. She pinched it gently, knowing from past experience that his nipples were as wildly sensitive as the tip of his cock.

'Oh, God, you remembered,' he groaned. She laughed against his mouth and felt for the other nipple as he fumbled for his shirt buttons. His chest was honey brown, lightly covered with crisp curly hair. She draped his tie over his shoulder and leaned over to give his nipples some undivided attention, warming them with her tongue, cooling the saliva left behind with tiny breaths, all the while with one hand on his cock, squeezing him gently through his wool crepe trousers. He was moaning continuously, out of his head with the merciless administrations of her tongue.

'Stop it. I'm going to come,' he gasped.

She stopped, kissing him lightly on each tingling tip before unzipping his trousers. His cock pushed through the opening, sheathed in wine-red silk boxer shorts. A darkened stain at the tip gave away that he was already oozing. She peeled away the shorts and let his cock spring free. It reared up from its nest of dark hair, swaying gently like an enchanted cobra. She daintily washed the salty secretion away with her tongue before getting into her stride, sucking lasciviously. She had forgotten how vocal he was, keeping up a stream of filthy commentary between prolonged grunts of pleasure.

'Shh!' she hissed suddenly. They listened with bated breath to the hard ringing footsteps coming towards them. Roberto ducked down as Richard walked past the car. He stopped and then, after a long, breathtaking pause, turned with a scrape of shoe leather towards his Mercedes parked on the other side of the car park. They heard the engine start with a throaty roar and its lights glare into the interior of the BMW. They kept their heads down until the scream of tyres receded into the distance.

'Shit, that was close!'

'Let's get out of here,' Pagan said. 'How would we explain to Clive that we lost the contract because we were caught shagging in the car park?'

They drove back to Hoboken and had a curry there before driving back to Pagan's house. On the way they stopped at one of the deserted viewpoints overlooking Warren Plains for half an hour of sensual foreplay, ending with a violent screw on the hood of Roberto's BMW. She knew he would not be back for more. They were both ending a chapter in their lives on a high note. From then on their relationship would be friendly but strictly professional.

Back at the house she kissed him goodnight. 'The combination of semen and pussy juice does have a certain artistic poetry, don't you think?' she asked innocently.

'I can't believe he actually said that,' Roberto laughed. He stroked her cheek affectionately. 'Thank you, but I still think you're marrying the wrong guy.'

'Remember our agreement,' she warned.

'Yeah, yeah. I've forgotten his name already.'

As he drove away she wished she could say the same.

The phone rang after midnight, waking her.

'Are you alone?'

'Of course I am! You made sure of that, didn't you?' She rubbed the sleep from her eyes and cursed Richard for being unable to leave her alone.

'We need to talk.'

'Oh, when have I heard that before? Piss off and let me get some sleep.' She slammed the phone down, then disconnected it before he could call back. If he was that desperate, he could drive over to see her.

But he did not come, and neither did sleep.

Don't think about how lonely you are. The thought swam over her large empty bed.

I am a woman. I have needs. Yes, but she needed Greg, not Richard, or Roberto, or any other man that she might choose to satisfy her. And what she definitely did not need was that feeling that grew every time she lay in the dark, stretching out, trying to ignore the fact that her whole being was alive and fizzing with energy that could not be expressed. One past night she had lain on the living-room carpet in the dark and the Wolf had come to her. She had felt him crushing her to the floor, his hands greedy and grasping, his arousal musky and thick in her nose and head. Then a groundhog had tripped the security light, sending a shaft of brightness across her face and she had jumped up, alone and breathless, wondering what the hell she was coming to.

But she felt the same way again. It was becoming a habit. One that she had to kick, and fast.

11

'Ever fucked on coke?' Renate sipped at the champagne Greg had ordered for them.

Greg shook his head. 'I don't need to, darling. I do just fine without it.'

'I'm sure you do. But what is life without a little adventure?' Renate reached into her tiny evening purse and drew out a small bag, which she dangled like a carrot in front of his nose.

Greg was wary. Uninhibited sex with strangers was one thing. Dabbling with class A drugs was quite another. He had seen a few of his former colleagues brought to their knees by the innocent-looking white powder and it wasn't going to happen to him.

'I think it's a shame you won't let me share a new experience with you,' Renate pouted, pressing herself up against him. 'Especially if you want us to spend the weekend together.'

Greg felt himself weakening under the influence of her hot body and Givenchy's Organza perfume. With Pagan safely away at the house that weekend he had been given the opportunity to indulge in two days of hedonistic pleasure and he had no intention of letting it slip through his fingers.

'Is it really that good?' he asked cautiously.

She smiled again. 'Close your eyes and think of the biggest hard-on you've ever had.'

'This one is pretty damned huge, just looking at you.' His warm hand covered the hand now palming his cock.

She pushed against it, releasing another surge of blood. He felt weak with desire.

'Good. Now triple it and make it last all night.'

Her face was inches from his own. Her long-lashed eyes were as deep as a siren pool, luring him into their depths. Her tongue snaked out from her glossy red lips and licked his mouth. For a moment they were joined in a flickering, pornographic kiss.

'Show me what you do then,' he murmured against her mouth.

She broke away and got to work with the powder and a gold razor blade on the low mirrored table. Expertly she cut the powder into four lines.

'Watch and learn.'

Tucking her hair behind her ears she snorted a line up one delicately curved nostril, then the other. Leaning back, her eyes seemed to sparkle twice as brightly as they had before. She giggled and shimmied as the coke hit, then lay back on the couch. Slowly she hitched her dress up past her thighs, boldly staring at him. She hooked one leg over the top of the couch, letting the other fall to the floor. Even though he was used to seeing her velvet, hairless pudenda all swollen and glistening, the sight still made him thirsty with lust.

'You have the most lubricious fanny,' he murmured, sliding one finger between her pussy lips. She felt all soft and pulpy, like an overripe mango.

'Eat me,' she commanded with a decadent smile.

Greg shuffled obediently down and gave her one long, slow lick, from perineum to clitoris. A shudder racked her whole body and she gave a soft scream, still soaring from the effects of the coke in her bloodstream. Greg zeroed in on her clitoris, strumming at it relentlessly between dipping deeply into her cunt with his tongue. Sweet floods of sticky juice began to ooze from her, soaking his face and the mock leather couch as she moaned with abandon. Greg looked up to see another man kneeling in front of her, by her head. She was frantically scooping out his cock and balls and sucking them greedily into her mouth. She looked like a society queen but had the manners of an alley cat, Greg thought, at once irritated and highly aroused by the sight of her chobbling enthusiastically at the other man's cock. He went back to her cunt, lasciviously probing her folds and teasing her clitoris as she bared her breasts from the exotic dress and stimulated her nipples, lost in wringing every ounce of sensation from her body as it was plundered by the two men. Greg felt her orgasm run through her lower body, her cries stifled by the penis forced into her mouth. The other man pulled out and came over her face, cock-whipping her mouth as he jetted over her lips.

Greg could not stand it any more. He had to get inside her but, as he moved to enter her, her eyes opened and she pushed the other man away, wiping his semen from her face.

'If you want me you'll have to try a little nose candy first.'

This time there was no hesitation. Greg bent down and snorted the remaining two lines, hard so it did not make him sneeze. At first, it seemed as if nothing had happened, but then he felt a soaring happiness; stress fell away like a mantle, replaced with invincibility. Renate had her hand on his groin again. As she squeezed, his cock seemed to explode into fresh life, making him want to roar with the sheer power of it. She carefully unzipped his trousers and his cock bulged through the opening like a ripe banana in the white bikini briefs.

'Suck it,' he rasped, though he would never have given such a demand to a woman like her before.

'Oh, no. First you have to go in the web like a good boy.'

The empty harness hung ominously on the stage like a medieval instrument of torture. The coke fizzing around his veins filled Greg with bravado.

'What do I have to do?'

Renate took his face in her hands and with a pointed tongue traced a warm wet path around his lips. His hard-on intensified and he moaned softly. Blindly he let her lead him to the stage.

'People will come to you and help themselves,' she explained as he stripped down to the white bikini briefs. 'We'll keep those on, I think,' she continued, hungrily eyeing the distended cotton. She buckled each strap of the harness, starting with his wrists, then his upper arms, extended in a crucifix position. One went around his chest and waist, then she spread his legs wide and buckled two further straps just above each knee. Finally she fastened the straps around his ankles, smiling up at him. From that angle his cock looked huge in the small briefs, his balls hanging heavy under his spreadeagled body.

People were still drinking, dancing, some just waiting, some rutting like dogs on the seats. It was a sleazy, shifty atmosphere, one he usually shied away from but, fuelled with champagne and cocaine he was fired up enough to welcome anything.

'Blindfold on or off?' Renate asked.

'Oh, on, I think.'

The last thing he saw was her smile as she tied the soft strip of silk around his eyes. He shimmered with excitement as the harness moved up until he was poised a few inches above the ground. Slowly the harness turned around and around until he was totally disorientated. He relaxed his body, resolving to enjoy whatever was going to happen. He began to feel hands on his legs, cool small hands that stroked his thighs, trailing upwards until they reached the base of his balls. Then other hands, massaging his shoulders, tweaking his nipples. Lips closed around them and tugged at the tiny buds until he bit his lip to stop from whimpering. Another tongue ran up the inside of his thigh, one side, then the other. No one touched his cock, even though each sensation made it throb wildly. He visualised it pushing out the cotton briefs and he waited for someone to pull them down, but instead he felt a hot tongue push underneath the cotton at the soft crease at the top of his leg. He tried to push his hips out towards the unseen mouth but it moved frustratingly away. His cock was huge now. Pre-cum oozed slowly from the dark teardrop slit in the red glans peeping out the top of the briefs, squashed by the thick elastic with Calvin Klein logo against his belly. Someone held something up to his nose and he heard Renate tell him to sniff it. He did, and the coke gave his urgency more fire.

'Someone suck me. Please!' He sobbed softly as he was lost in a sea of tongues, licking, tasting, flickering over his body, hands on his back, on his legs, in his mouth. He bunched his buttocks and thrust his pelvis upwards, begging for it to get some attention. Instead he felt the back of his briefs being pulled down and a hard smack on his exposed buttocks. He cried out as it happened again and again, but the warm sting was soon replaced by a numb anticipation. Then at last a hand palmed his cotton-enrobed cock, mashing it against his belly, before peeling the tight cotton downwards and hooking it under his balls so they bulged firm and proud. He was spanked again as two pairs of warm lips brushed against each globe and drew them in. Confused between pain and pleasure, his pelvis strained even more, making his back ache and then there was a third mouth, squeezing over the head of his cock, down, down to the root and back up, over and over. From his lips came words he had never uttered before; dirty, obscene words – words he barely knew the meaning of. He was blissed out on sensation, not caring if the givers were men or women.

'I'm coming,' he moaned, and almost immediately he felt firm pressure against the base of his cock, quelling the rising fever. A cool metal ring was slipped over his shaft and down to the root, keeping him hard as the torment went on. Hands forced apart his buttocks. He groaned again as a wet finger pushed against his rectum. His balls were still being sucked relentlessly. His hard-on was so intense it was painful, rocketing skywards. He felt something thicker than a finger between his buttocks but he was too far gone to want to stop it.

'Yeah,' he muttered, gyrating his hips. 'Give it to me.' He felt himself open up gradually, letting the huge thickness in, aided by yet another mouth over his cock. With every movement he was either impaled or taken to new heights of abandonment. He felt a huge scream building from the base of his chest; his balls tightened, ready to explode. As the cock behind him thrust deep the orgasm flared from his toes up, making his body vibrate, slowly at first, then with increasing urgency as a volcanic eruption of feeling burst through the top of his cock, making him roar, making him spit and grunt and lose all reason. The climax went on and on as his unseen tormenters gave too much, too hard, drawing out his pleasure until he was a shivering wreck.

Eventually he was lowered onto a soft mattress and released. He was covered with a silken throw and allowed to fall into an exhausted and well-earned slumber.

* * *

When Greg awoke he was on a different bed, sur-rounded by Victorian white lace pillows. It was morn-ing, judging by the sunlight streaming in through half-drawn brocade curtains and the noise of traffic outside the window. He was not sure what day it was.

He sat up, blinking, taking in his surroundings. They consisted of a dark mahogany sleigh bed and a plethora of country landscapes in ornate, gilt frames set on a wood-panelled wall. In one corner a collection of moon-faced Victorian dolls and china poodles stared blankly out from behind a glass-fronted display cabinet. There was a large oval mirror opposite the bed, giving him a top-to-tail view of his bleary-eyed, leaden body. On the bedside table a tray lay with a jug of iced, lemon-garnished water and a glass. His mouth was parched so he poured some water and drank thirstily. His backside felt sore but it was a dull sensual ache that he did not altogether object to. He lay back and closed his eyes against his surreal surroundings. For a while he was transported back to the night before.

He palmed his cock and rubbed it gently. Slouching amongst the snowy pillows he admired his body, tanned and buff, with hardly a ripple across his stomach and firm pectorals shifting under his skin. He liked how indecent he was being, like those models in the gay magazines he sometimes bought out of curiosity, som-nolent and lazy eyed and totally focused on their own pleasure. He gently pulled the foreskin back and forth over the swollen glans, watching how his face reacted with every new surge of blood into his cock. He aimed it at his reflection, admiring how bulbous and purple the head had become. Soon he was rubbing it with strong pumping movements, overcome with the eroti-cism of his reflected actions.

At that moment Renate walked in, looking gorgeous in a gold camisole and matching French knickers that complimented her dusky skin. She smiled at his face, which was showing shame battling with the need to finish what he had started. She crawled onto the bed and stretched out, gazing up at him, her hands roaming over her breasts and underneath the silky knickers.

'Don't stop. I love to see a man make himself come.'

He crouched over her and pumped against his hand, fixated on her hands roaming all over her body. His teeth gritted in an orgiastic grimace and with a loud grunt he shot his load, spilling it over her neck and face. She reached out with her tongue, catching the last few drops and massaging the viscous cream into her skin.

'That's called a pearl necklace,' he said, grinning and regaining his breath.

'That's called you being a very dirty boy,' she scolded gently. 'I'll have to punish you later.' She swung off the bed and kissed his cheek.

'I look forward to it.' He cast around for his clothes. They were nowhere to be seen. 'What's today? Where am I?'

'It's Friday morning and you're in my bedroom in my husband's apartment.'

'Your husband?' Greg practically bolted from the bed.

'Calm down. He knows you're here.' Renate retrieved his clothes from the closet and handed them to him. She pulled on a long scarlet kimono with handpainted Japanese fans, covering her semen-stained camisole, and rescued a packet of Virginia Slims and a lighter from the bedside table. Seeing her expel rich creamy smoke from between her rose-red lips made him shiver with renewed desire. 'Anyway, Rocco wants to talk to you. He has a business proposition.'

'What sort of business proposition?' Greg looked wary, pulling on his freshly pressed suit trousers.

'You'll see.' She waited until he was fully dressed before knotting his tie and brushing fluff from his jacket. She gave his penis one final squeeze and led him out into the cool white corridor.

Their feet made no sound on carpet, the walls studded with alcoves containing leering bronze animal sculptures and Japanese dancing girls. Greg knew from experience of antiques that these were imposters, bought to look the part.

The same went for the room he was ushered into. The fireplace was ornately carved mahogany, but that too had a faintly phony look to it, as if the Carlottis were striving for something they could never achieve. He wondered whose taste the apartment reflected and hoped with a cultivated shiver that it wasn't Renate's.

Rocco Carlotti sat behind a vast mahogany desk inlaid with hunter green leather. There were few items on it, apart from an inkwell, a large brown envelope and a gold penholder. He was physically a small man, built like a jockey but without the tensile strength and grit. His hair was slicked back with brilliantine from a sharp face and he had a Roman nose that dominated his features, along with pointed teeth and a chin like an elf. He was dressed in formal pinstripes, with a black tie.

Greg took the chair opposite him and Renate scooped up a small poodle in her arms. She called it Coochie and began to fuss its curly head.

'I'll come straight to the point,' Carlotti said, in a weasly whine of a voice. 'You have recently entered the employ of Wolfen Enterprises, of which Richard Mason is the owner, have you not?'

'Indeed I have,' Greg answered formally.

'Can you tell me, is this Mason in these pictures?' Carlotti opened the envelope and pushed over a sheaf of photographs, blown up to A4 size. There were six of them, showing a couple talking together, locked in an intimate embrace. The last two photographs showed first the woman stretched across the hood of an expensive sports car, the man's hand between her legs, and then, in a shot curiously more intimate than the one before it, the woman staring up at her companion, her hands touching his face.

The inside of Greg's mouth was slick. Carlotti smiled unpleasantly at the look of horror on his face.

'And I believe that recently Mason offered you a hefty sum of cash to sleep with her? A sum of five hundred thousand dollars, to be precise.'

As Greg opened his mouth to ask how the small man knew, the door opened and another man walked in; he was huge, and wearing a badly fitting Armani suit and a goatee beard. It was Benny from Richard's club. He stood the other side of Carlotti's chair and planted his feet squarely apart, staring impassively at Greg. Carlotti did not acknowledge him.

'Are you also aware that Mason is your fiancée's uncle? Which means you're practically related already. Benny, get the man a drink.'

Greg grasped the proffered whisky like a man dying of thirst. Carlotti smiled nastily.

'The trouble is, he's in love with her. Obsessed, even. And I don't think he's gone through this whole charade of employing you just to sit back and watch you marry her. Do you?'

Greg looked from Carlotti's fishy leer to Renate's triumphant smile, half hidden behind the poodle. At once the fortune he had been almost handed had been cruelly snatched back from his outstretched grasp.

'So ... where does that leave me?' he asked plaintively.

'Up shit creek without us,' Carlotti replied matter-of-factly, examining his small roundly manicured nails. 'But that's OK because we're willing to help you.'

Greg was aware of a surging rage towards Mason; towards Pagan for her duplicity; towards the whole unfairness of it all. If he did not marry Pagan, he would be a nobody. He would have to go creeping back to the accountancy profession cap in hand for a pathetic audit manager's job to tide him over whilst he waited another five years for a shot at the big time. All his former colleagues who had warned him about the lure of something too good to be true would be outwardly sympathetic but rubbing their hands with secret glee at his downfall.

'What did you have in mind?' he asked faintly.

'Firstly, these pictures are not enough. We need a videotape of Mason with the girl. He hates publicity, so he'll pay a whole lot of cash to keep this particular relationship with her quiet, given what it is. Plus you're in a strong position to sue him for breach of contract, employing you under false pretences, even emotional stress and adultery – with a really good lawyer.'

Greg's eyes narrowed. 'So why do I need you?'

'You can't take on a shark like Mason on your own. He'll squash you quicker than a carpet bug. You need protection.'

'Protection,' Greg repeated slowly. He took in the small, viperous man and the brick-built heavy behind him and began to feel very cold. 'What exactly is it you want?'

'What I'm talking about is a simple transference of funds from Mason to you, and from you to me.'

Greg felt the blood drain from his face. 'You want me . . . to blackmail Richard Mason?'

Carlotti coughed delicately. 'In a word . . . yes. And of what he gives you, I'll take fifty per cent.'

Greg's eyebrows shot up. 'What? That's outrageous!'

Carlotti bristled visibly. 'I'm not a charity, Mr Roscoe. Mason is a dangerous man. Two hundred and fifty thousand is a fair price for ensuring that he does not stop you marrying Pagan Warner. You'll be getting your money's worth and you'll soon get it back with dividends. As long as you remain married to her, he can't touch you. Harming you won't exactly help their relationship, will it?'

Greg took another gulp of bourbon.

'This is crazy,' he said hoarsely. 'If you have a problem with Mason why don't you deal with him yourself?'

'Because I don't particularly want to get that close to him, and you – once you marry Pagan – will be in a very strong position to get what I want, which is a very large chunk of his income.' He leaned forward again so Greg could see how serious he was. 'We both know you have just as many mucky secrets as he does. Do I have to spell it out, Mr Roscoe?'

Greg knew he was trapped. The only safe option would be to run, tell Pagan he no longer wanted to marry her and get out of the country. But then he thought of the hedonistic hours at the club, writhing on a bed filled with beautiful young bodies, of endless head in an alcohol- and cocaine-fuelled haze, knowing he could snap his fingers and screw any girl he fancied. And there was Renate, willing to shower him with gifts and pander to his greediest sexual desires. As their eyes met she trailed her tongue across her wet red lips and moved closer to Benny, slipping her hand inside his jacket to fondle him.

'Well? Do you understand?' Rocco demanded. Greg jumped, forcing his eyes back to Rocco's scowling face.

'Loud and clear,' he stammered.

'Just remember that you have more to lose than me.' Carlotti stood up. Greg followed suit and stuck out his hand by force of habit, his other holding the jacket closed. Carlotti shook the proffered hand wetly.

'You'll have the tape for me next Sunday. Renate will give you the details of when and where.'

Numbly Greg let Renate guide him to the waiting car.

'Meet me at the club at eight tonight,' she whispered. 'We'll get a couple of the girls and have some fun.' She pressed something small into his hand.

In the car he looked at what she had given him. It was a rectangular silver box with a lid on a tiny hinge. As he opened it a few grains of white powder dusted his trousers. There was enough for a couple of good hits. He carefully scooped out a tiny cone with the nail of his little finger and inhaled it gratefully, thinking he deserved it after the trauma he had been through. As the coke kicked in he started to grin stupidly. He was about to spend a weekend with three beautiful women, balling his brains out. Suddenly his troubles did not seem so great after all.

12

The same afternoon Pagan was packing her holdall for two days with her good friends Moira and Pam. They were escaping to the Jersey shore for the weekend, and she had been looking forward to it for months. It would be her last irresponsible gasp before the restraints of marriage took over.

Earlier that day she had spoken to Clive, who was eager to hear her feedback from her meeting with Richard the day before. She had adopted the stance she and Roberto had agreed on: non-committal, though all the good signs were there. Wolfen had a justifiable reason for employing Silverskin's services, but whether Richard would use it to further his case with Pagan remained to be seen.

A car pulled up and she heard the door slam with an expensive-sounding thud. Richard. It couldn't be anyone else. She walked out onto the balcony and looked down on him. He was wearing his usual relentless black, the only concession to the warmer weather being that the first three buttons of his shirt were unfastened and he was not wearing a jacket. But why she should note these small details was beyond her.

'You're not coming in unless you have a contract for me.'

'Not yet. My people are still considering the options. I was impressed by your presentation though. It was very professional.'

'I'm surprised you noticed,' she said archly. She folded her arms and waited for him to leave.

He looked around and saw Gloria Knapp lurking behind her roses. She was ostensibly pruning them but watching the scene before her with avid curiosity. He gave her a cheerful wave before looking up at Pagan again.

'Have you made any more cookies?'

She stifled a spontaneous smile. 'No, you cheeky bastard, I haven't.'

'I feel like a real jerk-off standing out here. If you don't let me in I'll climb up. Or I could just kick open the fucking door. You have ten seconds to decide.'

'I'd just love to see you climb up,' she said disbelievingly.

'If you insist.' He backed down the stairs and unbuttoned his shirt cuffs, rolling his sleeves up half way to his elbows. As she watched with dawning dismay he leapt lightly onto the balustrade surrounding the porch. Edging his way along he arrived under the balcony where she was standing and with comfortable ease hauled himself up onto the railings. With all his weight still on his forearms he planted a rapid kiss on her cheek, before swinging his legs over the railings. He dropped as lightly as a cat at her feet and straightened up, wiping his hands.

Pagan shrugged carelessly. 'So you work out. Big deal.' She went back to the bedroom to complete her packing, determined not to give him the satisfaction of seeing how disturbed she was. Too often recently she had wondered how he managed to maintain the physique of a thirty year old. At the gym she had even imagined him working out beside her, sweat dripping down his back, the tendons on his neck standing out like whipcord. Now she felt that familiar betraying pelvic fizz, the one that belied all her hot denials of her attraction to him.

'I have a personal trainer,' he said, reading her

thoughts with frightening accuracy. 'She's very good.' He sat on the bed and catapulted a pair of frothy lace thongs at her. She snatched the next pair out of his hands.

'How nice for you,' she said shortly.

'But I think she's a dyke,' he continued, watching Pagan's neat, rounded bottom in faded 501s and a small black FCUK T-shirt.

'Bad luck,' she said succinctly, pushing his feet off the clean bedcovers. 'You can't stay. My friends will be here soon.'

'That's OK, I'll leave when they get here.'

'Why? You think you can seduce me in twenty minutes?'

'It's been done before.' His cold blue eyes flashed wickedly, making her shiver. 'Or maybe now you'd prefer me in a tacky designer suit and BMW. I'm sure Roscoe would be very impressed with your idea of corporate entertainment, though even he would probably have preferred you to do it in a 5 Series.'

She stuck up a V sign and did not answer. He lay back on the bed to continue watching her, but after a moment he began to fidget. Feeling around under the duvet, he retrieved a hefty pink vibrator, with lifelike ridges and an enormous glans. He sniffed at it delicately and peeled a hair from the shaft, before it was snatched violently out of his hands and stowed away.

'I rest my case,' he said simply.

'I could have you or a chunk of quality latex. I've made my choice so I rest mine,' she retorted. Her face was flame red.

He waggled an admonishing finger at her. 'You'll pay for that. Anyway, I never did ask you where you were going. Somewhere nice?'

'Yes I am, but I've no intention of telling you where.'

He grinned at her. 'Don't worry, you're quite safe. I

won't be anywhere near Atlantic City. And before you ask, Roscoe told me last week where you were going. It's not quite my scene.'

'Really? I thought trashy hotels and throwing money around like water would be just your scene.'

'Depends who I'm with. This weekend I'm taking a lady friend up to Cape Cod. She has friends up there with a yacht, and the beaches are excellent for walking. Of course, that must sound pretty dull for a fly girl like you.'

She caught his sly, sideways look and smiled grimly to herself. It was the oldest trick in the book, to activate jealousy in a reluctant quarry.

'A lady friend? I didn't think you believed in such things. Does she know you're just using her to scratch an itch?'

Richard chuckled softly. 'You're beginning to sound over-confident in your power over me, my sweet.'

'On the contrary. I'm beginning to realise how your scheming mind works. Just remember that if I wanted a tumescent millionaire to keep my bed warm at night, I would have chosen one not related to me.'

'But you did, didn't you? Then you find out who I really am and suddenly you come over all moralistic. Which is pretty fucking rich when you've just been shagging *Roberto* under the nose of your precious golden boy.' He pronounced Roberto's name with an exaggerated Latino accent, loaded with venomous relish.

'So is this what you wanted to talk about last night? Or did you want to flaunt the fact you have some poor cow hanging on to your arm in a sick attempt to make me jealous? Message received and understood, so please leave.'

'There's something you should know, but however I say it, I know you're going to hate me.'

'I hate you anyway, so what is there to lose?'

'Fair enough. Roscoe's a piece of scum and he's using you.'

She laughed incredulously. 'And you're not?'

'I don't care how many dicks you suck to try and prove otherwise, but we belong together.'

'Oh, do me a favour!'

'I'm trying to! He obviously hasn't told you about the deal we've made for next Saturday night?'

'No, he hasn't mentioned any deal.'

'He intimated that he might be interested in sharing you with me. I offered him a substantial amount of money to make it happen and he agreed, with the proviso that he watches us. And this is the real gem. Apparently you like to be knocked around. Is that true?'

Pagan chewed at her thumbnail, not liking the sincerity on his face. He was so damned good at lying, it was difficult to tell what was real and what was not.

'How much did you offer him?' she asked eventually.

'Five hundred thousand dollars.'

It took a moment to sink in.

'You bastard!' She choked on the insult. It wasn't strong enough, but right then she was too angry to think of anything worse.

'Look, I know you're worth much more but it isn't as if he deserves it!'

'How is it going to work, then? You beat the shit out of me after Greg gives the nod over the port and cheese?'

'I don't fucking know! I thought he was going to discuss it with you!'

'Have you paid him yet?'

'How stupid do you think I am?'

'Oh, don't tempt me, Richard! I should be asking you the same thing! Greg's too shit-scared of you to even suggest anything like that and you expect me to believe you?'

'OK, I admit I led the conversation...'

'You mean you blackmailed him. Let me fuck your woman and I'll let you keep your job? Is that it? You're a piece of work, you really are. Get out of my house!' She flung a shaking finger towards the bedroom door.

'That is absolutely not how it was,' he said firmly. 'I'll go to any lengths to get you to see sense but blackmailing Roscoe is hardly going to help my cause, is it?'

'I don't want to hear any more! Just get out of my sight!'

'Hello? Pagan, are you up there?'

Moira and Pam were at the front door. She wondered how much they had heard as they stared curiously at Richard, who was now following her down the stairs and carrying her bag. She made awkwardly formal introductions, coughing to disguise the tremour in her voice.

'And now I'm leaving,' Richard said smoothly, dumping the bag at Moira's feet. 'Well done, ladies. Your timing is impeccable.' He strode past them out the door. They winced as it slammed shut, shaking the house. They watched him execute a neat, gravel-spraying U-turn and disappear down the road.

'Are you OK?' Moira asked, her dark eyes concerned.

'Sure,' Pagan replied brightly. 'He's an old boyfriend trying it on, that's all.'

'Boyfriend? He looked like a complete psycho,' Pam commented.

'Thanks a lot, Pam.' Pagan lugged her overnight bag out to Moira's black Thunderbird convertible, hoping she wouldn't be pressed for details. 'Hey, nice wheels.'

'It's Howard's. He said if we dented it we were dead.' Howard was Moira's ghetto-fabulous new boyfriend.

The yellow Jersey number plate bore the legend 'SUKONIT'. Pagan motioned to it, grinning broadly.

'Is this what you had to do to get it?'

Moira's white grin was very wide in her dark chocolate face. 'And the rest, honey. By the way, does Greg know this guy's trying to revisit your booty?'

'Nope.' Pagan slung the bag into the boot and slammed the lid.

'OK, I get the message,' Moira said wryly, holding up her palms in defeat.

'I'll tell you some other time when we're alone,' Pagan promised as Pam rejoined them from the bathroom.

As Moira drove them away from the house Pagan went over and over what Richard had said. It had the horrible ring of truth about it. Would Greg accept that kind of money? Of course he would. Richard wielded a huge amount of power over their lives. If he used it against him Greg would never find a decent career in Manhattan again.

It almost hurt, the hectic jumble of thoughts racing around her head. She pushed it forcibly to the back of her mind, stretching her legs out across the back seat and enjoying the cool wind in her face. She had been looking forward to this weekend for too long to have it spoilt by Richard's increasingly outrageous behaviour. She would deal with it when she returned home.

They snacked on Diet Coke and Doritos and sang along with Anastasia. The sky was a piercing blue and the Jersey shore was relentlessly grey with its cheap motels, bulbous water towers and long, wide strips of concrete highway.

The sound of a horn drew their attention to a yellow Mustang that had drawn up beside them. Inside were two young, glossy black males. They shouted and waved. The girls waved back and Moira's foot fell on the accelerator. For a few miles they raced each other, until the Mustang turned off towards Atlantic City. The girls were in fact going on to Cape May, to a beach house belonging to one of Pagan's work colleagues. It was fully furnished, with a Jacuzzi on the deck overlooking the beach. She smiled into her Coke, thinking of the small lie she had told both Richard and Greg. It was inevitable that Greg would tell Richard of her plans that weekend, which is why she had fabricated the story about going to Atlantic City. It did both men no harm at all not to know her real destination. For once she was truly free.

The beach house had been built in the style of Cape Cod, with grey slate roofing and wooden cladding bleached by the sun. There was stripped pine throughout, with comfortable fat sofas in blue gingham, cream linen curtains and soft plaited rugs under their feet. There was a distinctive maritime theme to the décor, with subtle displays of carved wooden seagulls and hand-painted lighthouses.

From Pagan's bedroom she had an uninterrupted view of the sea, glinting softly in the setting sun. She heard appreciative noises coming from the other two bedrooms before Moira came to find her.

'Respect to the girl,' she said, and they slapped palms. 'Have you checked out the Jacuzzi yet?'

From the lounge a wide glass door led to the wooden deck, large enough for a party. In one corner the Jacuzzi was large enough for ten people, with a rim wide enough to put wine glasses and nibbles. From it they would be able to watch the beach below. People were wandering along it, making the most of the gorgeous evening. Tiny waves licked at the silver sand and in the distance a band could be heard playing from one of the many bars.

'OK, who's hungry?' Pam said.

They chose a bistro overlooking the sea, watching the sky turn from vermilion to purple to black, and Pam recounted her adventures of the week before.

'I'm telling you, having three men spoils you for just having one.' She sighed longingly. 'I don't know how I'm going to cope.'

'I didn't think having two men in your puss at once was physically possible,' Pagan said, pouring more wine.

'Oh? So how do babies come out, halfwit?' Pam countered.

'That's different,' Pagan said defensively. 'Natural. As for having one in your ass as well –' she squirmed on her seat '– that almost gives me haemorrhoids just to think about it.'

'So what about tomorrow night? You looking for more of the same?' Moira asked.

Pam swirled her wine around her glass. 'Maybe.'

'Huh. I just hope you've got your haemorrhoid cream handy,' Moira retorted.

'You realise that if they get too big you have to have them lanced?' Pagan added.

'Oh please, that's disgusting.' Pam grimaced.

'And having three guys in your fanny isn't?'

The darkly handsome man at the table next to theirs choked on his wine. He had been eyeing Pagan up all evening, despite being with a very attractive brunette.

'I dunno. She could have had four, with one at the other end,' Moira suggested. 'Or five, depending on how big her mouth is.'

'That's just being greedy,' Pagan said seriously. 'Personally, I'm a one-man woman. The others just have to wait in line.'

The two other girls dissolved into laughter. Pagan winked at her admirer. It was the kind of flirting she thrived on, but right now she was too exhausted after her stressful week to play on it any more.

'He didn't notice me,' Pam said sulkily when Pagan told them about their eavesdropper.

'I guess not everyone goes for perfection incarnate,' Pagan said dryly.

'Especially when she's got a cunt like the Holland Tunnel,' Moira muttered darkly.

Pagan linked arms with them and they wandered back to the beach house, ending the evening with a skinny-dip in the Jacuzzi before falling gratefully into bed. For all of them it had been a long, hard week.

The next morning they breakfasted on coffee and pastries at a nearby beach bar. Sheltered from the spiky East wind, the sun was warm on their backs over a rich blue sky, the sea rising in choppy little waves around Cape May Point.

Afterwards they cruised around Cape May, finally coming to rest at Washington Street Mall, where Pagan bought a hideously expensive barometer in dark mahogany for Greg and a black skirt and top in flirty chiffon for herself. Moira found a handmade silver bracelet for Howard, to say thank you for the use of the car. As Moira was paying for it, Pagan's eye was drawn to a thick onyx and silver ring, which would look just perfect with a crisp white shirt cuff and long, elegant fingers. No, no, no, she scolded herself harshly. A pair of kitten-heeled, squared-toed shoes diverted her attention. She bought them to go with her outfit, thinking they would be good to go clubbing in that night.

They spent a luxuriously long time getting ready for their evening. Moira was resplendent in leopard-skin leggings, gold strappy sandals with clear Perspex heels and a cropped black V-necked T-shirt that strained dangerously over her ample bosom. That afternoon she had found a beauty salon and had her nail extensions renewed with zebra stripes. Her long crinkly hair was piled high on top of her head and finished off with a silver hair cuff, giving her an extra five inches in height.

'You can take the girl from New York . . .' she said.

'But you can't take New York from the girl,' the others chorused.

Pam looked stunning in a floaty, floral dress that wisped around her lean thighs. Two fat braids hanging down to her shoulders had tamed her golden hair. The only underwear she wore was a tiny pair of Victoria's Secret lace panties.

'The Pradas or the Jimmy Choos?' she enquired, as if the decision was one that would make or break the evening.

'The Choos. Hopefully you'll break your neck and make us look good for a change,' Pagan said good-naturedly. She was wearing the outfit she had bought that morning and was pleased with the effect.

'Huh! She'll get some millionaire coming to her rescue like a white knight,' Moira said, scowling fiercely. 'Both of you are too darned skinny. Any man worth his dick wants a woman with meat on her bones. So if you don't mind, let's go and get some.' She hiked her gold chain-link bag higher up her chubby shoulder and marched towards the door.

They found a lively roadhouse bar where the food was unchallenging and the clientele a good mix of locals and sophisticated city dwellers. They ate spicy chicken wings, ribs and blue-cheese dip to funky rhythm and blues, occasionally singing along with the music. Half way through the evening they were joined by four men that Pam had found at the bar. They were all dressed in artfully preppy long linen shorts and

Tommy Hilfiger sweatshirts, apart from one. He intrigued Pagan far more than his blandly handsome companions.

Paul and Tim were accountants from Philadelphia; Gavin, a tall, fresh-faced blond, worked in used-car sales; and Tom ran a deep-sea fishing business in Cape May for out-of-towners. He explained that they were on a college reunion, which accounted for why they were such an odd mix.

Tom was small and wiry, not much taller than Pagan, and his jaw was stubbled and dark. With his tanned skin he looked like a gypsy, wearing a black T-shirt and low-slung Wranglers and an earring in one ear. He was in his early forties and unmarried, but she guessed it was by design rather than fortune.

'Thanks,' he said, sitting next to her.

'What for?'

'For not saying, "*as in Tom Cruise*" when I was introduced and laughing like an idiot.'

'I was thinking of a sawn-off George Clooney, actually.'

He smiled uncertainly, obviously unsure whether to be insulted or flattered, but when he saw her wide smile he laughed.

'You English have the weirdest sense of humour.'

'At least we have one,' she shot back, and his grin widened.

He was more intelligent than his rough appearance suggested, and a good deal wealthier. His family owned a small restaurant in Santa Barbara, his home town. Every winter he went back there to escape the bleakness and lack of colour on the eastern seaboard. He also had a passion for the Mojave desert, due to having a Navajo great-grandfather. She had heard men claiming links with native races before, thinking it gave them mystique when in fact they had none, but this time she believed him.

'Hey, party girl! Are you going to talk all night?' Moira shouted above the music, which had suddenly been turned up. Pam leaned against Gavin, her hand stroking his thigh. It was clear that Pam and her trio of men would probably be having a private party of their own very soon.

Pagan would have been very content to listen to Tom all night, but she also wanted to dance. She and Moira hit the dance floor whilst Tom watched them with obvious enjoyment. He and Greg were both non-dancers, quite content to watch from the sideline with their beers.

Much later, Moira apologised and said she needed her beauty sleep. Pam was draped all over Paul, trying to decide who was wearing underwear and who was not. She seemed reluctant to leave.

'I'll walk you back,' Tom said to Moira. 'Pagan? You want some fresh air?'

He said it so casually, but Pagan felt a frisson of excitement.

'You go,' Pam said generously. 'I've got three white knights to keep me safe.' She fondled Tim under the table. He looked flushed and was not saying much.

When Pagan, Moira and Tom got back to the beach house Moira clumped up to bed, but not before whispering in Pagan's ear, 'Take what you can get, girl. I sure would.'

Downstairs, Pagan suggested a dip in the Jacuzzi, feeling idiotically shy.

'But you're getting married in two weeks,' he replied with mock severity.

'I know, but a dip is a dip. Nothing wrong with that, is there?'

'As long as you don't mind being with a naked man.'

'I've done it before,' she said lightly. 'But if it makes you happier I'll go get some beers. That'll give you time to get safely in the water.'

In the kitchen she retrieved two Buds from the fridge and put them on a tray, together with a bowl of salted tortilla chips and a pot of cheese dip. On impulse she went to her bedroom and put on her new silver Baja bikini. Two silver rings at each hip held the bottoms together; the balconette top cupped to support her full breasts but leaving an impressive shelf of bosom that there was no point in trying to hide. She tied a silver organza sarong around one shoulder to cover her modesty and took the tray out to the Jacuzzi.

Tom was already in the water, and for a moment she was shocked at how hairy his chest was. It was a real Sean Connery thatch, tufting up to his neck and, she presumed, down past his stomach as well. His arms were covered in the same dark hair, his tanned, muscled skin glowing through it. She stopped staring with an effort and put the tray down on the rim of the tub.

'I'm impressed,' he said. 'I didn't think it was possible for a woman to look as gorgeous as you do in less than ten minutes, and get the beers in as well.'

'Don't get smarmy. I hate that in a man,' she retorted. She slipped out of her sarong and stepped daintily into the tub, hurriedly hiding under the water.

He lifted his beer bottle. 'Here's to looking and feeling good.'

'Seconded.' She clinked her bottle with his.

'So tell me about your friends. You seem pretty close.'

'We are. Moira's got a man who adores her. She's my level head when I threaten to stray.'

'Oh? So where is she now?'

'Who says I need her right now?' Pagan stared challengingly at him over her beer.

'And the other one? Pam?'

Pagan grinned. 'Pam's the office bike, but she isn't ashamed of it. She's just getting her fair share before settling down with the right guy.'

'More than her fair share, it sounds like.'

'Shouldn't she have some fun?'

'Yeah, of course. I'm just an old-fashioned guy, I guess. Not into ditsy blonds.'

'You're underestimating her. She graduated *summa cum laude* from Princeton. Law. And she's the sweetest girl I know, so don't be rude about her.'

'And you're pretty loyal, aren't you? Does that extend to your fiancé?'

'Absolutely. I've always tried to keep the emotion out of a really good fuck.'

Immediately she said it, she realised that her thoughts had been laid bare. For some reason it mattered that this intelligent, articulate man respected her, and it wasn't going to happen now.

'I'm usually a little more discreet than that,' she said apologetically.

But he moved closer to her. 'That's OK. I'm glad you weren't.'

She felt his legs brush against hers under the bubbles. They felt warm and slippery. He slipped his arm around her shoulder and tilted her face towards his. She shivered at the tenderness of his kiss, lips closed at first, then his tongue tentatively exploring, searching for hers. The alcohol had washed away any lingering sense of guilt and she responded, shyly at first, then with increasing passion. His rough jaw felt strange, prickling against hers, but as he gathered her into his arms she forgot how alien it was and just enjoyed the continuing kiss as water popped and spat all around them. Underneath, his legs straddled her body, his chest pressing against hers. Her hands found taut bare buttocks. She gathered them together and squeezed, holding him closer, feeling the heft of his cock dig into her belly, almost bruising it with its fearsome hardness.

'See what being indiscreet can do to a man?' he said, smiling warmly.

'I certainly do,' she murmured. Sick anticipation had awoken butterflies in the base of her stomach. All her recent verbal sparring with Richard and the torment they were putting each other under, coupled with Greg's continuing refusal to touch her, was keeping her frustration at boiling point. It was all she could do not to grab Tom's cock and shove it inside herself right then.

Keeping his lower body locked against hers, Tom drew back and viewed her with obvious relish. The silver bikini top gave her a magnificent cleavage, almost overspilling the small cups. He unhooked the front fastening and let the bubbles pull the bra from her skin. Then he kissed her again, enjoying the delicate scratching of her nipples against his chest before lifting one heavy globe from the water and drawing the nipple into his mouth.

She gasped at the delight of his warm tongue, swirling against her cool skin. Using her elbows to prop her up against the edge of the Jacuzzi, she proffered the other breast. He took it greedily, like a baby desperate for nourishment, the stubble on his cheeks scuffing her tender flesh. As he pulled on her nipple she looked up at the stars and let her body float to the surface. It felt enervated and pliant, ready for him to do what he pleased. The cool air whispered over her skin, making it tingle, tugging at her nipples and hardening them into unbearably stiff points. She realised that he had turned off the bubbles and the green water now had a smooth, almost oily surface, their skin impossibly pale in the two spotlights underneath.

He supported her lower body, keeping it just under

the water, and removed her small bikini bottoms. Her tangle of dark red pubic hair floated like sea kelp in a secret cove as he opened her legs to stand between them. He lifted her buttocks so they were almost out of the water and, dipping his head, he plunged his tongue deep into her cunt to explore her from the inside out. The rush of hot, heady feelings his tongue aroused made her too weak to moan. She spread herself wider, letting the feelings wash over her, uttering a strangled cry when his slippery tongue finally played over her clitoris, already sensitised by cool air. Her fingers on her nipples added fuel to the fire of sensation radiating from that tiny, all-powerful bead of flesh. As he hit the groove and stayed there her orgasm expanded in a slowly increasing circle of pleasure, concentric rings in a pool of desire, sending their shock waves over her entire body. She screamed and did not care who heard it, her eyes on the galaxy of stars above, almost reaching them.

He let her rest for a moment, then drew her back into the warm pool.

'That was lovely,' she said, tenderly kissing his lips.

'Yes, it was,' he replied, grinning, and pushed himself away from her into the middle of the pool, letting his body drift out in front of him. His phallus reared out of the water like a mythical sea monster, the scrotum like the sac of a large jellyfish. Knowing instinctively what he needed, she opened his legs and stood between them, as he had done to her. Lifting his buttocks higher, she tongued his balls over and over, knowing that the heady mix of cold air and warm saliva would also drive him wild. His eyes closed and his jaw clenched as he obviously tried not to cry out, but he did when her lips finally closed over his cock, drawing him all in. His body moved from side to side as she traced every vein, every ridge with a pointed tongue, leaving him panting. She used the same elegant, seamless rhythm she used with all her

men, the simultaneous sucking and licking and squeezing that left them confused and crazy and begging for
more. To make the pleasure even more intense she
slipped her finger between his buttocks and pressed it
against his rectum, applying gentle but insistent pressure as she continued her loving worship of his cock.

'I've gone to heaven,' he groaned, spreading his legs
wider.

But she had waited long enough. She pushed his
body under the water again and pressed herself against
him, rubbing her breasts against his chest.

'I want you inside me,' she whispered throatily, nibbling his earlobe, her arms tight around his neck.

As he respected her demand she gave a soft, high
shriek of pleasure. His cock was scalding hot, searing a
path deep into her body. But the force of the water
worked against him, slapping noisily against their bodies, leaving him unable to thrust as hard or as deeply as
Pagan would have liked. He launched her out onto the
wooden deck, still buried deeply inside her, unleashing
a driving energy that left her breathless. The hard wood
dug into her shoulders but there was no respite. He
hammered her and she gave back, thrusting up at him
with all she had, a fresh burst of adrenaline charged by
wet skin hitting cool air.

'Stop!' she cried breathlessly.

'You OK?' He looked endearingly concerned.

She smiled lazily up at him. 'I'm fine, I just don't
want splinters in my arse.' And she squeezed his cock
with her inner muscles, making him sag with unexpected delight.

'God, that's good,' he said through gritted teeth. 'Do
you work out?'

'Three times a week,' she replied and squeezed him
again.

He gave her another penetrating thrust and matching kiss, deep into her throat.

'You'd better turn around so I can check that lovely ass for splinters.'

'That's very kind.' She smiled and turned to present herself to him. Her sex was all swollen and ready, and she gasped as he plunged his face into it, licking at every fold and crevice.

'Sorry, couldn't resist it,' he said behind her.

'Feel free,' she murmured, arching her back and readying herself for his cock.

'No splinters,' he said and rammed into her up to the hilt. As she took the sustained assault her head was suddenly filled by the single dirty image of Richard, his body slick with sweat, screwing her blind on the gym floor. She could almost see the wet heat collecting on their skin, glaring under the harsh strip lighting, and the smell of eucalyptus and hot bodies. She bit her lip hard to prevent his name from slipping out but he was still in her head, as real as the rampant cock invading her body.

'Come on, give it to me, you big fuck,' she muttered as her movements became wilder, her hair thrashing all over her face. She peaked noisily and incoherently, confused by the image and the reality. It sent Tom over the edge and he let go with a drawn-out 'yessss', shooting his seed way up into her depths.

Almost immediately he sagged on to her back, regaining his breath. For a moment they lay quietly, but then he saw the goosepimples on her skin and felt her shiver in the freshening sea breeze.

'I'd like to do that again,' he said.

'Come to bed and we can,' she replied, smiling in the dark.

* * *

He left just before dawn, after kissing her on the shoulder and pulling the sheet tenderly across her body.

'If you're ever in Santa Barbara between October and February, why don't you look me up?'

She smiled sleepily. 'I might just do that. Thank you.'

'No. Thank you.' They kissed lingeringly, rubbed noses and then he was gone. She curled up under the duvet and sank into a deep, untroubled sleep.

13

The next day the girls spent the morning on the beach, strolling along the silver sand before driving back via Atlantic City to take in the boardwalk. The smell of doughnuts and fried food was everywhere, together with the roar of amusement-arcade music and the ringing of one-armed bandits. In-line skaters dodged them effortlessly as they strolled along the herring-bone patterned boardwalk and perused the many stalls selling Native American crafts and other handmade gifts. How authentic they were, it was hard to tell. Nothing seemed authentic except the overall endearing crassness of the place, with its huge hotels with sparkling gold pillars and minarets. In the end it all got too much so they drove on to the relatively cool calm of Manhattan.

On the way Pagan called Greg. He was still in Manhattan, preparing for his trip to Atlanta and New Orleans. Richard had heard of two potential businesses to buy and he wanted Greg to check them out. He wouldn't be back until Friday morning. He sounded totally shattered and she resolved to have words with Richard to make him ease off on Greg's workload.

'I'm beginning to forget what you look like,' Pagan said, trying to keep the disappointment from her voice.

'Don't worry, darling. After we're married you'll be sick of the sight of me,' Greg replied, yawning widely.

'Why don't I get Moira to drop me off in New York and I can stay with you tonight? There's a direct train to Raritan from Madison Square Gardens tomorrow morning.'

'Well . . . I can't. I'm meeting Gareth tonight to discuss the trip. I didn't think you'd be back until this evening.'

He sounded defensive, which she knew from past experience was always the precursor to a row. And that was something she just didn't have the stamina for right now.

'Suit yourself. Have a good trip,' she said shortly and hung up. She slung her arms around Pam and Moira's shoulders and kissed them both on the cheek. 'Let's get wasted.'

She and Pam went to a club in Morristown, where they met two of Pam's girlfriends, who wanted to hear all the sordid details of Pam's weekend. Moira had gratefully gone back to Howard. She had had her fill of Pam's torrid adventures.

Pagan was soon feeling the comforting buzz that came with too much Grey Goose vodka and orange. She would pay for it in the morning, but for once she did not care.

'Hey.' Pam nudged her and whispered. 'It looks like your boyfriend's back.'

Pagan turned to see Richard lounging against the bar. He wore black leather trousers and a black silk collarless shirt, and he radiated a lithe predatory grace.

Her friends all wore the same expression, one of reluctant admiration. He had the same effect on some women that Jack Nicholson had: a deep-rooted sensuality that was at once repellant and alluring. Seeing him again so unexpectedly brought on a rush of confusing feelings: recklessness, hot excitement and panic.

'Just ignore him. Hopefully he'll go away,' she said unsteadily.

They began to talk Hollywood gossip. Pam knew it all, being an avid reader of *Entertainment Weekly*. Pagan preferred *Premier*, but Pam scoffed at it for being too highbrow. Then followed a heated discussion about the merits of various film magazines, but all the while Pagan was aware of Richard's constant vigil. Without even trying her body language had begun to scream sex, and once on that slippery slope there was no way of stopping it, however dangerous the outcome might be. Her eyes took on a new sparkle and the black leather miniskirt inched higher up her thighs. She was wearing a white figure-hugging strappy vest top and, every time she moved, the low neckline enhanced the deep jutting cleavage created by the balconette bra. Without even looking at him she knew that the combination of black leather and white cotton had set his primitive juices flowing. Because, damn him, he had done the same to her.

'He's still looking at you. I think he's too shy to come over,' Rachel said. She took out her purse and waved a cluster of notes under Pagan's nose. 'Fifty dollars says you can't go up there and kiss him.'

Pagan nearly choked on her vodka. 'No way,' she said immediately.

They all jeered good-naturedly at her.

'Afraid he won't go for it?'

'We won't tell your fiancé, honest!'

'You haven't got the guts!' Pam challenged her, grinning gleefully.

Pagan shot her a killing look. 'You're right. I haven't. Anyway I don't fancy him.'

'OK, I'll do it,' Pam said. 'Fifty bucks on the table says I can't get his tongue down my throat in less than five minutes.'

'You're on!' Anne, one of Pam's girlfriends, said gleefully.

'It's a really bad idea,' Pagan said warningly. 'You don't know what he's like.'

'It'll be fun finding out.' Pam stood up and stalked like a catwalk model towards Richard, her tight denim skirt stretched deliciously over her round bottom.

Richard sat up straighter as the lovely blond girl approached him.

'Hi,' she said, smiling prettily. She toyed with the laces of her red corset top, breathing in so her breasts puffed out from the restricting satin. 'My friend is taken, but I'm not.'

Richard leaned closer to her. 'I bet you are. Every day of the week.'

Pam stiffened at the implied insult. 'Screw you then!'

As she walked away Richard caught her wrist. 'Why don't you go back and tell the redhead that, if she kisses me, I'll give you girls five hundred dollars each.'

Pam's jaw dropped. 'You're crazy!'

Richard reached into his jacket and drew out a fat fold of one-hundred dollar bills held together with a gold money clip.

'Totally,' he said, and she could tell that he meant it.

As Pam walked a little unsteadily back to the table, Pagan dreaded what had been said.

'I guess all the drinks are on Pam,' Rachel said sadly.

'Well? What did he say?' Pagan demanded.

Pam told her. For a moment there was stunned silence. Pagan stared at Richard, who was laughing into his bourbon.

'It isn't going to hurt you, is it?' Pam said. 'I mean, we're talking five hundred bucks each! I could get those Manolos I saw in Macy's last week.'

'Baz and I are going to Long Island this weekend. It would be really handy for our bank balance,' Rachel, Pam's other girlfriend, said longingly.

'Honey, don't do it if you don't want to,' Anne said.

'But it's just one kiss,' Pam protested.

'Yeah, but not on the cheek. This guy is expecting the

full works. Tonsil-tickling, hands on your titties, fingers feeling your ovaries ... and what if he's a complete nutcase?'

'Oh, relax! It's easy money!' Pam said crossly.

'Calm down, I'll do it!' Pagan drained her vodka and stood up, smoothing her skirt. If he so much as looked at her anywhere else he would get it in the balls.

'Way to go, girl,' Rachel said admiringly.

'Go, girl,' Pam said. 'Earn that dough.' She rubbed her hands with anticipation.

Aware of their eyes on her back Pagan took a deep breath and approached Richard.

'You just can't leave me alone, can you?'

'Looking like that, I'm surprised any man is leaving you alone.' He gave her a boldly lecherous once-over from the top of her head to her pointed toes. She tossed her hair and thrust her breasts out to him, flashing a vivid smile. Her nipples were hard and very prominent. She walked her fingers up his shirt, toying with the buttons. One by one she undid them until his shirt was open almost to the waist.

'I've never had a sugar daddy before,' she mused, moving her hands down over his thighs, tightly clad in the supple black leather. She squeezed them gently, a slight smile on her lips.

'You're behaving very badly,' he chided gently but declined to move away.

'It must be in the genes,' she murmured, coiling her arms around his neck. It felt very comfortable as she moved in between his legs and planted her lips on his. In the distance she could hear cheers from her table. He floundered for a moment, taken aback by the unexpectedness of the kiss. Then he responded, pulling her closer and thrusting a snaky tongue deep into her throat. For an endless moment they were locked together, the inside of his mouth smooth and wet and sexy. The taste of him intoxicated her as she rubbed against him like a cat on heat. Her feet were attached to the ground only by the tips of her toes and she was acutely aware of the subtle pulsating of something large and warm and very alive against her stomach. For a few crazy seconds he was the only reality in the crowded bar and she did not want to let him go.

Suddenly her nipple tingled under his fingers and she tore herself away. They stared at each other, both stunned.

'You copped a feel. That's an extra hundred dollars each,' she said breathlessly.

'Kiss me like that again and I'll make it a thousand.'

'Screw you, Uncle Dick,' she replied, snatching the money out of his hand. She walked carefully back to the others, trying to quell the weakness in her legs.

'Now you can 'fess up. Who is he really?' Pam asked as she took her share.

Pagan could not think. It was as if his kiss had held some kind of narcotic that had reacted with the alcohol in her bloodstream. Distantly she thought it was probably time she went home before they asked any more awkward questions.

'It was a very long time ago,' she mumbled, rooting in her bag for her phone and Filofax to call a cab. She hastily said her goodbyes and went outside to make the phone call, relieved to be away from their curious stares.

Richard was waiting on the other side of the road, leaning nonchalantly against his stretch limousine, smoking a cigarette. When he saw her he got back into the car and left his driver to respectfully hold the door open for her.

The interior was dense black, at once inviting and vaguely sinister, like the lair of a wolf. There was never any question of refusing, but she strolled across the road, taking her time. She climbed in with careful dignity and after a moment the car imperceptibly began to move. Richard poured a glass of Talisker from the fully stocked bar but did not offer her any.

'Isn't it customary to offer a lady a drink?' she said.

'Yeah, it is.' He lit a cigarette and stared moodily out of the window.

She felt a vicious satisfaction at having needled him. She looked around at her otherworldly surroundings, which included wall-to-wall cream leather and a sophisticated television and DVD unit.

'It's like a sodding hotel,' she murmured. She felt as if she were cruising on air, the feeling heightened by the complete silence surrounding her. They bounced gently over a pothole in the road and she giggled softly, unaccountably filled with devilish glee. She was drunk but in control. Definitely in control.

There was certainly room to stretch. She shifted off her seat on to the lushly carpeted floor and flexed and pointed her toes between Richard's splayed feet. Humming softly, she kicked off one shoe and walked her bare toes up his shirt to tickle his chin. The action raised her skirt almost to her panties, but he did not respond. She slipped her big toe inside his shirt and stroked his nipple. Still nothing, though the tiny nub hardened under her touch. Slowly she walked her foot back down towards his stomach, trying to undo the button there with her toes. He grabbed her foot and removed it when it went lower towards his groin. His attention was still firmly on the velvet dark and his own grim reflection. He seemed to be stoking himself up for something, like the brewing storm in the West.

'By the way, is there anything you can't eat next Saturday? I'd hate to set off an allergic reaction,' she said innocently.

He turned his icy attention to her for the briefest of moments. 'I appreciate your concern. I'll eat anything

169

except anchovies. Damned things look like fish pussies.' He went back to staring out of the window. 'I also have an aversion to arsenic,' he murmured.

'Fish pussies? I always knew your sexual preferences verged on the exotic.'

'Unlike yours, then. I hear that deep-sea fishing is very good this time of year, especially off the waters of Cape May.'

'Really? I wouldn't know,' she replied lightly.

'That's because you were too busy fucking to notice,' he replied. An edge had crept into his voice for the first time, but he still would not look at her.

She took the dwindling Marlboro from his fingers and drew on it. There was no point in reacting to his accusation. It was what he had intended and, anyway, they both knew it was true. She crushed the Marlboro in a crystal ashtray and ran her hands along the insides of his spread thighs.

'Why do some men sit like this?' she enquired. 'Are their balls too big or what?'

'You should know,' he replied, carefully removing her hands.

'What about your lady friend? The one you took to Cape Cod?'

'You could ask her. It was Rachel Prosser.'

'Oh!' She felt oddly relieved. She was also feeling exhausted after the rigours of the weekend. She closed her eyes and let the smooth motion of the car lull her to sleep.

She woke up as the car drew to a halt outside her house. Richard took a bouquet of black tissue-wrapped red roses from the driver and led her to the door. She pushed the key in the lock and smiled sweetly up at him.

'Do you want to come in?'

His face softened and he smiled back. 'Yes, of course I do.'

'That's too bad. Because you can't.' She flashed him a bitchy little smile and slipped through the door, slamming it before he had a chance to push through. She pulled the curtain across, blocking his view, and went to the living-room to do the same. She saw the car move away but did not stop to watch, just in case he was looking at her.

After checking that all the doors and windows downstairs were secure she went upstairs to run her bath, pouring lavender essential oil into the steam to relax her aching muscles and clear her head, which had begun to spin slowly. She also took a healthy dose of very non-homeopathic Tylenol to prevent a threatening headache lurking in the background. Going over the past two hours, she was not proud of the way she had acted, but there was no use in fretting about it. The damage, if it really was that, had been done.

Half an hour later she heaved herself out of the bath and leisurely moisturised with lavender body lotion before pulling on a fresh vest top and cotton panties. She then padded out of the bathroom, straight into trouble.

'You scared the shit out of me!'

'That's a first, then.' Richard was on the bed, sprawled comfortably amongst the pillows. The room was intimately dark, lit by a single lamp, and he had put the roses in a square glass tower on the dressing table. He wore nothing more than the black silk shirt, unbuttoned, and a pair of black silk boxer shorts, and he still managed to look immaculate. She tried to quell the sickening thumping of her heart, all her senses on high alert.

'I assume you climbed in through the window.'

'Naturally.'

His legs were immensely long and elegant, the ankles and feet delicate sculptures of bone and sinew. The shirt had fallen from one shoulder, giving him an unnecessarily romantic appearance blunted by the obvious bulge in his shorts. It aroused a spurt of fresh panic.

'OK, time out, mister. You are not staying here, do you understand? No way, no how.' She noticed the bottle of whisky by his side. It was nearly empty. He swung his legs off the bed and approached her, stumbling slightly and steadying himself on one of the bedposts. Though it was dangerous she could not help goading him further, like a small boy prodding at a viper with a short stick.

'I guess it's the lot of every girl to have at least one lecherous uncle,' she said contemptuously. 'Good old Uncle Dick, he's such a fucking prick . . .'

The slap when it came spun her half way across the room. She landed hard on the wooden floor, knocking the lamp off her bedside table. It landed next to her with a loud clatter. The sting of his hand made her face glow. She tried to sit up but the shock had made her weak and she fell back onto her elbows. The pain and the crazed fire in his eyes told her that the game was finally over.

'Is this how you have to get women? You beat the shit out of them to get them to do what you want?'

'You're supposed to like it, remember?' He sounded bitter, advancing on her as she tried to scrabble backwards away from him. 'No more cock-teasing, Pagan. This is reality and it fucking hurts, doesn't it?'

'Screw you,' she whispered. Her fingers brushed against a hard object: the lamp. She snatched it up and swung it at his legs, pulling the plug from the wall. Taking advantage of his temporary loss of balance she dived for the door.

He caught her just as she reached it, slamming her up against the wood, his hands pinning hers above her head. Anticipating the knee in the balls he caught her leg with his own, and she was trapped. His breath was hot and whisky laden but the look in his eyes was one of cold determination.

'Get on the bed.'

'I don't think so.' She glanced frantically around the room, looking for likely weapons, and noticed the sharp-thorned roses he had left on the dressing table. As she yanked them from the vase it toppled over, sending water all over the floor. Viciously she slashed the roses across his face, spraying blood-red petals across the room. He cried out in pain as she sped past him. She would have made it but for the water on the floor. She slipped and lost her footing, giving him time to lunge at her. He dragged her down to the floor like a panther with its kill. As they landed amongst the scattered petals she could feel how excited he was, the bludgeoning force of his cock bruising her inner thighs. Distantly she thought it was just her luck that alcohol seemed to enhance his staying power, not deaden it. Finally he straddled her hips and captured her hands in his own.

She had wounded him. Long thin scratches streaked across his face and throat, oozing small beads of blood as if he had been wrestling with a ferocious animal. His breath was hot and heavy, a high flush blooming on his pale skin.

Her nipples tightened under his scrutiny, which had the effect of inviting him to suck one of them. His tongue sent a betraying tingle direct to the other, which hardened even more. She stared up at the ceiling, angry with her body for giving in so easily.

'Don't do this,' she moaned. 'Please...'

'If you insist.' He moved to the other breast, where the hard little nub was already waiting for his skilled mouth to work its magic. As he suckled her he stroked her stomach with the lightest of touches. His hand was at the top of her panties, tracing the edge round and down towards her moist, perfumed centre. Her musky smell renewed his hunger and with one movement he wrenched the panties downwards.

The crude action galvanised Pagan back to life. She brought her legs up and bucked, trying to get him away from her. It didn't help. He yanked the scrap of material over her feet, swatting her leg to one side to open her up entirely.

She had never felt so exposed and vulnerable before, with no one around but this primeval man who was going to have her, no matter what. His teeth sank into her throat, his fingers unleashing an overwhelming force that felt so damned good, despite being so wrong. She managed to twist her body around so she was on her front, but he pushed her against the bed and thrust her legs apart. Not stopping to check if she was moist enough to receive him he pushed hard into her, uttering a strangled moan when he felt her soft, wet warmth.

She cried out with the harsh excitement of feeling him so huge inside her, but when his finger pushed against her rectum she squirmed, trying to escape it. He held her down with his hand buried in her hair, pushing her face into the bedclothes and pushed his fingertip up her arse. With obscenely skilled co-ordination he began to ream both orifices at once, ignoring her mews of protest.

'God, you're good,' he murmured. 'Do you like that?' Another push, deeper into her depths. 'When did Roscoe last make you feel like that? Has his cock ever done this to you, Pagan?' He was talking almost to himself.

She could not respond. She felt too weak to do anything other than accept him though he was abusing her, using her need for release to punish her for teasing him so cruelly. She wanted him to go faster, harder, so they could both let go, make some noise, relieve some of the tension that had been building steadily between them. But he just kept the same maddening rhythm, fighting his own desire to lose control. When raw need finally defeated him he came with two huge lunges, a hoarse cry ripping from his very soul.

He withdrew and threw her on the bed where she stayed unmoving, as limp as a broken doll. His seed glistened between her splayed legs and her eyes were open and blank, but inside she was burning with the glory of finally accepting the need that had threatened to engulf her. She wanted his overpowering sexuality. She wanted his body all over hers. Roberto and Tom were imposters compared to his masterful understanding of her body. It no longer mattered what anyone thought; this man was the one she had been waiting for since she first discovered how good it was to be bad.

She listened to him in the bathroom, splashing water on his face, using the toilet. Excited anticipation made her quiver inside but she kept still. He came out and stared down at her, and behind his cold blue eyes she could see real regret.

'You raped me,' she said in a small, dull voice, her eyes haunted and huge.

He looked stricken, trying to find the words to justify what he had done but finding none. She watched him suffer for a few moments before giving him a totally feline smile.

'Do it again.'

He did not move, visibly struggling with the realisation that she had fooled him and exposed his anguish. Then came anger, incandescent and slow burning. She did not see it until he picked up the whisky bottle and deliberately tipped the contents over her sprawled body. As she shrieked with the cold shock of it he pinned her to the bed with his hand firmly around her throat. His smile was one of pure savagery.

'If you really want me, you damned well come and find me.'

And he walked out, leaving her amongst the liquid remains of their conflict.

14

Greg's weekend with Renate had cost him dear, both financially and physically. He could not remember how many people had been involved in the final orgiastic party they had gone to in Long Island, but he had left it feeling bloated with fucking, food and designer drugs, but still able to satisfy Renate in the limousine on the way back to Manhattan. His cock had become the centre of his being, a force he was ruled by, morning, noon and night. It even helped him forget the Damocles Sword hanging over his head. Each morning a pinch of coke woke him up enough to feel human again. It was only a pinch. Renate seemed to have a constant supply of the stuff but he barely used it. It was just nice knowing it was there.

Meanwhile Renate continued to taunt him. The night before he had gone to the club, only to find her being skewered by Benny from behind whilst her lips were wrapped around the club owner's cock. Tony was a small hairy beast of a man, all muscles and balls and buttocks like firm melons. Benny was using his full weight to force his mass of cock deep into her. They were like snorting bulls defiling a dainty gazelle, but her eyes were laughing at Greg as she jiggled the scrotal sac in her hand, her pretty mouth distorted by the fat penis pushing at the back of her throat. He had been revolted but totally transfixed at Tony's prodigious stash of semen oozing over her lips, her throat working as she gulped the viscous liquid down like life-giving nectar.

He was looking forward to the following Saturday

with equal degrees of trepidation and anticipation. Now he knew that Richard and Pagan were already lovers, it put a different slant on things. Had Richard persuaded Pagan to perform for Greg, or even agree to be shared by them? That scenario had kept him hard when it mattered over the weekend. Or was Richard just going to give him the money and disappear with Pagan, leaving him in an untenable position at Wolfen and with a great deal of explaining to do to his mother? Renate had assured him that Pagan wanted the wedding to go ahead, but the way Pagan had put the phone down on him on Sunday night had not augered well. Not that he had been bothered at the time, with Renate and Michelle licking at his cock like a strawberry popsicle.

The coke kept him from worrying about it too much. As a precaution he had hired a private detective to track Richard and Pagan's movements. He wanted as much incriminating evidence as possible, which he would use if Pagan decided not to marry him. He flew to Atlanta feeling that he was actually in control of the situation.

Pagan waited two excruciatingly long days before contacting Richard again. In that time she started packing for the following week and cleared her diary. She even dealt with an increasingly fraught Sylvia Roscoe with an air of serene calm.

On Tuesday just after lunch she dressed with ultimate care for her visit to Manhattan. As the late April day was warm she chose a simple voile shift that flipped around just above her knees. It had an indistinct floral pattern, not too fussy, in cream with the same green as her eyes. The elegant draped neckline was modest unless she chose to bend down, revealing an uninterrupted view right down to her navel. With it she wore a slim serpentine gold chain and pearlised sandals, two bars held together with three gold hoops, and pearly nail polish on her toes. And underneath she was wearing the cream Lejaby lace bra and panties she had bought the day before at Lord and Taylors at huge expense.

She had made two major decisions. Decision number two was the reason that she was looking so critically at her reflection, dabbing Christian Dior's Allure behind her ears and between her breasts.

'OK, baby,' she said finally. 'Let's go kick some family butt.'

An hour later she strode into Richard's office. Eleanor was there, taking dictation. She leapt from the chair, her tight-cheeked face horrified.

'Ms Warner! You can't just...'

'It's OK. We'll continue this later.' Richard closed the file he had been working from. Eleanor hovered, looking anxious.

'I said it's alright! Piss off and shut the door,' Richard snapped.

'There's no need to talk to her like that!' Pagan protested.

But Eleanor was already walking out, shutting the door behind her with quiet dignity.

Richard pocketed his Mont Blanc fountain pen. 'She's used to it. Been with me for over ten years. But I presume you didn't come here to make judgment on the way I talk to my staff?'

'It sounds like someone should.'

'OK! I'll apologise to her later and get some Godiva chocolates. Happy?'

'It's a start. Anyway, you're already in the doghouse. I object when a man walks out on me.' She tried to keep her voice level.

Slowly Richard rose from his chair. It was a huge black leather executive chair with padded armrests and a deeply dimpled back.

'Sit down and shut the fuck up,' she said.

Richard sat back down. He pushed the chair backwards to make room for her as she walked round the desk. From a safe distance she silently inspected him. He wore narrow black suit trousers, his shirt a pristine white under a buttoned waistcoat. His tie was discreet; slender silver and black horizontal stripes. And although his ebony hair was long enough to be caught in one of those hideous stubby ponytails favoured by small-time Italian gangsters and used-car salesmen, he chose to wear it slicked straight back. He looked nothing like the blood- and sweat-streaked animal he had been two nights before, though the four long scratches on his face were clearly visible.

'If you touch me I'll walk out. Understand?' Her voice was imperious.

He nodded slowly. She turned his face roughly to one side so she could inspect the damage, then moved close and ran her tongue gently along the length of each wound. The last one stopped within an inch of his lips. He was keeping his concentration firmly on a spot on the opposite wall, but she could almost hear his heart thumping. The plump leather armrests squeaked softly as he gripped them, his knuckles clearly showing white.

She lifted his left hand and licked it from palm to fingertip with a moist pointed tongue. This time his lips opened in an involuntary gasp. When she sucked the tip of his finger into her mouth his heavy upper lids drooped and he uttered a single grunt deep in his chest.

As he watched thirstily, she gathered up her dress and slipped a hand inside her panties so the smell of her sex was on her fingers. Pulling her dress back down primly, she traced a light line from the middle of his forehead down his nose to his lips. His nostrils flared at her scent and he tried to lick her fingertips as they passed, but she drew them away and sat back on the desk. She picked up the half-smoked cigar in the black marble ashtray and his lighter. Keep her eyes locked onto his she lit the cigar, drawing the fragrant smoke into her lungs and expelling it back out so it drifted in front of his nose. Her pretty dress and the insolent way she was smoking his cigar was packing a potent sexual punch, judging by his shallow, uneven breathing. She propped her feet, either side of his legs, on his chair.

'Great view,' she said, looking out of the window.

Richard was also enjoying a great view, right up to her silk panties.

'Is it? I mean, it is. A great view.' His voice was gravelled with desire.

She let him look for a few more moments before setting the cigar back down on the ashtray. She took his hands and put them on her warm, silky smooth knees. He moved stiffly as she pulled him towards her, his hands running up her legs. He squeezed her flesh involuntarily, overcome by her close proximity. She paused, waiting for the moment just before he decided to grab her anyway.

'Does this count as coming to find you?' she asked softly. The way she said *coming* was loaded with innuendo.

It was like lighting a blue touch paper. He launched himself at her with an animal cry, drowning her with his kiss. She was as light and dainty as a china doll as he pushed her back onto the desk, but there was nothing delicate about the way her legs wrapped around his waist, pulling him into her grasp. Lost in a madness of steamy kisses, any last scrap of doubt she had been clinging to went flying from the room. Their kiss became breathless and greedy, drowning out all sound. She tugged at his hair and the collar of his shirt, breaking the kiss to rub her cheek like a cat against the fine wool of his waistcoat and inhale his unique aroma. He smelled as a real man should; of cigars and woody aftershave and the bourbon he had with his lunch earlier. It was a heady mix that made her drunk with longing. As he bit her tenderly on the soft curve between neck and shoulder she began to undulate beneath him, her body feeling for the hardness in his pants.

'I want you so much,' she whispered, running light fingers over his face. He was haunted and beautiful in close-up, his pale eyes darkened with untamable passions.

He tried to reply but could not, such was the emotion she had evidently wrought in him. His breath was hot and moist, the tremble in his body told of terrible restraint. She pulled him to her again, kissing his mouth, his nose and finally his eyes, licking the salt away. He laced his fingers with hers and stretched out her arms across the dark mahogany, rendering her totally unable to move. A stack of in-trays fell to the floor with a loud crash but they hardly noticed as he ground his pelvis against hers in a slow, lascivious dance so erotic she felt paralysed with lust.

'No more games, Pagan. This is for real,' he warned her, pushing his cock so hard against her needy pussy lips that it felt almost as intense as real fucking.

'No games,' she answered softly, hugging him closer with her legs and rocking him gently. He eased the small dress up past her buttocks and whimpered with pleasure at the wisp of cream lace covering her pubis. Then his hands were on her inner thighs, pushing them apart, his tongue working between her swollen labia. She cried out at the deliciously warm, wet, probing feelings, the inside of her thighs slick and cool from his saliva. Stretched out across management reports, bar charts and memos she experienced an orgasmic surge at this arrogant, powerful man reduced to slavering over her cunt. The first flutter of his tongue over her clitoris was enough to set her body vibrating, so needy had she been after their violent encounter three days before. As he responded to her body's desires, Pagan was sucked into a vortex of ever-increasing joy, crying out for more and more until she was sure the whole office could hear her. As the last sporadic pulses faded away he stared down at her, wild eyed and wet from her juices. They kissed again, stickily, flavoured with her musk. She licked him clean, liking her smell and taste on him.

'Get inside me, you crazy fuck,' she growled.

It was as if her voice had been a slap on the face. He suddenly hauled her to her feet, straightening her dress. She felt bewildered and lost and near to tears, until he kissed the hurt expression from her face.

'I'm taking you home. When we get there, I'm going to make love to you. But I need your guidance. It isn't something I'm very good at.'

'Not very . . .' She suddenly realised what he meant. 'I'll teach you,' she said softly.

They left via the security entrance so no one would see them. In the car he kissed her again; a short, ferocious burst of emotion that left her in no doubt that she was now committed to what she had started. He steered with one hand, the other tightly holding hers as he drove to the Upper Seventies and stopped outside a palatial apartment building.

A doorman opened the door of the Mercedes and helped her out. Richard handed him the keys and they walked into the building. The floor was marble and the chandelier huge, sparkling in tall gilt mirrors. It was a step up from the brownstone loft he had taken her to before. They entered the lift and the doorman pressed the button marked 'PH': penthouse.

He did not touch her as the lift took them skywards. She sensed the tension tightly coiling within him, holding him back, his eyes fixed to her hint of a smile.

They were a long way up, with Central Park stretching like a green velvet quilt below them and, in the distance, the Upper West Side, a fairytale jumble of old New York skyscrapers. The penthouse suite was chic and spare, similar in style to his other apartment but it was obvious that a lot more care had gone into it. An interior designer had obviously been in and filled the whole apartment with black leather and stainless steel. A plush white carpet ran throughout, except in the kitchen and bathroom, where the floor was a glossy black marble, and the stairs, which curved in a graceful black spiral to the next floor. Slender futuristic lamps perched on glass tables; a copy of *Forbes* lay on one of them.

He captured her around the waist, his breath feathering through her hair. She turned to kiss him, sharing the sweetness of her tongue as it slid against his own.

'Do you have any champagne?' she whispered. 'First rule of lovemaking: always have champagne.'

As he went to the kitchen she examined the contents of his bookshelves. He had an eclectic taste in books, from Dostoevsky and Maupassant to the complete words of James Ellroy, plus a collection of vintage *Playboy* magazines. The mix of sensual and violent literature did not surprise her. Knowing what she did of him, it seemed his personality was fairly represented by his preferences.

He came back holding a bottle of Krug and two crystal flutes. He was frowning at the label.

'1989. I'm told it was a vintage year.'

'You're not an expert then?' She grinned at him.

'Is that the second rule of lovemaking? If so I've failed at the first post.'

'Relax. The second rule is to get very comfortable.' She put the magazine on the table and stretched luxuriously, making the supple leather creak softly. Richard expertly removed the foil and cage from the bottle. The cork came out with the gentlest of pops, just as it should do. She took the offered flute and toasted him. 'This is pretty acceptable.'

'That's a relief.' He came to sit on the floor next to her, wrapping his arm comfortably around her waist and kissing her stomach. 'There's something gloriously decadent about drinking champagne in the middle of the afternoon, alone with a beautiful woman.'

'I guess you're used to it.'

He shrugged. 'With whores, yes. Or with someone else's wife. It's an illusion, that's all. Like playing at being alive. With you it feels –' he nuzzled her stomach again whilst he searched for the right word '– like coming home.'

She palmed his face in her hand. 'Talk to me,' she said softly. 'Tell me who you are.'

He turned away from her, so abruptly that for a moment she thought he was angry with her. But when he looked at her again his eyes were unmistakably moist.

'What's wrong?'

He laughed deprecatingly and refilled their glasses. 'Nothing. You're just the first woman who's ever bothered to ask, that's all. All the others were only interested in my money and my dick.'

'Having both does help,' she replied seriously.

He laughed again, moving down to slip her sandals

off. 'I agree. But I can only tell you what I know. If you want any more you'll have to ask my therapist. I've made him a millionaire, too, you know,' he added dryly.

Unknown to him Richard had passed a crucial test. If he had dodged the issue Pagan would have been disappointed, but it seemed that her question had given him permission to justify why he was the way he was. For an hour he talked, in a way he had never talked to a woman. After the way he had been treated by women as a child it had taken him over forty years to trust one again. All the while she stroked his hair and pressed comforting kisses on his forehead when the memories became too painful.

'I always wanted to be able to throw my hard-earned cash in Arthur's face and tell him to go fuck himself,' he said finally. 'When I finally did, it felt so fucking good.' He had removed his diamond cufflinks and had been using them as worry beads for the last hour. Now he dropped them into her champagne glass. 'There you go. Champagne and diamonds. Don't say I don't know how to treat a woman.'

'What did you do to celebrate making your first million?' She retrieved one of the cufflinks and trailed it against his lips. He sucked the precious liquid from it and she dipped it in the champagne again, feeding him slowly, tiny jewels of liquid falling on and around his lips. He licked them away.

'I started on making my second. You know, thinking back about it, I was a pretty dull fucker back then.' He smiled, a pure Machiavellian grin that belied his words.

'I hardly think so.' She kissed his forehead.

'You understand me too well, my sweet.' He sighed contentedly, nuzzling her stomach. 'What's the third rule of lovemaking?'

Now they had stopped talking seriously, the room seemed too quiet. 'Music,' she said decisively, heaving him off her lap so she could get up. Flipping through his CD collection she found several surprises. The jazz and opera were a given, but not The Verve, Tracey Chapman and the Eels. Then she picked one up and looked incredulously at him.

'ELO? Shame on you!'

'That's an old one,' he said defensively.

'It can't be, it's on CD. Ah, here's one.' She had chosen Aretha Franklin. She looked at the sleek blank machine and frowned. 'How do you get the darned thing open?'

Richard went over and waved his palm over the Bang & Olufson music centre. It opened without a whisper. By the time Aretha starting singing, 'You're no good, heartbreaker...' Pagan was back on the sofa. She lay down and stroked the leather next to her.

'Rule four. Always make out.'

'I definitely like the sound of that.' He crawled onto the sofa, straddling her and settled down half on top of her, trapping her against the back of the sofa. 'Caught you, you little minx,' he murmured, before sliding his tongue deep into her throat. She began to squirm as his hands roamed over her body, pushing up the thin dress and cupping the creamy swell of her buttocks. He was still fully dressed and it was intensely erotic to fumble through his expensive clothes to stroke his bare back. It was smooth and warm, each vertebra a tight little knot. He moaned and pushed against her, taking her hand and pressing it against his cock. She unzipped him and palmed the swelling organ in her hand. He was wearing boxer shorts made of silk as light as gossamer, allowing her to feel every vein, every ridge, pubic hair rasping crisply against her fingers. Subtly she worked her fingers up one leg of the shorts until she came into contact with bare skin, velvet smooth in the crease of his thigh. He growled with pleasure and began fighting with his tie. She brushed his hands away and unknotted it for him, casting it aside before fiddling with the buttons on his waistcoat and shirt for the second time that afternoon. She took her time, kissing each inch of skin as it was uncovered, but made him leave the garments on, enjoying the shambles she had made of him. She ran her fingers through his hair, messing it up and wiping the residue of hair gel onto his handmade shirt. She opened the shirt and sought out his nipples with her teeth, tugging at them gently, feeling his gasp of breath in her hair.

He lifted her dress above her head and threw it over the back of the sofa. Her lingerie followed after he had given it due admiration, ripping her panties in the process.

'I don't have any underwear left, thanks to you,' she protested.

'Now it's off, you might as well let me take you to bed,' he said mildly.

'I thought you'd never ask.'

His bedroom was at the top of a spiral wrought-iron staircase. His bed was at least seven feet wide, covered with a deep red silk throw; a dramatic statement in a room that was predominately white. On the wall opposite was a watercolour of a young woman posing in a chair, her legs drawn up in front of her. Her smile was shy but her eyes were bold, and behind her dainty feet one could just see her young, plump sex, barely covered in red-tinted pubic fluff. Behind her, in black and grey, was the sketch of a wolf with pale blue eyes; eyes that seemed to follow Pagan around the room.

'Oh my god, that's me!' Pagan exclaimed softly.

'That's right,' Richard said behind her. 'I commissioned an artist and gave him a photo of you that I'd found in your father's effects.'

She should have been angry with him, but she could feel the love that had gone into the painting.

'It's beautiful,' she admitted, thinking it looked better than the real thing.

'Actually you look better than that now,' he said, again reading her thoughts with disturbing accuracy.

'I wish you wouldn't keep doing that. Reading my mind all the time.'

'Can you read mine?'

She beckoned him to come closer. When he was within reach she spread her palm and placed it over his face. 'Let me see. You're thinking ... why am I here?'

He kissed her hand and moved it away. 'Clever girl. Are you going to tell me?'

She slipped the shirt and waistcoat from his shoulders as one and discarded them. She ran her hands over his broad chest and wide angular shoulders, thinking how strange it was that his size did not overwhelm her, but filled her with a deep-rooted sense of belonging and maybe even love. But she stuffed that last thought firmly in the box where it belonged, right at the back of her mind. She'd get raw lust out of the way first, before clouding it with more heavy emotional issues. There would be plenty of those soon enough.

His face changed and she knew that hesitation in answering him had given him the wrong impression.

'No more games, Pagan, just tell me! Why are you here? After all the denial, the fighting, the bad words. Why? And now, before you have the chance to lie about it. Quickly!' He rapped out the last word, snapping his fingers in her face.

'I don't know! I can't find the words so please don't ask me to explain. Not right now, anyway.' She stroked his face, hushing him, letting him know with her eyes that she was for real. He gradually relaxed and the tension left his body.

'Thank you,' he said quietly. 'Now can we get on with it?'

'Fifth rule of lovemaking: take your time,' she said lightly as he removed the remainder of his clothes. He turned to her, naked and fully erect. His cock was as long and thick as a broadsword. The crude splendour of it aroused her to the point of weakness.

'I say fuck the rule book. I think we've waited long enough, don't you?'

15

Pagan woke up the next morning to tuneful male humming and the smell of freshly roasted Java coffee. She buried her face in his pillow, inhaling his animal scent, then sprawled out to wait for him. He loped silently into the room, carrying a tray with the coffee and pressed orange juice. He was wearing a black silk robe, unfastened so she could see his nakedness underneath. As he set the tray down beside the bed she watched him, thinking curiously that she had not actually seen him without an erection before. His skin was very pale, emphasising the blackness of the hair on his body. Not that there was much, and it was soft and silky, concentrated in a glossy nest between his legs. His cock was impressive even in repose, framed by a pendulous pair of balls that had felt divine smacking against her thighs late the previous night.

When he saw her watching him he slipped off the robe and stood next to the bed. She rolled onto her back and shifted her body so she could see up under his scrotum. It hung down like a succulent ripe fruit. His cock began to twitch as she ran her hand down between her legs and stroked herself, spreading her labia wide so he could see how pink and wet she was amidst the soft fluffy hair. She reached up for his cock with her other hand and pulled him down so she could draw him into her mouth. His cock thickened almost instantly as he kneeled on the bed and nuzzled between her legs. He tasted clean and soapy, swelling and filling her mouth as he moved gently up and down, growling deep in his throat.

Her clitoris felt numb from all the attention it had received the previous day, but his skilled tongue knew just how to pleasure her. She moaned and churned, muffled by the thickness in her mouth that seemed to grow harder every time she made a sound. She worked her hand up to scratch gently at his balls. He seemed close to coming but, using mutual understanding, they timed the moment perfectly, he bolting deep into her throat as she lost herself in a series of sharp, almost painful peaks. They pressed their bodies close, wanting to feel each orgasmic moment, their sounds of pleasure vibrating through each others' bodies.

After a moment of rest he turned around and kissed her.

'Good morning,' he said cheerfully, as if the previous erotic five minutes had never occurred. 'Would you like a warm bagel to go with that?'

She giggled and stretched luxuriously. 'I'd love one.' As he went away she savoured the creamy taste of his semen in her mouth. It was something she was normally repulsed by, but not with him. Even anal sex was pleasurable with him, despite his size. She clenched her tender backside and was relieved that she still had some muscle tone left.

They ate the bagels with butter and strawberry conserve imported from Fortnum & Mason, drank the coffee and then drowsed around until mid-morning. Another passionate lovemaking session spiked her hunger enough to walk to the Plaza for brunch at his table at Le Regence. He went there most days for breakfast, he said casually, but tended to avoid weekends when it seemed full of wealthy tourists. Afterwards she reminded him that he owed Eleanor an apology for his rudeness the previous day, so they walked to Godiva

Chocolatier, where Pagan picked out a lavish selection of the exquisitely formed confections.

'She's going to think I've flipped,' Richard said mildly as they waited for the chocolates to be gift wrapped and topped with a gold voile bow.

'Not at all. After ten years she'll already know you're nothing more than a big pussy cat,' Pagan replied, reaching up to tickle him under the chin.

'Make that pussy lover,' Richard grinned, taking the sumptuous parcel from the shocked assistant and winking at her. They went out of the shop laughing.

Pagan browsed in Saks whilst Richard delivered his apology along with the chocolates. He had given her orders to choose some underwear to replace the items he had ruined, but her mind was not on shopping. When he found her again she kissed him deeply, ignoring the fact that they were standing in the middle of the store.

'Let's go back to bed,' she said.

The next day they worked at the apartment, catching up on phone calls and e-mails, enjoying the companionable normality of life in between sumptuous meals and slow, voluptuous lovemaking. Pagan had one message from Greg in Atlanta, but she erased it without bothering to reply. After all, he regularly did the same to her.

They went to Dean & DeLuca to order groceries for Saturday night. She had been surprised that Richard wanted the evening to go ahead, but he seemed excited by the prospect.

'Don't you get it? Fucking you in front of Roscoe is the ultimate power trip. I want him to see exactly what he's throwing away.' He kissed her hard, bruising her mouth, and the depth of his feeling was enough to trigger her own excitement. Guilt wasn't an option. She had watched in disbelief in the hushed offices of Chase

Manhattan bank as Richard wired half a million dollars into Greg's Swiss bank account without even blinking. If Greg was prepared to sell her for five hundred thousand, she might as well have some fun.

They went back to her house that night and tested the four-poster bed to its limit. She made him park the Mercedes in the large double garage as a token act of discretion, but anyone with keen hearing would have known that she was not with Greg. She had called him earlier, just to make sure he would not turn up unannounced in the middle of the evening. He said he would be flying back from Atlanta the following afternoon, and he sounded peeved that she had not returned his earlier message.

On Friday morning she woke before Richard. For a while she was happy just to watch his long, dark lashes flicker softly against skin as pale as parchment, and the slight smile on his lips shift and change like dappled sunlight. She tenderly kissed the prominent vein on his temple, the one that throbbed when he was aroused. He mumbled and turned, but the physical excesses of the past few days had finally caught up with him and he sank again into slumber as deep as quicksand.

Downstairs she made a cup of English tea and put the television on quietly, curling up on the sofa to watch a sycophantic interview with Joan Rivers and the Duchess of York. Then she realised that the Duchess of York was doing the interviewing. That was weird. But then so was her own situation, with her uncle upstairs in her bed and her future husband about to receive a very large amount of money for her services.

After a while she heard movement upstairs so she went to the kitchen to prepare breakfast. She jumped when he appeared in the doorway, fully dressed. He looked more serious than he had over the past two days.

'What's wrong?'

'The spare room door was open. I saw your case, half packed. From the look of the shoes and the fancy underwear anyone would think you were getting married soon.'

Pagan cursed silently. She was sure she had kept that room shut to avoid awkward questions.

'I started packing over a week ago. A lot has changed since then.'

'You're damned right.' Richard opened the back door and lit a cigarette, leaning in the doorway so the smoke drifted out into the balmy spring morning. 'When are we going to tell him about us?'

'I'll talk to him on Sunday when we're alone.'

'No way. Whatever you say can be said in front of me.'

She waggled a stern finger at him. 'Now listen, mister. Just because I sleep with you it doesn't mean you can start dictating how I run my life.'

'You *sleep* with me? Are you saying I'm just an itch that needed scratching? Someone to spice up your wonderful relationship?'

She stood her ground, unfazed by his sudden change in mood. 'My relationship with Greg is a mess, Richard. I thought you might have noticed by now.'

'I've noticed it's over, if that's what you mean.' He continued to smoke, watching her with speculative eyes. He looked good in the cream pleated chinos and white linen Paul Smith shirt she had chosen for him the day before, his feet bare, the arms of the shirt rolled half way up to his elbows, showing off his lean sinewy arms. In fact he looked so good that she forgot their difficult conversation and wanted him again right then.

Seeming to take in the hunger written plainly on her face, his tension visibly melted away. He flipped the cigarette into the sink and drew her into his arms.

'Which rooms haven't we fucked in yet?'

She thought for a moment. 'The garage and the downstairs loo.'

Wordlessly he led her to the door leading into the large garage. The Mercedes gleamed like quicksilver in the gloom. The air was cold and she shivered as he rescued his big cashmere coat from the passenger seat. He wrapped it around her shoulders and pushed her back onto the wide expanse of bonnet, opening the robe to expose her long white thighs. There was a strong smell of oily grass clippings and other grubby, dusty garage odours but he knelt down on the filthy floor, spread her legs wide and began to lick at her with a hot probing tongue. She cried out with the shock, trying to stop from slithering downwards on her bed of cashmere and silk lining whilst he tried to hold her up on the car bonnet. It was hideously uncomfortable, but she could feel her orgasm building as her fingers brushed against the car's silver three-point emblem. She grasped it, triumphant in the scene they were making: Richard slavishly worshiping her cunt on that luxurious symbol of his wealth. Her climax was sudden and noisy, taking them both by surprise. Then she threw away the coat and hastily pulled at her chemise. She pressed her bare breasts against the big cold car, feeling her nipples spring to life. It was almost as if she had forgotten Richard was there, pulling her undulating hips back so he could lunge into her. She was revelling in the feel of cold hard metal under her body, coupled with the hot throbbing flesh and blood challenging her inner muscles.

'Oh, yes,' she whispered, drunk with dizzying, lecherous thoughts. Nothing mattered except the fuck, the explosion of feelings, the desperate need for more, and more and more. He rammed inside her, coming with a loudly sobbed curse. Afterwards he braced himself against her, regulating his breathing. She stretched like a cat beneath him and kissed the Mercedes lovingly.

'Thank you,' she murmured.

'You're welcome,' Richard said above her. She smiled secretly and did not disillusion him.

The table looked perfect; silver cutlery gleaming under a soft candlelight, reflecting simple white and gold bone china. Pagan had made a long, low arrangement of waxy lilies and shiny laurel leaves around three fat church candles, as yet unlit. The Beaujolais breathed on the sideboard, along with a large platter containing English cheddar, stilton and a meltingly ripe Camembert, all coming up to room temperature.

Nina Simone's smoke-laden voice floated from the sitting room as Pagan put the last garnish on a simple Caesar salad. The beef Wellington was in the oven, smelling meaty and delicious, accompanied by potato dauphinois. Tiny French beans waited to be steamed on the hob. The *jus* for the beef had already been prepared, dark and wine-rich and waiting to be warmed in an elegant white gravy boat. Pagan prided herself on her entertaining ability. Her range was not wide, but she had a knack for presentation.

She had dressed just as carefully, in a fabulously expensive Gucci dress Richard had bought for her the day before. She had not let him see her in it, but she knew he would approve. It was the latest style: strapless and figure-forming in fine black tulle over flesh-coloured silk, the seams accentuating the pointed bra top. She had seen it on Sarah Jessica Parker, but had not expected it to look so good on herself. Her uplifted breasts had a playful 'look at me' air about them, nestling in the low-cut bodice like white chocolates in a box, but without being too over the top. After all, Greg was the corporate tart, not her. With it she wore sheer black stockings and Manolo Blahnik stilettos with fetishistic straps around the ankle, and around her neck was a simple black choker studded with small chips of jet. The final touch was a dab of Paloma Picasso perfume behind her ears and between her breasts, and a slick of Estee Lauder's Black Wine lip colour.

Richard arrived precisely at eight o'clock, looking every inch the millionaire playboy in his black silk shirt and the tight leather trousers. Only this time he had left the buttons of the shirt half undone, presumably to save her time later and to display the slender platinum choker chain around his neck. When she walked in the room he and Greg were discussing the fifty-year-old cognac Richard had brought with him. Richard had sampled a bottle the previous week, he said as if casually mentioning an admittedly fine Californian Cabernet Sauvignon.

But they stopped talking when they saw her. Greg's mouth dropped open. His gaze dropped to her breasts and stayed there. Richard's facial expression did not change but his eyes suddenly lit with a flame that made her shiver. As she moved the light played tricks on the fine tulle and gave it a shimmering, whispering life of its own.

'It's good to see you again,' she said in a low sultry voice, proffering her cheek for a kiss whilst shutting Greg's mouth with a finger under his chin.

'You're more lovely every time I see you,' Richard said plainly. For a moment they were aware only of each other, before Greg coughed and offered aperitifs.

Behind the kitchen door she saw Richard pass a slim white envelope to Greg, and Greg's satisfied smile. She should have been angry, but when he had arrived home that lunchtime she had looked at him with fresh eyes. He was as stunning as a Greek god, and the thought of him watching her with Richard and getting turned on by it had kept her shivering with moist anticipation all afternoon.

She was adding the last coriander garnish to roses of smoked salmon when he sneaked up behind her.

'You look very tasty.' He slipped his arms around her and cupped her breasts, palpating them gently. For a split second she was confused. Which man was it? Then she saw Greg's wide, spatulate hands on her stomach and she experienced a power rush that was almost orgasmic. Two men, both stunning, both focused solely on her. What more could a girl ask for?

She turned and twined her arms around his neck. 'You look pretty scrumptious, too. Can I have you for dessert?' She ran her finger down his gold and grey polka dot silk tie. His charcoal grey suit was Hugo Boss, very new. She wondered whether he had bought it especially for that night. She manipulated her hipbone against his cock and felt it shift as Richard appeared in the doorway.

'God, you're hot tonight,' Greg muttered. 'I'm as hard as rock. And so's Richard.'

'I noticed,' she whispered, laughing silkily and smiling at Richard over Greg's shoulder. 'And I think he's hungry, too.'

Greg noticed Richard and flushed pink. 'Sorry, Dick. I've been away from her too long.'

'Don't mind me,' Richard said wryly, shooting a murderous look at Pagan. He stayed as Greg went back into the living room. 'What the hell are you playing at?' he hissed.

Her eyes widened innocently. 'I'm just having a little fun. Girls like to do that, you know.'

'Not at my expense, you don't.'

She moved close and closed her hand around his cock. It was as hard as stone and plainly obvious under the skin-hugging black leather. She gave it a tiny squeeze and drew away again.

'You love it really,' she whispered with a knowing smile.

The meal went even better than planned. The beef was moist and still slightly pink in its golden crust of short pastry. The mango and lime mousse that followed was fluffy and tangy, complemented by papery almond wafers.

'By the way, I've given Silverskin the contract for updating our software system,' Richard said casually.

Pagan paused from stacking dessert plates. 'Seriously?'

'I don't joke about executive decisions. The letter went out late last night.'

Pagan was speechless. In between hours of exuberant lovemaking, she had not noticed him doing any work. Besides, she had dismissed their previous meeting as a ruse.

'Well, what do you say?' Greg prompted her.

She hated him then for making her feel like a little girl. Richard instantly picked up on her irritation.

'Don't say anything. Your presentation was very professional and I believe in giving the underdog a chance.'

Greg spluttered into his wine. 'That's hardly the way to do business, though.'

'Which is why I'm a multi-millionaire and you're not.' Richard's glacial stare squelched him flat.

Pagan thought it was a good time to make the coffee. As she arranged thin parmesan cheese biscuits on a dainty Royal Doulton plate she heard Richard challenging Greg to an argument on the impending presidential election, and how it could, theoretically, affect Wolfen's future. Greg was floundering out of his depth, just as Richard knew he would. He had been exposing Greg's shortcomings at every opportunity, and Pagan was getting just a little annoyed with him. She was already aware that Greg had little that was new to say. They had heard all his university stories and there wasn't much of interest that one could say about accounting. It did not need Richard to underline something that was already painfully obvious.

'I hope you're not still talking shop,' she said, leaning over Richard's shoulder to put the cheese and biscuit plate on the table, together with a bowl of marinated Greek olives. She let her breasts press against him. If he turned his head he would be close enough to lick the tops of them, rising out of the low-cut dress. Her other hand rested lightly on his back. 'One thing to remember: if you're mean to my future husband, I'll be mean to you,' she said flirtatiously, shifting away. Greg looked too relieved at her intervention to pick up on the fact that she did not have to be so close to Richard to put the plate on the table.

'That sounds like incitement,' Richard said, taking an olive and winking at Greg.

'Maybe it was,' Pagan replied provocatively over her shoulder as she went back into the kitchen.

As they moved into the living room to drink the coffee she sensed that the mood of the evening had subtly changed. Richard had a slightly glazed, dissolute look that hit the bottom of her chest every time his eyes met hers. He lit a cigar, notably without asking first, and she watched him smoke it. He even managed to give that action lewd meaning; his heavy-lidded reptilian gaze stuck to her like a magnet.

Greg was in ebullient mood again, bringing out a bottle of vintage port that he had been holding on to since his twenty-first birthday.

'You realise we must finish this tonight,' he said,

struggling with the cork. 'This stuff doesn't keep and it's a crime to waste it.' He poured the tawny liquid into three small glasses. Richard sipped at it and grimaced.

'Too sweet for me,' he said. He went into the dining room and came back with the bottle of Laphroaig that Pagan had bought to replace the one he had finished last Sunday, plus a glass. It was too obvious that he had done it many times before.

Pagan caught Greg's frown and knew exactly what he was thinking. When he wasn't looking she slapped her forehead silently at Richard and mouthed 'idiot!' Richard gave her a sardonic smile in return. He obviously found the whole situation rather amusing.

She had put the platter of cheeses and biscuits on the coffee table so everyone could continue helping themselves at their leisure. Richard cut a portion of Camembert and smeared it on a cracker and handed it to Pagan.

'The most erotic food in the world. Taste it and tell me what it reminds you of. Don't hold back.'

Greg was watching closely as she ate the morsel. She swallowed and took a sip of port.

'The fresh semen of a hot man after a dip in the ocean.' She stared challengingly at him. He gave her a glimmer of a smile and toasted her description.

'One assumes you're an expert.'

Greg laughed good-humouredly. 'For God's sake, Richard, don't ask her what she thinks of the Stilton.'

Pagan took another cracker and more Camembert, allowing the men a good view of her cleavage. 'Of course, it's better when it's melted and warm, oozing out of a crust of breadcrumbs. It heightens that Mediterranean sailor effect perfectly,' she continued. 'Not that I'd know, of course, never having had a Mediterranean, or even a sailor.'

'How about a deep-sea fisherman?' Richard asked pointedly.

She smiled sweetly. 'I wouldn't know. Anyway, I like accountants. They have a very smooth texture.' She idly stroked Greg's knee. He squeezed her hand and looked smug.

'There's an endorsement for you.'

'Not everyone can differentiate between smoothness and blandness,' Richard countered tersely.

Greg excused himself with an inane comment about needing the little boy's room. As soon as he had gone Richard moved in on Pagan with the speed of a heat-seeking missile, throwing her legs apart and burying his face in her breasts, drinking in her lush womanly fragrance.

'God, I want you,' he muttered, his voice rough with desire.

'You'll just have to wait,' she whispered, stroking his hair.

He looked up at her with blatant lust. 'I don't think I can take being this hard for much longer.'

She laughed throatily. 'You're going to have to, for as long as I choose.'

'You're being a total cunt this evening.'

Hearing Greg coming back down the stairs, she pushed him violently away and rearranged her dress. Greg smiled benignly at them as Richard relaxed back on the sofa.

'I was just saying to Pagan that she's an excellent cook as well as being beautiful,' Richard said.

'She's a pretty good all-rounder, really,' Greg replied, patting her on the head.

'You need some lessons in how to treat a woman, Roscoe. What you should be doing is this.' In one movement Richard had left his seat and was pulling Pagan out of hers. They met in the middle and he planted his lips on hers. They were locked in a passionate clinch for what seemed like a lifetime before Richard let her go.

'I assume you're an expert as well,' Pagan giggled. It was a deliciously girlish sound that came out of nowhere. She had not intended to get drunk, yet there was no mistaking that bubbly yet languorous feeling that came with slightly too much alcohol. 'Let's see if you can do better,' she said to Greg.

His eyes met Richard's over her shoulder. She sensed that a tacit agreement had been reached between them. Greg pulled her close and kissed her with considerably less finesse but, as their tongues met, he relaxed into it and in seconds they were kissing more passionately than they had for weeks, even months. Then she was aware of another looming presence behind her, warming her back, lips velvet on the back of her neck, stealthy hands stroking her buttocks and thighs. Greg broke the kiss but kept her in his arms.

'Do you think she's expert enough to take both of us?' he asked Richard.

Pagan felt like hitting him. How he thought he could get away with this was beyond her. But she smiled adoringly up at him, trying to convey that she trusted him implicitly.

'She certainly looks the part,' Richard replied. 'But we won't really know if we don't test her ability.' From the sound of his voice Pagan knew he was enjoying every minute. She had a good mind to tell them both to go and fuck themselves but she had been so sexed up all afternoon, waiting for this moment. Both men were circling her like hungry predators and she was getting wetter by the second, the anticipation almost killing her.

'What is this?' She feigned a protest, knowing that even if it had been for real, the alcohol fizzing around her veins had made her too weak to fight them. She remembered Moira's words: *take what you can get, girl.* She rested her head against Greg's shoulder and smiled compliantly up at him, letting Richard swoop and give her one long slow lick over the tops of her breasts.

'I've been wanting to do that all evening,' he said.

'Hmmm, I don't think I can handle both of you.' She stumbled slightly and Richard steadied her with his hands on her waist. She reached up and laced her fingers around Greg's neck, tacitly inviting the men to explore her.

'I'm sure you'll find a way,' Richard replied softly.

Their hands were large and warm and gentle over her body; Greg's as clumsy as bear paws, Richard's as accomplished as a concert pianist's as he reached down to stroke her from ankle to thigh, exquisitely slowly, avoiding her sex, which was rapidly becoming unbearably heavy with desire. She whimpered and undulated as he worked up her other leg, pattering her skin with the very tips of his fingers. Greg's hands were on her breasts, squeezing and kneading them, his breath hot in her ear. He obviously had no intention of explaining what was suddenly happening to her, but she no longer cared. Having two men exploring her body was something she had never experienced before. She felt like a goddess, able to exert control over her lovers but choosing not to. Richard bent to kiss the base of her throat, his lips setting the whole surface of her skin shimmering.

'Magnificent,' he murmured and sucked a creamy portion of skin just above her nipple so hard it was red and bruised when he let go. She heard Greg sigh behind her. The sound also alerted Richard to his presence.

'I'll take over from here, Roscoe,' he said softly.

There was no question of argument. Greg went to sit on the sofa. He reached for his replenished glass of port and settled back to watch. Richard pressed small kisses from one shoulder to the other, pushing her hair to one side so he could taste her neck on the way. Distantly she hoped that it would not be too obvious that they were already lovers. He cupped her breasts, his thumbs hooking into the bodice and exposing her firm dusky nipples. When he pinched them gently a bolt of pure pleasure ricocheted to her clitoris and back up, hardening the nipples even more. Then she felt him unfastening her dress and peeling it away from her body so she stood in stockings, heels and panties. His fingers continued their exquisitely slow exploration, down around her deep well of a navel to her panties. He eased them over her hips and they joined her dress on the floor. She had trimmed her pubic hair so it formed a small dark triangle between her legs. Her hands hovered coyly in front of it, but her pretence at shyness did not fool him. His fingers delved between her sex lips and found her moist and wanting.

'I'm going to eat that later,' he whispered hotly.

'I didn't realise the chairman was still so hungry,' she said huskily to Greg. 'But if he wants me it'll cost him.'

For the first time Greg looked alarmed. He looked at Richard for guidance.

'How much?' Richard asked into her ear, following the question with a moist kiss.

'Hmmm, I'm very, very expensive,' she purred, enjoying Greg's growing panic. 'Say, a million dollars?'

Greg splurted into his port, but Richard just kept caressing her pussy, his body moving with hers in the gentle rhythm she had set.

'Two fifty,' he murmured and pushed the tumid length of his cock hard against her lower back. She reached back and sheathed it in her hand, feeling it pulsate against her palm.

'Five hundred,' she countered, giving his cock a hefty squeeze and staring boldly at Greg, silently conveying that she had rumbled him. Richard sighed throatily into her ear.

'Done. Get down on me before I change my mind.'
He let her go and she sank down onto her knees before
him, winking at Greg as she did so. Carefully she eased
his zip down, exclaiming softly as his erection suddenly
smacked her in the face. Richard planted his legs wider
apart for balance and scrunched her hair in his hands
as she drew him between her full wide lips.

'Oh, God,' Greg moaned, seeing her taking Richard in
hand like an expert. Richard bit his lip and stared at the
landscape of Henley-on-Thames above the fireplace.
Pagan sensed he was struggling to keep control and
drew away, leading him stumbling to the sofa to sit
next to Greg. She stood back and placed her wickedly
pointed shoe directly over his crotch, making sure he
could see right up into her plump juicy sex.

'Take it off,' she commanded. She was enjoying herself immensely, seeing these two expensive men hanging on to her every word and movement. Richard dealt
with the shoe's tiny buckle, unwrapping the slender
black straps from her ankle and easing the shoe away
from her foot. Cautiously he reached for her suspenders
and unfastened them, rolling the stocking down her leg
and over her foot. She swapped legs and proffered the
other to Greg. He fumbled with the buckle, managing
to snag her delicate nylons in the process. She threw
the suspender belt contemptuously into his lap and
straddled Richard, moving his clothes so she could rub
her lubricated mons against his naked cock. She beckoned to Greg to move closer and her hand fell into his
lap, seeking out his erection and quickly finding it,
trapped excruciatingly in his pants. As she manipulated
him he grunted softly, pushing his hips up against her
hand. As he went to unzip his trousers she slapped his
hand away, still moving against Richard and enjoying
the cocktail of lust and anger on his face. His hands
were on her buttocks, holding her hard against him. She

toyed with the knot on Greg's tie. He helped her undo it, the barest slither of silk lost under his quickening breath. He rapidly undid the top shirt button, letting her do the rest, but she was not ready yet. She turned her attention back to Richard, her green eyes penetrating his as she did the same to him. She could tell he was angry but too turned on to express it. She grasped him by the shirt collar and pulled him to her for a deep tonguing kiss. Then she did the same to Greg, her fingers slowly unfastening the rest of his shirt buttons.

'My idea of heaven, having two wealthy executives at once,' she sighed happily, giving Greg's cock an extra squeeze. With her hand still on him she wriggled down between Richard's legs and began to fellate him; long slow licks, smelling her own excitement on him, tasting the sweet clear liquid that had begun to appear right at the very tip. She heard him moan as her lips closed fully over his entire length and felt his body shiver as she continued her smooth motion, up and down, until she felt him tense and pull her away. Smiling seductively she turned her attention to Greg, unzipping his trousers like unwrapping an anticipated gift. The black bikini briefs were packed to bursting and she softly exclaimed with delight, knowing it would anger Richard even more. Carefully she peeled the briefs away and his cock sprang out like a Jack-in-the-box, to be immediately caught in her mouth. She lavished the same attention that she had on Richard. If a job was worth doing it was worth doing well and, from the noises Greg was making, she was doing very well indeed. She was aware of Richard moving off the sofa but did not expect the hard, stinging slap on her backside. She cried out and whirled around to confront him.

'I didn't pay to watch you suck someone else's dick,' he snarled, sliding his fingers into her hair and forcing her to suck him instead. She drew ferociously on his cock as he messed up her hair until it was wild and tangled, half concealing her face. She sucked him harder, wanting to hurt him, but he pushed her away, sending her sprawling onto the carpet. He prodded her with his hand-stitched shoe.

'Get on your knees, bitch.'

She rolled over so she was on all fours, her bottom stuck high in the air. Greg groaned with pleasure. Pagan looked up at him through the curtain of her hair, her face half hidden. Richard knelt behind her and spanked her bottom, once on each buttock, raising matching blooms of redness.

'Say you're sorry,' he said coldly.

'Screw you,' she replied boldly and received another hard slap for her insubordination. His roughness kept her wet but also fearful. Latent violence was an integral part of his complex personality, but he had sworn never again to use it on her. He roughly pulled her hair back so she could receive his kiss, wet and superheated all over her mouth.

'It's OK, I won't hurt you,' he whispered, eerily reading her mind yet again. He licked his fingers and worked them around her swollen sex. She squirmed in response, reassured by his words and wanting him to finger her more deeply. Instinctively he understood and sank two fingers deep inside her, slowly withdrawing them and plunging them in again, stretching her, probing her as she panted and sighed and pushed back against his hand. He withdrew his fingers and smeared her sticky love juice all over her face before licking his fingers clean, rapture breaking through his usually implacable facade.

Greg watched it with glazed eyes. His phallus was thick and ridged and impossibly hard. He reached out to grab Pagan by the hair but Richard pulled her back with a warning growl. Licking his fingers again to make her sex ready – although there was no need as she was already drippingly receptive to him – he slipped inside her with punishing slowness, making her wait, making himself wait. His hand was in her hair, holding her back so she could not get at Greg, all the while screwing her with long elegant strokes, showing the man in front how it was supposed to be done. Greg was watching with an overblown, half-inebriated look that she had never seen before, masturbating slowly. It both sickened and excited her. Richard diverted her attention by sinking his teeth into her shoulder. She panted with delight.

'This is just so Discovery Channel,' she purred richly. He continued to knaw at her, alternately licking long cool trails up her back. Then he withdrew and bore her down onto the carpet, pulling her on top of him. He was still fully dressed but his black silk shirt and immaculate hair were in total disarray. She slapped him not too lightly across the face, hearing Greg gasp in the background.

'Bastard,' she said coldly. 'Thinking you could buy me like a whore.'

'You are a whore,' he said and received another slap, harder this time. She pulled his shirt apart, spraying tiny bone buttons across the carpet, and ran her fingernails down his chest to his stomach, leaving white and then red trails in their wake. Her pussy lips were wrapped around his cock, the friction eased by her wetness as she slid up and down. His gaze became fixated on her full firm breasts, the nipples dark pink and rigid. He swallowed visibly as she teased them to their full length, as dark and red as raspberries. She smiled, knowing the power she could wield over him, acknowledged by every throb she could feel reverberating up through the very centre of her being.

His hands came up to touch her. She caught them and pinned them above his head. Her breasts swung achingly close to his face. She snaked over him, just out of reach, letting her nipples brush against his lips.

'Ride me,' he said hoarsely. He let out a deep rasping breath as she lifted and impaled herself with consummate skill. She reached back for his balls and raked them with her fingernails as she fucked him, slowly and sinuously. With a growl he rolled her over until he was on top, still buried deep inside her, and began to imprint deep punishing kisses over her body, starting with her throat, leaving reddened bite marks that throbbed and burned. He moved down, pulling out of her and smattering her breasts and stomach as she shifted underneath him, her fingers ruffling through his hair. She knew where he was going but it did not seem right, not in front of Greg.

'No. Stop it!' She tried to bar his way into her cunt with her fingers but his tongue worked its way inexorably through. She gasped raggedly as he began to lavish attention on her cunt; long, slow licks ending with a teasing double flick to her clitoris. It felt so good that she instantly forgot about Greg and abandoned herself to Richard's tongue, spreading herself wide and letting him feed off her. Then he changed his pace, strumming her clitoris so delicately that she felt need building up in her like the anticipation of the edge of a waterfall.

'Go on,' she urged him. 'Please!' She felt that merciful swoop into oblivion, then the soaring into white blinding light, over and over as she flung her arms out in a crucifix dive and let it take her at will.

As her orgasm ebbed away he showed her no mercy. Within seconds he was really fucking her, not just playing at it, her back chafing against the pure new wool carpet, his feet slipping on her delicate dress until he impatiently kicked it away. A thin sheen of sweat glistened on his smooth forehead, his hair in black strands over his face. He was a feral creature acting out of physical need, uttering deep-felt, guttural sounds of pleasure. The pulsating of his cock as he came deep inside her sent her off again, into swirling realms of ecstasy. She clung to him, shrieking softly as he gave her every last drop, whispering loving obscenities into her ear.

When he was finally spent, she shifted to distribute his weight more evenly over her body. They lay like that for a while, bathing in the afterglow. Then she remembered Greg, who had not spoken for some time. With difficulty she moved her head and looked up at the sofa. He was still in the same position, but his penis was flaccid and he was snoring heavily.

She struggled to her feet and stared down at Greg in disbelief. Richard had a look of studied innocence on his face.

'I guess it can get boring, watching everyone else have a good time.'

She patted Greg's face, none too lightly. He did not even shift. She turned accusingly to Richard.

'What did you give him?'

'A Mickey Finn. I didn't want him getting in on the act.' Richard pulled on his shirt. Pagan wished she had a robe to cover herself. She did not like the feeling of sordidness that was beginning to pervade the atmosphere now the deed was done. She turned back to the recumbent Greg. He looked ridiculous, with his limp dick lying in his lap like a newborn puppy.

'How long is he going to be like this?'

'Until the morning. He'll have one hell of a headache, especially after you've told him you're through.'

'Get him on the sofa. He can sleep in here tonight. I'll get a blanket.'

She went upstairs to slip on her robe. In the second spare room she went to the wardrobe to fetch a blanket for Greg. She reached up to the top shelf and tugged at a brightly coloured throw. It tumbled on top of her, catching on an empty cardboard box that also fell to the floor. Behind it on the shelf sat an unfamiliar grey box bristling with knobs and lights.

'What the hell . . .?' It took her just a few moments to realise she was looking at a sophisticated piece of camera equipment. On the tiny screen she could see Richard standing by the mantelpiece, relighting his cigar. Greg lay on his front on the sofa like a felled log. A wire led from the camera down through the wardrobe floor. Pagan immediately realised it must then lead to the light fitting in the ceiling below, where the living room was.

For a moment she felt so choked with rage she could barely move. She had been a blind, stupid, trusting fool. Richard's greed for vengeance had not stopped with her father. He intended to wreck her life as well and had recorded the evidence for his own enjoyment. Now he was regarding the unconscious Greg with a supercilious sneer, as if he had finally completed what he had set out to do over forty years before.

Downstairs she slapped his face as hard as she could, forcing him to drop the cigar.

'Get out!'

'What the hell's got into you?'

'You're disgusting! I gave you my trust and you abused it just like you did the first time! Just get the hell out of my sight!' She picked up the decanter of cognac and threw it at him. He ducked as it smashed against the wall.

'Jesus! What is this, post-coital depression?'

'Get out of my house!' she heard herself screaming, out of control. As he slammed the door she finally broke down in a flood of tears.

16

Late on Sunday evening Greg slipped unseen into a black stretch Cadillac with darkened windows. It was a very much downmarket version of Richard's, with door-to-door fluffy grey carpet and an inferior bar tucked into one of the passenger doors. No television or video. In the gloom he could see Rocco and Renate Carlotti sitting side by side, the poodle between them. It wore a pink diamond collar. As he sat opposite Renate she opened her slim tanned legs just enough to reveal her lack of underwear.

He grimaced and looked away. She no longer interested him. He had seen Pagan's wild side the night before and, now he knew which buttons to push, he intended to exploit it for all it was worth. He suspected that Richard had drugged him towards the end of the evening, but to his eternal relief the video equipment had remained undiscovered.

As for Pagan, she had been subdued that morning but affectionate, which had reassured him greatly. They agreed not to discuss what had happened the evening before, and he thought it best not to mention the money unless she did, which she did not.

The Cadillac parked snugly up against a ramshackle warehouse on the edge of the East River. The stink of gently lapping oily water mingled with the almost overpowering odour of rotting fish. Carlotti kept the windows shut and lit a slim cigarello, ignoring Greg's obvious coughing and hands flapping around his face.

'Well?' Rocco demanded aggressively.

Greg silently handed over the video.

'And my two fifty?'

'I don't have it yet.'

Carlotti scowled, his dark straight brows almost meeting above his nose. 'I thought you said you'd have it by now.'

'I said no such thing. Mason wasn't going to pay until afterwards. He isn't that stupid. If you want it you'll have to come to England. I'll have it at the hotel next Saturday.'

'Now listen, you little shit –'

'I can't give you something I haven't got, can I?'

Carlotti cursed loudly and smoked ferociously for a few moments. 'Renate and I will be at the hotel on Saturday and you will have my money ready. Don't try to screw me, Mr Roscoe. If you do the only safe place for you will be on the moon.'

'And Mason? He might try to stop the wedding.'

Carlotti smiled nastily. 'No he won't.'

On the forty-five minute journey from New Jersey to Manhattan Richard had finished off a three-quarters full bottle of Jack Daniels. When Thomas opened the door outside his apartment building he fell out of the car onto the pavement and had to be helped up to his penthouse. There he stayed in a semi-comatose state until Sunday evening, when he left to wander the streets and clear his head.

No one was about. After a while he was not even sure where he was. He lit a cigarette with shaking hands, aware that he must look like some kind of tramp. His hair was unkempt, his clothes rumpled. He had not showered since early on Saturday evening.

'What a fucking mess,' he muttered, critically observing his reflection in a dark window. 'No self-respecting whore would look at you right now.'

He was dazed and confused by Pagan's outburst, but there was no point in regretting not staying and forcing her to tell him what the problem was. There was still time to get some sense out of her. He groped for his mobile phone, dropped it, and with an effort stooped down to pick it up again, cursing loudly. He stared gloomily at the phone, his fuddled brain too slow to work out which buttons to press.

He had noticed the black stretch Cadillac parked on the other side of the street, but he did not hear the footsteps behind him, or sense the bulky body until it pulled a black sheet over his head. Thick arms pinned his arms to his sides and he lashed out blindly with his viciously sharp boots. As he was regretting the alcohol slowing his defences his assailant bundled him into the Cadillac, which tore away from the street with a screech of tyres.

The sheet was roughly removed as they drove along, and he found himself flanked by Benny, his own body-guard, and another heavy called Ronny. Rocco Carlotti sat opposite him together with Renate and a small poodle. Carlotti had read the gangster's handbook and was following it step by step. Richard would have laughed had it not been for the grim look on Carlotti's face. The man had all the presence of a goldfish but even in the state Richard was in he knew it would not do to underestimate him.

'What the fuck is this? I thought you'd left town weeks ago.'

'I said we were leaving. I didn't say how long for or where we were going,' Renate said, laughing lightly. She fussed the poodle's ears lovingly.

Carlotti leaned forward. In the gloomy car interior his teeth were Dentine-white, with a mint-smelling mouthwash that made Richard's stomach turn over. 'Don't worry, Mason, we're as good as gone. But I waited a long time for this opportunity. Not that I need to do much. You look like shit warmed up.'

'Get to the point, Carlotti.'

'The point is that I'm being paid to do something I love, which is to cause you pain. Greg Roscoe resents the fact that you only employed him to get at his girlfriend, and that his career is on the line because of your devotion to your dick.'

'Greg Roscoe?' He had to be drunk. How could Carlotti have joined forces with Greg Roscoe? Carlotti chuckled at the astonishment on his face.

'And in case you're wondering, he is marrying Pagan Warner on Saturday, whether you like it or not.'

'What if she doesn't want to marry him?'

'She adores him. That's what she told me,' Renate said. She scratched the poodle's furry head. 'She did, didn't she, poppet? She loves her man very much, faults and all.' She smiled cruelly at Richard's sick expression. 'I'm surprised at you. I didn't think fat little *Hausfraus* were your style,' she remarked cattily.

'I like to feel what I'm fucking. When was the last time you could?'

A vicious pistol-whip to the side of his head made him grunt with pain. After a moment he shook his head to clear it and turned evil eyes upon Benny, the treacherous thug he had trusted.

'You're dead, asshole.' But his words came out sluggish and indistinct. He heard Carlotti laughing softly in the background.

The car stopped in a deserted stretch of ground just over the Brooklyn Bridge. Richard was hustled out and taken into a disused storage shelter. Grassy tufts pushed through the crumbling tarmac, and the only signs of recent human life were two rusting beer cans and a broken bottle of cheap whisky. The lights of Manhattan Island looked like a distant magical kingdom floating in the inky blackness of the Hudson, as if on a dense starless sky.

Carlotti nodded to Benny, who pistol-whipped Richard on the temple, raising another angry bruise on his pale skin. As Richard slumped, half-conscious, Ronny headbutted his nose. The blow brought him to his knees. There was a spurt of warm blood and a kick to his ribs, followed by another, and another. Then he was lost in a sea of hard fists and steelcapped shoes. The pain never seemed to stop, the grunts of effort from the two men as they laid into him muffling his own stifled sounds of agony.

Carlotti ordered them to stop just as he felt consciousness slipping away. He collapsed on the filthy ground, gagging on the taste of his own blood. Footsteps sounded behind him and his head was yanked viciously back, forcing him to look into Carlotti's satisfied face.

'This is much better,' he heard Carlotti say from way above. 'On your fucking knees, showing some fucking respect,' he added, crudely mimicking Richard's own accent.

'Go fuck yourself, Carlotti,' Richard managed to croak. His head was as light as a helium balloon but his eyes were murderous. Renate was smiling spitefully down at him. She kissed him lightly on the forehead, delicately avoiding the blood.

'Have a nice life, Richard. Pagan deserves you.'

Carlotti nodded at Ronny, who gave Richard another savage kick, this time in the groin. He folded, teeth gritted against making a sound. Benny lashed out with his right fist, connecting with his abdomen. This time he did cry out, though the wind was taken out of him, and it came out more like a whispered groan. Ronny and Benny held his sagging body up by the arms. Carlotti smiled at the damage they had done. He reached into Richard's coat and drew out his wallet, then removed his Rolex and the Celtic wedding band. He handed them all to Benny.

'Your bonus for services rendered,' he said. Benny looked in the wallet and grinned stupidly. It contained over six hundred dollars plus several cards, one of them a Platinum Amex.

Finally Carlotti found the silver flask Richard habitually kept in his jacket pocket. He unscrewed the lid and emptied the contents over Richard's head. Richard flinched as neat bourbon came into contact with raw flesh.

'A piss-drunk, wealthy businessman on the wrong side of town. Mugged because he was too stupid to take a cab. It'll be days before anyone finds you. Then it'll be too late to save your niece from marital bliss. Too bad, isn't it?'

He gave Richard's face one final hard slap. He collapsed like a pack of cards on the cracked concrete. A fresh cotton handkerchief was handed to Carlotti. He fastidiously wiped the blood from his fingers.

'Get rid of him.'

17

Pagan felt curiously detached as the beautician completed her French manicure. Her hair had already been done, held back behind her ears by two simple diamond clips. The weather was promising for the wedding service at 1.30 p.m., with fluffy little clouds studding an endless azure-blue sky. That would please Sylvia Roscoe, who had been anxiously casting her eyes to the sky for the last three days. Amelia, Greg's younger sister, was Pagan's Matron of Honour, but they had hardly exchanged a word. Pagan had not wanted any bridesmaids at all, so it had taken negotiations of Camp David proportions to sort it out, with Pagan backing down just before open hostilities broke out.

Outside the air was sweet and warm, drifting through the lilac hedge that formed one side of the Roscoes' huge back garden. A thrush hopped about on the perfectly striped lawn and the smell of coffee wafted up from the kitchen below, mingling with high, excited voices.

A crunch on gravel signified the arrival of the cars. The leading white Daimler was Pagan's. Because Pagan had no one to give her away – another custom that she thought unnecessary in the light of there being no one obvious to do the job anyway – she would be accompanied by Sylvia Roscoe and Amelia. Fortunately the church was only two miles away. The reception was being held at a large hotel on the banks of the River Thames, a mile up from Henley. It was the venue many wealthy people in the surrounding villages used when they were obliged to spend copious amounts of money on their offsprings' weddings.

Sylvia burst into the room. 'The car's here,' she said briskly. She nodded in approval at Pagan. 'Oh yes, that colour does suit you after all.'

Pagan had refused to wear white. It looked glaring next to her pale skin and, anyway, the symbolism was a joke for most women in their thirties. Sylvia Roscoe had not approved. She preferred the Daz-white meringue look but, then, she did not have to wear it.

Pagan stood up to let the beautician attach the gossamer-thin veil to the hair clips. It fell in a foamy waterfall down her back. The dress was a slim column of oyster satin that clung to every curve, the décolletage a cloud of voile interwoven with delicately embroidered leaves. It skimmed her upper arms, leaving her shoulders and back bare. To enable her to walk the skirt was slit deeply up the back, almost to the lace webbing of her sheer silk stockings. The same leaves traced around the hemline formed the only other decoration. If she leaned too far forward the vicar would get an eyeful, but as he was gay it hardly mattered. She struck a Gina Lollabridgida pose with her final cigarette and smiled grimly. She should have been nervous but inside she felt hollow.

Sylvia picked up Pagan's oyster satin high-heeled shoes. 'Come on. We don't want to keep him waiting, do we?'

'It's the bride's prerogative to be late,' Pagan pointed out. Sylvia tutted and huffed away.

The tiny village church was filled to bursting, not helped by the vast array of millinery fighting for attention. Pagan handed over her bouquet, a simple sheaf of waxy lilies, glossy green laurel leaves and variegated ivy. Greg looked almost impossibly dashing in his tails and dress shirt, the top hat on his chair along with his father, who looked swamped by the exaggerated suit and waistcoat. Four ushers, all Oxford cronies, sat behind, grinning inanely at one of their pack being captured by mankind's oldest institution. Behind them, and on the other side as well, the women's floral dresses competed with the pew posies and large sweeping arrangements on either side of the altar. Sylvia Roscoe had gone to town on fluffy cerise carnations, white freesias and pink day lilies. The resulting smell reminded Pagan strongly of her parents' funeral. By design the lilies were the exact match of Amelia's dress, which was a shorter version of Pagan's own. Unfortunately, being chunkier all over than Pagan, Amelia looked like a Tesco economy sausage. If she had smiled it would have been better, but her petulant mouth was fixed in a down-turned pout under her curly blond hair, frothing around a simple circlet of flowers.

The vicar smiled down from his lofty position, saving the real warmth in his eyes for Pagan. He was young, in his thirties, and handsome, unlike the crusty old fart who had been indisposed very suddenly by an alleged bowel complaint. Sylvia Roscoe had paled and did not want to hear any more when the replacement vicar explained his presence. She only hoped he would not produce a guitar and tambourines and encourage people to hold hands.

Pagan found she was holding her breath as they went through the inevitable 'if anyone sees a reason why these two people should not be married' routine. She felt faint, the heat of the church and the people and the smell of lily pollen making her head spin.

Then the door opened.

As one the entire congregation turned around. Within a whisper of passing out, Pagan caught Greg's arm. She turned just in time to see a small man slip into a pew at the back.

'Who's that?' she whispered to Greg.

'Someone I used to work with,' he whispered back.

'Tell him his timing is crap.' Pagan tried to regulate her breathing so that no one would notice how shaken she was. Or how empty she suddenly felt. The vicar made some gentle joke that she did not hear but it obviously amused the congregation and eased the sudden tension. Sylvia Roscoe sat bold upright, unsmiling, as if someone had shoved a broomstick up her backside.

The vicar gave Pagan a reassuring smile before continuing the service. Eventually Greg slipped the simple gold band on her finger and kissed her chastely on the cheek, obviously mindful of his mother's baleful stare.

After the exhausting barrage of photographs they were swept away to the reception in a shower of rice and confetti. Greg did not kiss her or even hold her hand. After all the impassioned pleas and promises, it was business as usual.

They were welcomed at Chandlers House with Buck's Fizz, and the tedium of greeting and meeting began. Pagan knew hardly anybody, and by the time they were half way through the seemingly endless line of well-wishers she had begun to feel a little lost. At the end of the line was Uncle Johnny, the burly black sheep of the Roscoe family. He gave her a wet kiss on the lips and patted her bottom when he thought no one could see. His third wife, Ruth, had dyed ginger hair, sharp nails and an ample bosom. She gave Pagan a totally insincere air kiss and moved on quickly. Pagan did not mind. By then she too had become a master of the false platitude.

'Are you OK? You look exhausted.' Steve Jones had divested himself of his cassock and dog collar and now looked startlingly contemporary in a green silk shirt, black trousers and black brogues.

'Thanks. This is supposed to be the happiest day of my life, remember?'

'Hey, come on, we discussed this. What happened to all your positive thinking? An opportunity? A fresh start?'

'I know, but . . .' She let out a deep breath. 'I look pretty damned good and the one person who should appreciate it doesn't. Which isn't great for one's ego.'

Steve took another flute of Buck's Fizz and pressed it into her hand. 'Come on, kid. You can do this. You were the bolshiest cow in our class, remember? Scared the pants off all the boys, even me.'

She grinned at last. 'You hid it pretty well. You always were a good actor.'

'And I'm especially good at playing vicars.' They clinked glasses. 'Oops, you're getting the evil eye from the dragon lady. I'll see you later on the dance floor.'

Rocco Carlotti caught Greg as soon as the crowd had dispersed onto the veranda.

'Where's my two fifty?' He kept his voice very low and tight.

Greg looked coldly down at him. 'Go away. I'm at my wedding reception for Christ's sake!'

'I want that money, goddamnit!' His hand was claw-like on Greg's arm. Greg brushed him away.

'Keep out of sight. I'll deal with you after the speeches.'

Carlotti stalked back to his room. Greg watched him go, smiling superciliously.

The three-tier cake stood resplendently in the middle of a large square table on an S-shaped stand trailing with freesias, carnations and variegated ivy. Around it long white linen-swathed tables ran along three sides of the room, with the other end being kept for the dance floor and the 60s and 70s tribute band that was playing later. White-aproned staff stood around; young girls holding heavy silver trays loaded with sherry and Buck's Fizz.

Pagan felt sorry for them, wilting in the afternoon sun. She was still feeling stupidly sorry for herself. She wanted to be out there, relaxed and enjoying herself, not under the constant eye of Sylvia Roscoe, seemingly waiting for her to put a foot wrong.

Soon the party had moved into the reception room and out on to the veranda, leading down the vast striped lawn to the river below. Those who wished could sit by the curvaceous swimming pool, cerulean blue with dark blue mosaic picking out the entwined letters 'CH' on the bottom. Greg kissed Pagan quickly and said he had to go upstairs to their room, where they would be staying for the next two nights.

He stopped outside room 103, the room next to theirs. After a quick glance up and down the corridor he knocked softly on the door. It was immediately opened and he was grabbed and pulled inside.

Kiki and Honey, a blond bombshell that had recently joined his harem, lay draped on the bed and over each other like lazy young lionesses. Kiki wore a black latex mini dress zipped up at the front, and black fishnet stockings. Her spiky black stilettos scissored behind her as she lay on the bed on her front, smiling sweetly at him. Honey was simply edible looking in a cream chemise that was so sheer that he could see the dark shadow between her legs. She stretched out on the bed, her hands gathering her mass of blond curls behind her head. Her breasts almost billowed out of the tiny scrap of organza silk, leaving only her areola and nipples covered. Michelle walked around Greg, admiring his dove-grey morning suit and silver cravat. Her fetish bra and panties made tiny clinking sounds as she moved, the garments simply comprising of silver rings and leather straps. Her thigh-high black plastic boots squeaked softly.

With his windfall from Richard he had paid for the girls to fly to England and stay at the hotel. They would be sharing a room, and each other, for two nights before flying back to New York. He liked the feeling of being able to splash cash around in such a fashion. It gave him power and a hard-on, like nothing he had ever experienced before.

'Aaaah!' He gasped as she suddenly grabbed his crotch. They had been waiting since their arrival that morning, and now they were hungry for him.

'Very nice,' she said, running her hand down between his legs. He buckled, checked himself, and stood up straight again, planting his feet apart so he did not wobble when her hand curved around his penis.

'Uh,' he grunted, feeling her unzip him. Outside he could hear the wedding reception going on, voices drifting through their open window. He could see the guests chatting, laughing, unsuspecting. A cool wetness swarmed over his cock. Michelle was licking him, then immediately blowing on the moisture left behind. He was fully erect now, his cock sticking out of the grey trousers like a beacon. Honey turned around and presented her backside to him, using long gold-tipped fingers to spread her labia so he could see right into her dark, wet tunnel. She looked cheekily over her shoulder as he stumbled towards her. In a moment he was inside her hot sweet depths, pumping hard, watching Michelle unzip Kiki's dress just enough to nibble at her breasts with small white teeth. Underneath her, Kiki fingered Michelle's rosy puckered hole through one of the rings making up her panties. Greg reached over, still buried deep inside Honey, and slid two fingers inside Michelle's soaking wet pussy. He slid them in and out in time with his own thrusts, feeling her muscles tense against him. Michelle panted and squirmed and told Kiki to stick her finger in her ass so she did, she and

Greg finger-fucking both orifices. Then Honey wanted to join in. Michelle moved so that she could reach Kiki's pussy. She nuzzled it through black gauzy panties, working her tongue underneath and poking it between Kiki's labia until Kiki started to moan as well, spreading her legs wide, using her free hand to agitate her clitoris. Greg's balls bunched and he came with a series of grunts, thrusting hard and slow into Honey's warm depths, only withdrawing when every last drop of semen had been expelled.

Carefully he withdrew and zipped himself up, grinning down at the girls still writhing on the bed.

'I'll leave you to it for now,' he said, patting Kiki on the bottom. 'You're next, my sweet,' he grinned at her and slipped quietly from the room.

Barely ten minutes later he was back at Pagan's side, sinking Buck's Fizz as though it were lemonade. He was thinking of five hundred thousand in his bank account, soon to be bolstered by twenty million. Now he was married into the Warner clan he could behave as badly as he pleased without anyone being able to touch him.

In between the beef tournedos and vanilla terrine, Greg excused himself again. Tummy trouble, caused by nerves, he whispered confidentially to Pagan, ignoring his mother's scowl.

On the way to room 103 he spotted Renate at the bar, sipping a martini cocktail. She wore a black Versace dress held together with what looked like cock rings. It clung to her slender body, giving her more curves than she actually possessed in real life. Underneath she wore sheer black hold-up stockings, the wide webbing ornate with flowers. As she sat down Greg could see past the scalloped edge to her white skin above. Her ebony hair was pulled back in a sleek French plait, and her patent handbag and tall stilettos were crimson. In her large, graduated sunglasses she looked the epitome of Italian chic.

'Hey, lover,' she called out softly. 'Going for another quick screw?'

'Keep your voice down!' he hissed. She had obviously been drinking and from the slightly crazed sparkle had been hitting the coke as well. 'Shouldn't you be in your room, coping with jet lag?'

'I am coping with it. I could even cope with you right now.' Her pointed toe toyed with the crease on Greg's suit trousers. She speared a black olive with a cocktail stick and placed it between her cherry red lips. It disappeared with a soft plop. 'Too bad you're married now, isn't it? Even I couldn't fuck the groom at his wedding reception.' She smiled conspiratorially at the young barman, who flushed crimson. As Greg stalked away he heard her ordering another martini cocktail.

He wasn't unduly worried about Renate's implied knowledge. She was steadily drinking herself into oblivion and was likely to embarrass herself long before she succeeded in embarrassing him.

Ten minutes later he left the women as they were losing themselves in an orgy of their own, lubricated with his semen. From his room he ordered two more bottles of Laurent Perrier and a Black Forest gâteau to be sent to room 103.

'Are you OK?' Pagan stroked a strand away from Greg's glistening forehead.

'Fine! It's just this bloody penguin suit and it's so damned hot in here.' He ran his finger around the edge of his collar, noticing that Uncle Johnny had already dispensed with his jacket and had undone his waist-coat. Ignoring Sylvia's silent disapproval, he did the same.

The speeches were mercifully short. No one really

knew Pagan well enough to say much about her, and the best man had been put under special instruction by Sylvia Roscoe to keep it clean or else. However he did manage to sneak in a few slyly bawdy jokes to appeal to the more juvenile element of the party before moving on to the telegrammes. One had come from Michael and Rachel Prosser; another was from Pagan's colleagues at Silverskin. The last one was from a man simply known as Wolf, simply saying *Best wishes to the happy couple. Tell the bitch she broke my heart.* There was much nervous laughter and curious looks at the bride, but Pagan simply shrugged and smiled. Then Greg stood up and started his speech with the obligatory 'My wife and I', and went on to expound her virtue to such an extent that she as well as everyone else wished he would be quiet. The applause was loud and prolonged when he sat back down.

As the waiters served coffee and wedding cake the string quartet struck up and people broke out of the rigid seating to form their own smaller groups. The tribute band would be starting up at six o'clock, with a light buffet at seven. Staff milled about, clearing tables and replenishing coffee cups. Because of the warm afternoon most people had moved out into the open air. The women in their finery looked like exotic flowers studding the sweeping, closely mown lawn.

With Pagan safely on the mingling treadmill Greg sneaked out again. He strutted into room 103 like top dog. When he gently closed the door on his way out again ten minutes later he was suddenly sprung upon.

'Got you, you old bastard!' The two men pushed him up against the wall.

'Spill the beans, Roscoe. Have you got a woman in there?'

'We've been watching you all afternoon. What are you up to?'

Greg relaxed. Nigel Potter and Peter Smith had been with him at Magdalen. They leered at him gleefully.

'OK. If you tell, I'm dead meat.'

'We won't tell, as long as we can have a share,' Peter said.

Greg hushed them and they looked up and down the corridor like children up to no good. Then he knocked on the door again.

He wished he could preserve the astonishment on his friends' faces as they saw Michelle, Kiki and Honey on the bed. They stared at the luscious young women like children in Santa's grotto.

'You sly old fox! How did you manage it?' Pete said when he could move his lower jaw again.

Greg smiled smugly. 'The benefits of living and working in the Big Apple, old chap.'

The girls moved slinkily around the men, feeling their shoulders, their buttocks. The two men in turn did not dare touch anything, lest it disappear into a cloud of nothing.

'You got any Charlie as well?' Nigel whispered. The girls looked at each other, puzzled.

'Charlee?' Kiki enquired in her divinely exotic accent.

'Over there. Help yourselves,' Greg said magnanimously, motioning to a small porcelain bowl filled with pure white powder. It had been an impulse buy, but the looks on his friends' faces justified it completely.

'You're kidding!' Nigel said, staring at the coke.

'Can you get me a job as well?' Peter added as he was engulfed in Honey's generously padded limbs.

Greg glanced at his watch. 'I'll leave you single fellows to it for a while. Save some for me.'

Pagan had also begun to wonder why Greg was disappearing so often, so she went up to their room to see if she could find him. She could not, but she found her cigarettes. She put them with a lighter and her lipstick in a small cream bag and went back downstairs, but not before she had paused outside the room next to theirs. Someone was obviously having a good time, judging by the steady banging of a headboard against the wall, coupled with loud male grunts. It seemed an odd time, at just before six in the evening, but that was just sour grapes, she chided herself. Already she was thinking just like a Roscoe. And all because of that wretched telegramme. It had been like a wake-up call; one that had torn her apart inside.

Deliberately she waited until she was downstairs again before lighting up, putting the cigarette in a small bone holder she had acquired at an antique shop in Wallingford two days before. It gave her a certain chic, but Sylvia was giving her frosty looks. *Give it a rest, you tight old bitch*, Pagan thought irritably and went over to George, who was talking to one of the old aunts. She slipped her arm through his, kissed his cheek and thanked him for his speech. He was a sweet man and she felt sorry for him, being dominated by Sylvia all the time.

'I just wanted you to know how much I appreciated your help,' she said.

'That's very kind, my dear. But it's Sylvia who's been under the most pressure...'

Pagan squeezed his arm again. 'We both know that isn't true,' she said firmly, holding eye contact so the tacit message would be received, loud and clear, 'and that's the last I'll say about it.'

George Roscoe's ruggedly handsome features broke into a wry smile. 'Thank you, my dear. I think Greg is going to have his hands full with you.'

A tap on her shoulder made Pagan look around. It was Greg.

'The band is just starting. We're needed for the first dance.'

As they reached the dance floor the band struck up with 'It had to be you.'

Renate had been drinking more as the afternoon progressed. She had moved on to Pimms and had been seduced by its innocuous fruitiness. Now she was flushed, her eyes sparkling, her French plait slightly wispy. She stumbled into the toilets for a wee and to reapply her makeup. Whilst rooting in her handbag she found the small bag of cocaine that she had purchased that morning while Rocco was negotiating a price on a handgun. She cut a line. It wasn't very straight, but nothing looked straight after four Pimms. Swaying slightly she snorted the white heaven into one delicate nostril. Then the other.

'What the hell are you doing?'

The loud male voice made her jump, dropping the handbag on the floor. A florid handsome man was standing behind her, waiting expectantly for her explanation. From his dress she could tell he was one of the wedding guests. She tried to gather the contents of her handbag together.

'Oh, you know, just powdering my nose!' She giggled shrilly, standing up. The floor looked a long way down. She had a touch of vertigo, and swayed into his arms. Uncle Johnny caught her.

'Powdering your nose, eh? That's illegal in this country.'

'Well, what would I know? I'm from New York,' she said airily.

'So is a lady being in the men's toilets.'

'I didn't know I was a lady.' She giggled again, trying to stifle it with her hand. Her companion was a very big man, burly and coarse, despite his dress shirt and smart trousers with diamond-sharp creases. He had thick sensual lips and deep-set shifty eyes under dark curly brows. 'You won't tell anyone, will you?'

Johnny's eyes became narrow and speculative. 'That depends on you, doesn't it?'

'You want me to suck your dick?'

'That's the best offer I've had all day.'

He pushed her back into a cubicle, where she sat down on the toilet lid. The words had come out cruder than she had intended, but there was no going back now. He closed and locked the door behind them. She tried to fumble with his trouser button but could not manage it, so he did it, unzipping his trousers and pulling down his black cotton briefs. He was semi-erect, a heavy mass of flesh bobbing gently up and down. She drew it into her mouth and closed her eyes, shutting out the man above it, but revelling in the feeling of flesh and blood rolling around her tongue.

'Oh, lady,' he moaned, leaning back against the door.

The main door opened again and two men walked in. Renate did not let up, pulling at Johnny so relentlessly that he had to bite his lip to stop from grunting. The men used the urinals and rinsed their hands, talking loudly. As their voices faded again Johnny heard someone mention 'three hot girlies in room 103'.

Renate reached in and scooped out his balls, tickling the underside of his scrotum. His soft grunts became more animalistic as she lapped at his balls then sucked on his cock again with fluid practice, stroking his scrotum with sharp fingernails. His large hands cupped the back of her head and held her fast as he began to pump at her, making her gag. But when she looked up at him with wide violet eyes and tried to smile, he came right then, all the while watching her wring him of every last drop.

'Don't get it on my trousers,' he rasped, so she didn't,

swallowing and licking and sucking until he thought he could get hard enough for her to do it all again.

They shuffled out of the cubicle one at a time. He used the urinal as he had originally intended, and she went back to the bar to get another drink.

By 7.30 p.m. the night had almost drawn in and the party was in full swing. Enough alcohol had been consumed to dispense with the prim atmosphere, and it was only a matter of time before someone ended up in the pool.

Word had been getting around amongst the men about the libidinous treats on offer in room 103. The temptations of free sex and free coke proved too much for the younger members of the party to ignore, and one by one they sneaked upstairs, coming down ten minutes, or sometimes half an hour, later, slightly tousled, their eyes glazed.

Sylvia Roscoe was growing increasingly distressed at the deterioration of her elegant gathering. The men were spoiling it with their loud laughter and crude jokes, but when she complained to Greg he told her sharply to relax and let him enjoy himself for once. Confused, she retreated to where Amelia was sitting, looking bored.

'I don't know what's got into him,' Sylvia said pettishly. 'He isn't being very nice at all.'

'You've noticed then? It's only taken thirty years, mother.' Amelia stomped off into the garden.

Renate had wandered out into the garden, collecting another Pimms on the way. No one took any notice of her as she weaved unsteadily towards the summerhouse on the riverbank. Jetlag and the Pimms was catching up with her and she wanted to find a quiet spot to snooze for a while.

There was no one by the summerhouse. The three sunbeds looked very inviting, facing out over the river. She lay down and closed her eyes, sipping the Pimms through a straw and thinking that life in England was infinitely preferable to pollution-stained Manhattan. For a while she drifted away in the warm, darkening night.

'Hello, who's this?'

Her eyes flew open. Two flushed young men, obviously the worse for drink, grinned down at her. One of them held a full bottle of Bells scotch.

'We thought we could have our own party,' one said.

'Beat it, guys. This is my spot,' she drawled.

Nigel and Peter looked at each other. Another American hooker. The hotel was full of them. They sat either side of her and Peter took her drink out of her hand.

'Hey! Leave me alone!' Nigel stalled her protest with a wet, drunken kiss. He tasted of beer. As she tried to push him off Peter ran his hand up her thigh and opened her dress to the waist.

'You're a hell of a lot more classy than the others,' Peter said, admiring her wine lace panties. He undid the button at her waist so her dress fell apart completely. 'Oh, lovely little titties,' he continued, covering one of them with a clumsy paw.

'We'd better go inside,' Nigel said. 'Don't want anyone else wanting a share of you before we've finished.'

Renate gave up and smiled languidly. Why was she fighting off these two rampant young animals anyway? Struggling to her feet, she shrugged her dress from her shoulders and trailed it along the floor, luring them into the summerhouse. Stumbling, they followed her, shutting the door behind them.

18

Amelia was sitting on the riverbank, moodily plucking the petals off daisies. It seemed that she was the only one not getting chatted up, and she put it down to the loathsome dress she had been forced to wear.

It was then that she heard sounds coming from the summerhouse. As she drew nearer she could see flickering shadows thrown by a single fat candle on a wrought-iron stand. The noises were female moans and male grunts, the unmistakable sounds of sex. For a moment she listened outside the door, daring not to peep in. She felt jealous and strangely stirred by the vigorous rutting that was happening inside. It had been ages since she last had a shag. Whoever the woman was, she was getting double her share. At last Amelia hazarded a look.

The tableau was just like a porn film she had once seen at college, with the woman being corn-cobbed by two men. One of them was Nigel Potter, a friend of Greg's whom she had known since she was fourteen. The woman's lips were wrapped around his penis, which was far larger than she had ever imagined it. He was drinking from a bottle of Bells scotch, his lower body moving in time with the woman's bobbing head. Peter Murray banged her at the other end with a vigour that made Amelia's own sex moisten with sympathy. Peter took the bottle from Nigel and drank, never breaking rhythm. Amelia licked her lips, transfixed at the sight of those two fat cocks brutalising the skinny bitch. Amelia already hated her for being slender and beautiful, because only those women seemed to get the best men, the best sex, the best everything. She backed away, but as she did so she tripped over a lifebelt that had been propped against the wall. Nigel looked up and saw her. She was about to run like hell but he was out of the door in an instant, catching her arm.

'Come on, Millie. Join us,' he said breathlessly, leading her back towards the door.

'No!' She tried to release herself but he was already steering her into the warm shadowy room, where Peter had pushed the sunbeds together. He was lying across them with Renate, and they were kissing with open mouths. They looked up.

'Come on, Millie. Don't be a spoilsport,' he grinned. He had removed his trousers and his penis stuck straight up like a huge salami sausage. Renate simply smiled and bent down to take it into her mouth. Peter's head hung back and he groaned loudly, lifting his hips. Amelia felt Nigel unzipping her dress.

'Come on, Millie, have some fun. You're a big girl.' He eased the dress down past her breasts. They were aggressively restrained in a cupped strapless bra that pushed them together so high and tight they felt like a shelf to rest her wine glass on. 'A lovely big girl. Big and blond, just like Marilyn Monroe.' He hefted her breasts in his hands. 'Look at these huge melons, Pete. Isn't she one hell of a woman?'

Peter feasted on her through heavy-lidded eyes. 'Yeah. Take her undies off. Let's see her for real.'

Renate stopped sucking on his cock. 'I'll do it,' she said, standing up.

Amelia was horrified. 'No way!' But as she backed away Nigel prevented her from escaping.

'Enjoy it,' he whispered hotly in her ear, nudging his erection into her buttocks. As Renate removed the bra Amelia's large breasts swung gratefully free. Renate eased the dress down over her wide hips. Her stomach swelled over the edge of her panties but suddenly she was no longer ashamed. Peter was still sprawled on the chair, his cock harder than ever, staring right at her, not the black-haired woman easing the panties down and telling her to step out of them. When she was standing just in her stilettos Renate embraced her with limbs as slim and soft as silken ropes. After a moment of tense awkwardness, Amelia realised how nice it felt. They were opposites, one willowy and dark, the other blond and Rubinesque. Renate tenderly placed her lips on Amelia's, and it did not seem wrong at all. Amelia opened her mouth under Renate's kiss and tasted Pimms. It intoxicated her more than the four gin and tonics she herself had consumed that afternoon.

'Go on, Millie,' Peter urged, as Renate led her towards the makeshift bed. She hesitated, but in the cocooned unreality of the summerhouse all taboos had been broken. She lay down, entangled with Renate, and Nigel lay down next to her, spooning his body around hers. Peter did the same to Renate, pushing his cock into her molten opening and screwing it slowly. Amelia gasped as Nigel explored past her labia with two fingers.

'God, you're wet,' he muttered, slipping his fingers in and out, feeling her muscles suck at them. She thrust her bottom out, the natural progression being feeling his cock, so huge and fat, inside her as Renate bent her head and gently sucked on her fat pink nipple.

'Oh!' She moaned as Nigel pushed himself fully inside her. Renate's soft lips sent electricity straight down to her clitoris and made it throb and swell. With an understanding only women have, Renate zeroed in on the sensitive little organ, agitating it with her fingers whilst still pulling on Amelia's nipple.

The men's thrusting became more urgent, mashing the women together, forcing their bodies to rub against each other. Renate put Amelia's hand on her breast, at the same time forcing her tongue deep into the younger woman's throat. Amelia loved the feel of Renate's breast in her hand, the nipple hard and scratchy, surrounded by soft flesh. She stroked it and ran the nipple through her fingers, then found she wanted to let her hand drift down towards Renate's shaven pudenda, feeling it as soft as velvet, the tiny clitoris hard and swollen. As she touched it Renate moaned and bucked, and Amelia realised that she too had the power to please. Not just men, but women as well. She strummed Renate's clit gently, as she did with her own sometimes. Renate's head fell back and she was gasping, unable to continue her seduction of Amelia, realising it was not necessary.

Peter manoeuvred himself so that he was lying underneath Renate with her back to him. She was wide open, Peter's fingers teasing out her nipples.

'Go down on me,' Renate urged Amelia.

Amelia hesitated again. Nigel still pumped her gently from behind, rolling her breasts around in his hands. Renate reached down and spread her labia, which glistened as darkly as a sweet plum.

'Go on, Millie,' Peter urged. 'We'll take you out to dinner tomorrow night if you do. Le Manoir? The Compleat Angler? The choice is yours.'

'And we'll fuck you afterwards,' Nigel added, nibbling her ear.

'All night,' Peter said, pushing up into Renate's swollen cunt. 'Come on, eat me too. Get those lovely red lips around my balls.'

The thought of having both men to herself the following evening was too much to resist. Amelia knelt down between Renate's spread legs and shyly poked out her tongue.

The barest hint of her breath on Renate's distended

clitoris made her thighs quiver, so much that it encouraged Amelia to go further, pressing her lips against Renate's sex lips as if kissing a mouth. Renate tasted sweet and musky and not unpleasant. Underneath, Peter's cock was still, buried half inside her. Boldly she licked it and heard him say 'yeah' in a low, abandoned way that gave her further confidence. She probed deeper into Renate's pussy, her tongue along side Peter's cock. Peter's hips began to move slowly up and down, screwing Renate slowly. Renate moaned loudly, spreading her legs further. Galvanised by the sound Amelia began to lick her like an ice lolly, up and out, up and out, stopping just before her clitoris, saving that delight until she sensed the woman was desperate for the touch of her tongue. Instead she tickled the underside of Peter's balls, feeling him jerk and curse with joy. Enjoying her new skill, she began to tease, fluttering her tongue along Peter's cock as it moved in and out, faster and faster, then using her tongue as a humming bird's wing against Renate's clitoris. Nigel watched with an open mouth and dry throat as Renate and Peter groaned and writhed, totally under her spell.

'Jesus, Millie, you're fantastic! Do it to me.' He pawed at Renate to extract herself from Peter. Renate clambered onto Nigel and Peter watched Amelia do the same, rolling Nigel's balls around her mouth, pulling on them, delicately teasing Renate's clitoris with mouth and fingers. Peter knelt behind Amelia and shoved his cock into her, slick with Renate's juices. He reached for Amelia's breasts, hanging down like heavy fruit swaying in a high tree. She was the main focus of their pleasure, driving the other three to new heights whilst losing herself in a lust she never knew she had. Renate came first, vibrations shuddering through her whole body. Amelia strung out the pleasure, a past master at doing it to herself, until Peter also began to buck and grunt with new intensity, and she could see first-hand how his cock swelled and pulsed, and his balls jumped as he came. His grunts became a prolonged roar as Amelia wrapped her warm tongue around his balls, exquisitely timing each lap with each new spurt of semen.

As they recovered, Nigel stretched out on the sunbed and beckoned Amelia to him. Renate immediately understood and knelt down between their legs. Within minutes they were experiencing the same hedonistic joy, their orgiastic moans ringing loud around the garden to the tatters of the genteel gathering above.

Greg went to room 103 again when he was sure that the girls were alone. He sat on a small, armless chair and unzipped his trousers. His cock was standing to attention, swollen by the sight of Honey's pink shaven pudenda.

'Just a quick one this time, darling,' he said, pushing the organ up at her. 'I'll see you right later.'

'You better.' Michelle sank onto his lap, guiding his cock into her entrance, watching his eyes roll as she impaled herself onto him. With his hands on the chair seat for support, he fucked up into her hot little body with all his strength while she bore down onto him, her hot, breathy moans sandblasting his face. The coke he had taken was wearing off and he rasped at Kiki to give him some more. She held a delicate little cone of powder to his nose and he sniffed, all the while screwing Michelle. This time he came with a roar, not caring who could hear him. Afterwards his eyes were crazy and his hair was no longer neat and tidy. The girls retreated to the bed, giggling at his attempts to compose himself. It took longer this time as he blundered about like a drunken elephant, zipping up his trousers and trying to straighten his hair. He took a final tiny sniff of coke to get himself back to normality and staggered back down the stairs to the reception. The first person he met was his mother.

'You're drunk!' she snapped disgustedly.

He gave her a smacking kiss on the cheek. 'Of course I am! It's my wedding reception, you daft cow!' And he went, leaving her open mouthed with outrage.

Sylvia looked around. People were dancing, kissing, laughing together, but the gathering had taken on a distinctly bawdy, Bacchanalian air. By the pool at least two couples were openly kissing and caressing on the sunbeds. Pagan was talking earnestly to the vicar, yet again, and Johnny was holding court with three young women, all giggling drunkenly at his filthy jokes. Johnny's wife, the Essex trollop, was nowhere to be seen. And neither was her own husband.

As she was wondering what to do, two of her oldest friends came up to thank her for a delightful day, adding pointedly that the party was getting far too lively for them. They looked happy to leave, and Sylvia wanted to cry. But she painted on her brightest social smile and, when they had gone, she went to find George.

'I don't think she's smiled once today,' Steve said to Pagan as they sat on the wall outside overlooking the lawn.

'She doesn't like me, that's why. Thinks I'm not good enough for her darling boy. Usual story.' Pagan picked at a cushion of soft moss on the weathered limestone brick. She had stayed longer than planned simply because she had been waiting. Waiting for someone who wasn't going to show.

'Why don't we leave now? No one's going to notice.'

She laughed ironically and looked around her. 'It seems a shame. The party looks like it's getting interesting.'

Things were getting out of hand. There was a drunken female shriek and a loud splash, followed by prolonged cheering. Two girls were in the pool, being chased around by three men. People lurched drunkenly around, giggling uncontrollably. Some were snogging on the lawn. Half empty glasses, beer bottles and plates of half-eaten food were tossed carelessly around. She could see Sylvia Roscoe talking animatedly to the hotel manager. From the snippet of conversation that could be heard, some of the other hotel guests had been complaining about the noise. And there had been some mention of drugs.

Pagan grinned gleefully when she heard that. She didn't understand what was going on, but it would serve Sylvia right for being such an uptight old bag if her genteel gathering turned into drug-fuelled screwfest.

'I'll go and get changed,' she said to Steve. 'I'll meet you outside in fifteen minutes.'

'I'll make sure the engine's running.'

They parted and she made her way up the stairs.

Rocco Carlotti caught Greg as he was about to knock on the door of room 103 again.

'Where's my money, you sonofabitch?'

Greg looked down at him and laughed with amused contempt. 'I'm sorry, do I know you?'

Carlotti grabbed his lapels but Greg swatted him away like an irritating fly.

'We made a deal, Roscoe! Where is it?'

'A deal? Sorry, the only deals I make are in writing.'

'I put my ass on the line for you!'

'That was your choice, not mine. You've got the video, so what's the problem?' Greg said coolly, continuing down the corridor. Carlotti ran after him. 'I'm married now and I can deal with Mason very adequately by myself, thanks very much.'

'You'll pay for this, Roscoe! She isn't going to want anything to do with you when she finds out what you've been up to at that nasty little club of yours. Or what you're doing right now under her nose with those whores you've been poking all afternoon!'

Greg spun on his heel and slammed the small man up against the wall. 'No, I'm warning you. Keep out of my face. Pagan is a very understanding woman, and after what she's been up to recently I don't think she'll have any cause for complaint. You've had some fun with Mason but that's between you and him, not me. Now I suggest you leave before I inform him that you've been trying to use me to embezzle money from him. I don't think he'll take too kindly to that.'

He gave Carlotti one final hard shove and continued on his way.

'You're a fucking dead man, Roscoe,' Carlotti screamed after him.

'Not before you,' Greg called back, not turning around. Carlotti did not have the clout to hurt him. He was a small-time crook, nothing more. Richard Mason, on the other hand, was a formidable opponent, and now he knew that Greg was onto him. But he could still turn it around with Pagan to shield him, which she would because she was too stupid and devoted not to. His grin was smug as he walked into room 103 yet again.

In a dark doorway Pagan pressed her hands to her mouth, trying not to hyperventilate. She sank deeper into the shadows as Greg walked past. He knocked on the door of room 103.

'Hello, ladies,' he said in a sickeningly oily voice, before closing the door again.

Pagan wondered why she was so calm. She had made a terrible mistake, blaming Richard for something that was Greg's doing all along. No wonder he had not tried to reach her. He had finally given up and had gone out of her life for good.

She thought fast. It was definitely time to go, but she wasn't going to let Greg get off lightly. Get off. She laughed softly at the excruciating pun. Well, he could get off if he wanted to, as much as he liked, but he wasn't going to do it thinking he had her fooled.

She took a deep breath and knocked on the door of room 103. After a moment it was opened by a voluptuous blond. She stared coolly at Pagan and let her in. Greg was lying on the bed, his shirt and trousers undone, being sucked off by a tiny Oriental girl. For the first time Pagan noticed he had put on weight. His stomach was bloated with champagne and rich food, his face ruddy and corpulent. He opened his eyes and grinned at her.

'Hello, darling. Come to join in the fun?' He sounded stoned. She saw the implements of cocaine use on the table by the bed, but the three girls looked as if they had been supplying rather than taking the drug. Pagan smiled slightly, respecting their shrewdness.

'Maybe later,' she said calmly. 'I need to attend to our guests.'

'You go and attend to them then. Watch out for Uncle Johnny. He's hung like a donkey.' Greg giggled, a horrible, childish sound.

'I'll do that,' Pagan said and walked out again.

Trembling, she locked herself into the Bridal Suite and began to strip off her wedding finery, starting with her ring. Her fingers shook as she struggled with the hair clips. They caught in her hair and pulled it painfully but she hardly felt it.

'I guess you've found out about him, then.'

The calm voice from the shadows by the window

made her whirl around, her heart thick in her throat. The man stood in the balcony; he was very tall, with a black leather trenchcoat.

'Richard!' Her first instinct was to run to him. She got half way and hit the brakes fast. Round, wire-framed Hugo Boss sunglasses disguised the yellowing discolouration on his face, but the hollows under his eyes and cheekbones gave him a hunted cadaverous look, as if all the angels of Hell were after him. 'Jesus, what happened to you?'

'You don't know?'

'Don't give me that. What is Greg up to? Is he blackmailing you?'

Richard nodded slowly. 'And he thinks he can get away with it because he's married to you. I won't say I told you so, you dumb bitch.'

'You should have been here earlier!' she flared at him.

'You shouldn't be here at all!'

She flung her arms around him. 'God, I'm so glad you came. I should have known the video equipment wasn't anything to do with you.'

'What are you talking about?'

'The hidden camera, filming us making love last Saturday. I thought . . .'

'That I'd do something like that? Why?'

'To get more revenge on my father.' The moment she said it she realised how stupid it sounded.

'He's dead,' he said simply. 'What kind of sick bastard do you think I am?'

She bit her lip and let the first hot tears run down her face. He carefully removed her hair clips.

'Let's have a look at you,' he said. He captured one tear on his finger and licked it away, then drew her into his arms and held her tightly as the rest followed. They did not last long. Already she was drawing strength from the heat of his body pressed limb to limb against hers. She wiped the moisture away with his handkerchief, taking most of her make-up with it.

'God, I must look a sight,' she sniffed, peering in the mirror. Her mascara had stayed intact, at least.

'You look beautiful,' Richard said behind her. 'One hell of a lot better than me.'

She reached up to remove his sunglasses. The swelling had subsided under his eye but it still showed every shade of purple and black, highlighting the translucency of the skin surrounding it. He jerked his head away from her touch, but her trusted fingers drew him back, stroking each damaged piece of skin with her fingertips.

'Where else does it hurt?' she whispered.

'Everywhere,' he answered huskily, appearing turned to stone by her alluring nearness, the smell of her perfume drifting up from somewhere just below her breasts, barely veiled with a cloud of sheer voile. The dress accentuated her slim waist, curving hips and long legs. Hesitantly he placed his hands on her waist as she shrugged the leather coat off his shoulders. It spread around their feet like a pool of oil. Then she unbuttoned his shirt. His body was a mass of lurid bruises, concentrated around his ribs. His left shoulder was strapped to support a cracked collarbone. She stroked him so lovingly that his whole being was suddenly aflame.

'Anywhere else?' she asked, her eyes wide and enquiring. She lightly stroked his penis and his bruised balls underneath his black trousers. His mouth opened in a silent gasp and he backed away.

'No. Don't do that. It'll hurt. It'll . . .'

She continued her gentle massage. Unbelievably he was getting an erection. It pulled at his balls, making them ache, but it was a sweet, heavy ache full of need.

'You're a witch,' he muttered. 'A pagan witch, born to drive me crazy.'

She turned her back on him, giving him a come hither look from over her shoulder. 'The zip is at the back.'

He unhooked the tiny hook and eye and pulled the concealed zip tab down smoothly and slowly.

'What if Roscoe comes in?'

'He won't. He's fucking someone else.' She shrugged at his quizzical look. 'Long story. I'll tell you when I'm in the mood.'

'So what mood are you in right now?'

No words were needed. The way Pagan peeled her wedding dress away from her body and let it drop to her feet was answer enough. His need for her was written all over his face as he drank in her small curvy body, long legs in cream lace-topped stockings and a smooth satin basque, pulling in her neat waist and flaring out at her hips and breasts, just resting in half-cups barely covering her nipples.

'My god,' he said, swallowing hard. Her waist looked small enough for him to encircle it with his hands, her feet tiny in cream satin court shoes. 'Is this what a wedding night is supposed to feel like?'

'I don't know, but it's the nearest you're going to get,' she whispered, pushing him back towards the bed. Carefully he lay down. Instinctively he drew in his breath as she worked her fingers into the waist-band of his trousers. She hit his hardened stomach lightly.

'Don't be so bloody vain. This is me, remember?'

She pulled his zip down and removed his trousers. He was wearing snug black Calvin Klein trunks, the ridge of his cock long and plump against his stomach.

'These look good on you,' she said, fondling him gently.

'Yeah, well, my balls feel like Mount Washington. I'm very protective of them.' He could not look down at her, because of his damaged collar-bone; he could only guess what she was about to do next.

He made a deep, animal lowing sound as she raked her fingernails very gently up and down his shaft and cupped his balls, hot and tight with unshed seed. Pagan kicked off her shoes and climbed on the bed, straddling him. Pushing her panties to one side she guided him in. It did not matter that he was damaged and weakened, seeing him again had driven home just how much she wanted him. It wasn't just lust; something more complex had nurtured itself over the last fifteen years into a need that only he could satisfy.

Her hiss of pleasure clashed with his as they made contact. Her mouth dropped open as she felt his big blunt cock easing into her slowly moistening pussy. She had not had the time to make herself wet and welcoming, and after a week without him her pussy felt stretched, almost like the first time, all over again. Before he was inside her all the way she lifted herself and slid down on top of him again. This time she was much slicker. Again and his expression changed. His eyes rolled back and his jaw tightened.

'Pagan . . . my love . . .'

'What is it?' She leaned right over so that he could see her face without straining his neck. The movement thrust her breasts forward against his chest and made him pulse in appreciation inside her. She eased a pillow under his head so he could see her properly.

'I may not . . . be able to hold back.'

'Then don't,' she replied, smiling radiantly down at him. 'Save the niceties for later and let's just fuck.'

It did not take Greg long to feel hard again and unsatisfied. Bored with the girls he went back downstairs to find Pagan. He had always known she was a hot piece of work. Now it was time he had his share.

The first person he saw was his mother. She saw his stained shirt and unkempt hair and launched into a tirade about what a disgrace he had been that day. He pushed her out of the way.

'Hey, watch it!' Steve Jones steadied Sylvia. He had also come back to find Pagan. Greg veered round to see who had spoken. When he saw Steve he remembered how often he and Pagan had been seen together that afternoon. His eyes narrowed and he lashed out with his fist.

The unexpected punch landed squarely on Steve's nose and floored him. People gasped in shock and ran to help, one calling for ice cubes and a towel. They stared at Greg in horrified disbelief. It had to be a first, witnessing a bridegroom punching the vicar. Sylvia Roscoe bustled behind him at a safe distance as he blundered on through the room.

'Where's my wife?' he roared, staggering out onto the veranda. No one heard him. They were all too busy enjoying their own small parties, some draped over chairs and flowerbeds, totally stoned. Then he was aware of soft female cries, growing in urgency. Blearily he looked up towards the direction of the sound. It was coming from the Bridal Suite.

Sylvia Roscoe had also heard the cries. George was with her, looking slightly dishevelled, but she was too distressed to ask him where he had been for the last nightmare hour. The hotel manager had also joined them, and was starting to tell the Roscoes he was calling the police. Punch-ups in his hotel were simply not acceptable.

They all looked at Greg, then the balcony above, then back at Greg again. All were thinking the same thing: someone else was doing his job.

Enraged Greg grabbed a half-full bottle of Laurent Perrier and hurled it up at the window. The smash was deafening. People scattered to avoid the shower of champagne and broken glass, and the noises abruptly stopped.

After a long pause Richard appeared at the balcony, fully dressed and only slightly ruffled. He pointed an aggressive finger at Greg.

'You're fucking fired,' he said.

19

The air of expectation was intense as Richard walked into the remaining crowd. They moved aside to let him through. His imposing height gave him an authority that no one was willing to question. He went in for the kill immediately, using the calm voice he usually saved for giving everyone a bollocking in the boardroom.

'I apologise for being late. Courtesy of Mr Roscoe here, I was detained in hospital.' He glared at Greg, who took a stumbling step backwards. 'Shall I tell everyone why?'

Greg glanced around at the crowd. His mother stood at the front, her mouth sagging open with horror.

'You married Pagan Warner to get at me –' Richard continued in the same neutral tone, '– and her money. You wanted a share. It's as simple as that. You don't love her. You never have. Now you're blackmailing me with something you think I want kept secret.'

He walked a menacing circle around Greg. Greg turned with him, keeping him in view. The crowd kept their distance but did not leave. Richard addressed them.

'She's my niece. There, I've said it. I fell in love with her years ago, not knowing who she was, and when I did find out it was too late. But we're not going to make a Greek tragedy out of it. If people want to pillory us for it they can, and then they'll move on.' He turned his wolf-pale eyes on Greg once more. 'What you have failed to realise, Roscoe, is that people don't give a fuck. And neither do we. So what is it you think you actually have over me?'

'You lied to me,' Greg said thickly. 'You employed me . . .'

'For a very generous salary, which you took. For a cushy position, which you took.'

'And you were going to take it all away at the first opportunity, leaving me with nothing! You were prepared to destroy my life just so you could get into her knickers!' Greg sounded like a petulant child. Sylvia whimpered and groped for George's arm. Richard glanced at her and smiled slightly.

'Not true, Roscoe. I also offered you a reasonable amount of money for me to sleep with her. Five hundred thousand dollars, ladies and gentlemen. Sitting in his bank account as we speak. I'm too much of a gentleman to say whether or not it was a bargain. Oh, and I was going to give you this.' He produced an official-looking document from his jacket and held it out to Greg. His father snatched it away and read it out loud.

It stated that Gregory Roscoe should receive ten million dollars, plus a home of his choice, in the location of his choice. In return he was to leave his position at Wolfen and agree to no further contact with either Richard Mason or Pagan Warner. If he sought to gain more funds by causing adverse publicity or any other means, the money and the house would be withdrawn.

There was a short silence after George Roscoe's voice trailed away. Greg looked as though he was about to throw up. Richard plucked the document from George's fingers.

'If you had waited instead of turning to some non-entity to get money out of me, I would have given it to you. It's legal, it's binding, but right now it's worth jackshit, because you've just blown it.' With a flourish he produced his Gucci lighter and held the flame to a corner of the paper.

'No!' As Greg lunged for it he stumbled to his knees. Sylvia Roscoe pressed her hands to her mouth, her face grey. George put his arms around her and she huddled against him, hardly daring to watch the crashing humiliation of her only son.

Richard let the delicate remnants of the document float down to Greg's feet. He followed it with Pagan's gold wedding band. It tinkled softly as it hit the ground. Greg grubbed for it as it disappeared into the darkness.

'I guess this must be one of the shortest marriages in the history of England,' Richard said mockingly.

'No it isn't,' a muffled voice behind them said. They all looked around as Steve Jones shuffled through the crowd, holding a bloodied face flannel to his nose. 'Pagan and I are old school friends. She asked me for a favour and I was happy to help.' A dark slug of blood started to ooze from his left nostril. He dabbed it away.

'What are you talking about!' Sylvia demanded shrilly, close to collapse.

'The marriage is void. I'm not a vicar. I'm an actor with the Royal Shakespeare Company.'

Sylvia Roscoe fainted.

A glass of water was hastily produced. As she regained full consciousness George gathered her in his arms and stood up, staggering slightly under her weight. He had lost his hunted expression. In fact, a new mantle of confidence made him almost unrecognisable.

'I'm taking my wife home. This is your mess, Greg. You deal with it.' And he left with his quiet dignity intact.

People began to disperse, avoiding Greg's eyes. Even his Oxford cronies didn't want to look at him. Just then, Amelia lurched around the corner, supported by two very drunken men. Her hair was like a crow's nest and her dress was shredded.

'Hi bro, what's going on?' she slurred. 'I've just seen Pagan leaving without you.'

'Where?' Richard demanded, grabbing her shoulders. She looked owlishly up at him.

'Ooh! You're big, aren't you?'

Richard shook her. 'Just tell me where she is, you stupid bitch!'

'Hey, leave her alone!' Nigel made to wade in, but Amelia had been shocked into semi-sobriety.

'Going towards the river. There was a little man with her.'

Richard began to run as fast as his bruises would allow. As he reached the riverbank he saw a small white boat speeding away. Pagan looked tiny and defenceless. He heard her calling his name but it was a reedy, hopeless sound.

'Carlotti, you cocksucking bastard!' he screamed.

'I'll call you!' Carlotti shouted cheerfully back.

Pagan was thinking fast. The seat Benny had put her in was only a foot away from the side of the boat. The inky black water looked like sweet freedom if only she could move faster than Carlotti, who was pointing a gun at her heart.

She had begun to pack as soon as Richard left the room. She had already dressed in her going-away outfit; a bronze linen shift dress with matching Prada sandals with wooden stilettos. Richard had advised her to keep a low profile and for that she was glad. She had wanted to make her departure as discreet as possible and, although that wasn't going to happen now, she had seen no pleasure in rubbing the Roscoes' noses in their humiliation.

The bag she had packed was pathetically small as she had intended to walk out with nothing more than her passport, a single plane ticket back to New York and spare underwear. She did not want her wedding dress or any of the trappings that went with it. She had left the note she had written almost a week earlier in a prominent position on the bed, where Greg would see it. She thought the knock on the door had been from Richard, but it had been a horrible mistake.

On the way to the boat they had passed Amelia Roscoe, swaying with two inebriated men like elms in a gale. They had not seemed to notice Pagan. And just as they were pulling away from shore she saw a familiar shadow, but he was moving as if in pain and there was no way he would be able to get to her. Her single anguished cry sounded too much like a final farewell.

Carlotti took over the controls and snapped at Benny to find the duct tape. The boat had slowed to avoid attracting attention but she was running out of time. If she was to do anything it had to be before they bound and gagged her.

A blowsy, over-made-up woman was sitting opposite. Pagan recognised her instantly. It was Carla, from the gym, not looking quite as chic as she had before. As comprehension showed on her face, Carlotti grimaced at his wife in disgust.

'I believe you already know Renate.'

'Unfortunately, yes.' Pagan tried to keep the fear from her voice, but the cold and the gun and the horrible enjoyment on Carlotti's face made her shiver violently. 'What's going to happen now? Before Richard kills you, that is.'

Benny placed his jacket around her shoulders, but Carlotti snatched it away and threw it back at him.

'She's merchandise! You're not supposed to be nice to it! Where the hell is that tape?'

'I'm looking, boss. I can't find it.'

'Idiot!' He turned back to Pagan. 'It's easy. He pays up and he gets you back.'

'How much am I worth?'

Carlotti picked a nonexistent speck of dirt from his fingernail. 'Twenty million. But don't be flattered. You don't mean shit to me. You're a commodity, that's all.'

'That's OK, because you don't mean shit to me, either.'

'Hurry up and gag that bitch, Benny.'

Benny had found the tape. He was peering at it, searching for the end with his blunt thumbnail. Carlotti snatched it impatiently from him and told him to mind the wheel. Pagan's eyes met Renate's.

'How do you like screwing my cast-offs?'

It was an educated guess but it had more than the desired effect. Renate's smirk disappeared and she stared at Pagan with such hatred that Pagan was glad Carlotti was sitting between them. Carlotti also saw the look and realisation showed on his face that the comment had not just been a cheap shot. He rounded on Renate.

'What the fuck does she mean?'

Pagan knew it was her only chance. Whilst Carlotti's attention was on his wife she twisted and threw herself overboard.

The shock of the cold, musty-smelling water closing over her head knocked the breath from her body. As she broke the surface she pushed her hair frantically from her eyes, trying to orientate herself. The boat was frighteningly close as it began to turn. Carlotti was shouting at Benny, telling him to go faster. It was too dark to see much, but she started to swim downstream, working out that the hotel was on the left bank. She headed towards it, hitching her dress up to her waist to give her legs added freedom. She wasn't a great swimmer and the breaststroke seemed woefully inadequate for escaping kidnappers. The river grew colder as she drifted into the deep middle section. When she glanced back her vision was filled with a sharp white prow, bearing down on top of her.

Then her foot brushed against something soft, sand or mud, and the branches of a weeping willow scratched at her face. She grasped it and scrambled for the bank. Carlotti was shouting and pointing from the boat. The riverbank was steep and slippery with mud. She tried to heave herself up, failed and slid back into the water. Desperately she tried again, this time finding a thick tree root to give her purchase. The tree branches tried to pull her back into the river as she clawed her way up the steep, slippery bank, using her delicate Prada sandals as crampons in the mud. As the boat bumped against the bank she was up and away, kicking off the shoes and running for her life through an open field that smelt of cows. Stinging nettles and thistles assaulted her as she ran, sobbing and gasping for breath, her chest raw with effort, the dirty river water clagging at her throat.

'There she is!' The voice sounded too near. She could not hear footsteps above the pounding of her eardrums, but she cried out as the bulky body launched at her and brought her down.

They rolled together, Pagan fighting and kicking with waning strength. Benny clamped a porky hand over her mouth and told her to shut the fuck up.

'I've got her!' he called to the Carlottis, who were both standing on the deck of the boat.

'Make it quick, goddamnit!' Carlotti yelled.

'Yeah, yeah. It'll be quick, all right,' Benny muttered. Still holding Pagan down, he felt for something in his pocket. With mounting horror she knew he was about to rape her.

'Please don't,' she sobbed quietly.

'Why? They deserve it.'

She saw the small black box in his hand, and the red and green LED buttons.

'What's taking you so long?' Carlotti shouted. Renate stood on the deck beside him, peering into the darkness.

'Just stay there, I'm coming back!'

The night exploded. Benny covered Pagan with his body and hid both their faces from the searing blast. They were showered with burning fragments and fibre-glass. Pagan's ears rang with the noise. As she cautiously looked up at the devastation there was a smaller explosion, the fuel tank this time, rupturing under the heat of the original bomb. She dived back down as the heat rolled over them, bringing thick grey smoke and the choking smell of diesel oil.

At length they sat up. Benny told her to stay where she was and he went over to inspect the damage. There was one charred body littering the remains of the boat. The other was floating face down in the water, the clothes ripped off its back. He smiled grimly and went back to Pagan.

But she was running again, back towards the distant lights of the hotel and the old Tudor beams she could see spotlit amongst the trees. He easily caught up with her, and she screamed as he grabbed her again.

'Hey, I'm not going to hurt you!'

It took a further minute of frantic struggling before his meaning filtered through. He held her tightly as she gradually calmed down.

'It's OK, lady. You're safe now.'

She could not see his face but his voice sounded sincere. And there wasn't any other feasible alternative to trusting him, locked in his bearlike embrace.

'How come?' she asked between deep heaving breaths.

'It's complicated.'

'Try me.' He helped her to her feet and they started to walk, or rather hobble, in Pagan's case. Benny scooped her up and carried her as if she were a Ming vase.

'OK. Carlotti's been a pain in the ass for years. Mr Mason has always been good to me, so when Carlotti approached me to go turncoat I saw the opportunity to show my appreciation.'

'Appreciation? You beat the shit out of him!'

'Yeah, well . . .' Benny sounded sheepish in the dark. 'That was the hard part. I didn't realise how involved I'd get with Carlotti. And if I looked like I was going soft he'd know what I was doing.'

'So how has Richard been good to you?'

'My father was fired on some bullshit issue when his company was taken over. He'd been there almost thirty years. They didn't want to pay his pension or his layoff money so they tried to make out he had been fiddling the books. We're poor people; he couldn't have financed a claim for unfair dismissal. But Mr Mason did. He won and he gave my father a job at the end of it. He's one classy guy.'

'And I suppose you want me to stop him killing you now.'

'Well, ma'am. I would . . .'

'I'll do it. Just don't call me ma'am.' He set her gently down and she gasped gratefully at the cool, dewy soft grass, soothing her battered swollen feet. She had just seen two people die, but all she could think about now was a hot bath, a cigarette and a steak sandwich.

As they walked up to the hotel there was a horrified scream from the pool.

When Greg had been left amidst the ruins of his wedding party he had no idea what to do. He was finished, washed up, his friends and family all witness to his greed. He had to find a way to rebuild his life with the money left in his Geneva account, which did not amount to much after his recent elaborate spending.

He slumped in the corner, drinking flat champagne from a bottle he had found on one of the tables. He was a mess. His shirt was hanging out and his eyes were bloodshot. He took the small pillbox from his pocket and scooped up a pile of cocaine, snorting it up his left nostril, thinking that he should find the energy to get up and go to room 103. At least the girls there would be grateful to him.

But as he staggered to his feet again he noticed Richard standing by the poolside, smoking with quick, palsied movements. He was staring out towards the river, looking desolate. A small muscle twitched sporadically under his left eye, as it always did when he was stressed.

'Don't tell me she's left you as well,' Greg sneered.

'Go screw yourself, Roscoe.' Richard continued to smoke, not looking at him.

A large bloom of light coming from the river caught their attention, followed by two solid blocks of sound. The few guests left in the hotel started running onto the lawn like rats flushed from a sewer to see what was happening. As Richard went to join them Greg swung the champagne bottle at his head.

The blow sent Richard sprawling into a small glass-topped wrought-iron table. It collapsed under his weight and he landed amongst long shards of broken glass. Greg pulled him up by the shirt so they were eyeball to eyeball.

'You've ruined me, Mason,' he snarled, his eyes red-rimmed and insane.

'She chose me. Bad luck,' Richard whispered hoarsely.

Greg thrust him back onto the ground and aimed a kick at his stomach. Richard grabbed his ankle and brought him down. They scuffled, rolling dangerously close to the edge. Richard's bruised ribs and cracked collar-bone were hindering him as Greg worked his way on top of him and pushed his jaw back so his head dangled over the cool blue water, underlit with green spotlights. Richard's forehead, then the bridge of his nose, brushed the water. He finally mustered the energy to bring his knee sluggishly up between Greg's legs and kidney punch him at the same time. Greg fell away and Richard rolled onto all fours, coughing and choking up pool water. He was in agony, his head hanging down as he panted like a sick dog. His body felt as if it were moving through molasses as he dragged himself to his feet. Just as he drew upright again he felt a hard blow to his neck, followed by a sharp, stinging pain. Warmth spread over his shoulder. Stiffly he looked at the blood blooming on his shirt and the reddened shard of glass in Greg's hand.

'Sonofabitch,' he whispered. He staggered, swayed and caught hold of Greg's shirt. Greg grabbed his wrist and gave him one final stunning blow to the jaw. Richard relaxed his grip and fell backwards into the pool. Blood clouded around him as he sank slowly to the bottom.

Greg watched him for a moment, breathing heavily. People were beginning to filter back on to the veranda, talking about the strange explosion, but Richard did not reappear. Greg slunk into the garden before anyone saw him. Soon it was pitch black, fingers of light from the hotel only reaching so far down the lawn. He fumbled in his pocket for the silver box of cocaine and opened it up with his thumbnail. He snuffled into it, drawing up what there was into his overworked veins. Fizzy lights behind his eyes blinded him to the riverbank. Then he was falling, falling. There was a distant splash and intense cold. Then darkness.

The angel was lifting him up, through the thick and hazy sky towards a bright ball of fire that hurt his eyes. Muted and hollow sounds became sharp and loud as they burst through into glorious fresh air.

'Pagan,' he said. But he could not say it, because his lungs were full of water. There was an insistent thudding in his chest and distorted words he couldn't understand.

'Breathe, you stupid motherfucker.'

Deep kisses that forced air into his lungs. He tried to fight it but could not.

'Breathe, goddamnit.' And again that pressure on his chest, becoming painful, forcing the water out. He convulsed, coughed, the water replaced by sweet air. He took huge, greedy breaths, retching to rid himself of the horrid liquid. When his eyes flickered open it was very dark and it felt as if he were lying on concrete.

'Pagan,' Richard said again and the effort brought on more violent retching.

'Don't worry. You haven't died and I'm not the Virgin Mary,' she said dryly.

'Thank Christ for that,' he muttered and passed out again.

20

The room was quiet and more like a hotel room than one in a hospital. Richard had been there for nearly a week, recovering from both severe beatings he had been given. If the glass had gone in five millimetres further up he would have been a dead man, the doctor had said severely, as if it were his fault. His hostility was partly due to Richard's refusal to tell him exactly how his injuries had occurred.

When Pagan arrived at the hospital that morning he was still asleep. His complexion was still very wan, his skin as white as the sheets he lay in. He looked battered and bruised and strangely vulnerable as she pressed a soft kiss on his lips. Apart from an incomprehensible mumble he did not stir.

She decided to let him sleep for a while longer and went to the café for coffee. On one of the tables was a tabloid newspaper with a small picture of Greg, unshaven and haggard, with the news that he had been charged with grievous bodily harm and drug possession with intent to supply. Looking at his unrecognisable hollow-eyed face, she felt nothing. He was part of a life that she had never felt truly comfortable with, and she had no intention of seeing him again.

Her agenda that morning was clear. She had dressed in a clinically white, short summer dress with a thick silver zip that fastened all the way up the front, sheer black stockings and shiny patent stilettos. The wickedness of what she was about to do to him had kept her awake the night before, sleep only coming after a prolonged session of self-pleasure that had left her gasping and exhausted.

'Is he awake yet?' she asked the ward sister.

'Unfortunately, yes,' the stern woman replied tersely. 'He's been asking for you. And wanting coffee. But "not that shit we serve in England", apparently. He's been giving my staff merry hell.'

'Ah, he must be feeling better.' Pagan glanced through the small window. 'I'll give him a wash. That should cheer him up.'

'Rather you than me,' the sister said, pushing the trolley towards Pagan. 'There's hot water in the room. See if you can persuade him to get up. Some exercise will do him good.'

'Thanks. I'd ... prefer it if we were not disturbed for a while.'

The ward sister's hard face cracked into a smile. 'That is absolutely fine by me.'

Pagan watched Richard through the small window for a moment before going in. He was watching, of all things, Kilroy, and she could sense his boredom from the other side of the door. She opened the door and backed the trolley in. Her slender heels clicked on the wooden floor.

'It's time for your wash, Mr Mason,' she said briskly.

'Fuck off.' He turned his head to the wall.

'Come now. Don't be like that.' She put her hand to his cheek and made him look. 'Don't tell me you've finally decided you don't want me?'

His face changed dramatically. 'Hey, you,' he drawled, pulling her towards him. They kissed deeply.

'The sister says you've been misbehaving,' she chided him gently.

Richard grimaced. 'That dried-up old hag has been on my case since I first woke up. I think she wants my body.'

'Personally I think she'd prefer to give you an enema, followed by colonic irrigation. You need to learn how to be nice.' She sat on the bed and stroked his hair. He was still showing the effects of sedation in his sleepy eyes and slightly slurred voice.

'That isn't why you like me, though.' He managed a lewd glance at Pagan's luscious curves and toyed with the ring holding the zip tab. It dangled temptingly just below the first two inches of swelling cleavage. 'I'm sure these aren't standard issue, even in the private sector.'

She laughed lightly, leaning forward so he could take a better look. The white cotton stretched invitingly over her bad boy's dream of a figure.

'It's time for a wash,' she whispered.

She ran hot water and mixed it with liquid soap. She dipped a sponge in the soapy water and squeezed it out. She started with his face, being very gentle so as not to disturb the fresh stitches on his temple. She tilted his head back so she could reach his throat, his neck, down to his shoulders. Dip, squeeze, wipe, avoiding the dressing on his neck. The silky hair under his arms and on his chest was flattened against his skin. She patted him dry with a soft towel as he watched her. He lifted one leaden hand and touched one of the scratches on her cheek.

She moved the crisp white sheet down past his feet. He was not wearing anything underneath. His penis nestled comfortably on the generous bed of his scrotum. It looked so warm and pink and velvety that she wanted to take it into her mouth but she restrained herself and continued to wash him. As she gently rubbed his toes dry he broke the swollen silence.

'You missed a bit,' he said huskily.

'Oh! How careless of me.' Her green eyes were luminous as she admired his cock. It had started to swell during her gentle ministrations and now it was lying to one side, still quite soft but waiting, expectant. She tucked her hair behind her ears and bent her head, giving it a closer examination.

'This needs special attention, I think.' She grinned at him. 'A professional valet.'

His reply became a stifled moan as she scooped up the swelling organ with her tongue and drew him fully into her mouth. She lay with her head on his stomach, letting his cock fill her mouth and pattering her fingertips over his balls. His lower body moved out of instinct as she began to suck him gently, holding back from succumbing to her own terrible lust. He tasted salty and musky, his distinct scent intensified by hours in the hospital bed. She lapped slowly at his balls, like a mother cat with her kitten, feeling him move and moan. His fingers laced through her hair, massaging her head in time with each lavish lick.

'Pagan,' he breathed, so softly she barely heard him. She slipped her hand into her panties and felt how damp she was, oozing nectar over her fingers that she held to his mouth. She felt him suck greedily and saw his cock spring into life, the bulbous end strained and tensed to exploding point. With an effort she remembered what she had come to do, though the temptation was to jump on him right then and ride his cock like a merry-go-round horse. Instead she fondled him slowly, then grasped him just tight enough to make him stiffen with the anticipation of pain.

'Just because Greg turned out to be a complete nightmare doesn't let you off the hook, mister,' she said mildly.

'All I did was fight for something I really believed in. How could I know that avaricious little sod was going to blackmail me?'

'If you want forgiveness you'll have to do better than

that.' Another squeeze. He pulsed against her, the one area of his body that was in full working order and getting harder by the second.

'I'm not going to apologise, if that's what you're after,' he said.

Her heart was racing. He was playing right into her hands. Or maybe she was playing right into his. It no longer mattered, she thought, as a secretive smile turned up the corners of her mouth. Ever so slowly she pulled the zip holding the short white dress together down to her waist, past juicy breasts in a small burgundy silk push-up bra.

'You've been a bad, bad boy,' she whispered. 'I think you need to be taught a lesson, don't you?'

He nodded, his throat too dry to speak. He shuddered as she scratched him slowly with plum-red fingernails, leaving white and then red trails from his chest to his stomach. His body was a patchwork of purple and yellow bruises, but his cock was a dark menacing red. It pulsated sporadically as she turned and lifted the hem of her dress so that he could enjoy her stocking tops and the peachy globes of her buttocks. She stood just out of his reach, her fingers playing lightly over her skin, bending forward slightly to display her plump, satin-encased cleft. She was so turned on that a patch of lubricious juice showed dark on the wine-coloured satin.

'I hope the doctor doesn't come in,' he said lightly.

'He won't. And the nurse asked me to make sure you had some exercise.'

'Is that right?' He licked his lips as she eased out of the dress, leaving it on the floor. Her bikini briefs were held together with two cheeky bows at each hip. She moved deftly away as he reached for one of them. From the trolley she produced a thick gold vibrator. His erection was rampant by the time she slipped the vibe inside her panties and caressed herself with it. His lips were half open and his breath was hot and needy.

'Put it in your cunt,' he said hoarsely.

She smiled and shook her head. 'I could make myself come while you watch, jerk you off until you're just about to shoot and then walk away. Would that be punishment enough for you?'

'Perhaps.' He tried to sound cool and failed miserably.

She ran her hand under his nose so he could smell her. He tried to bite at her fingers but she moved slinkily away and reached for the hook on her bra, letting her breasts fall free. The nipples were already hard little kernels of flesh. She leaned down to kiss him, letting them scratch delicately against his chest. Her scent was too close to ignore, too remote to drink in. His sigh was soaked with longing as she moved down and visually feasted on his sex. She sensed him tensing, his whole body rigid with suspense.

'You've put me through hell,' she said conversationally. 'I really do think it's time you apologised.'

His gaze on her was lascivious. 'Never.'

'You sure about that?' She began to wash him like a cat, long sensuous licks along the insides of his thighs. His balls flinched as she drew nearer, his breath becoming shallow as she ran a wet figure of eight around each plump globe, again and again, blowing gently on the moistness she left behind.

'Never,' he gasped again. 'If you want an apology you'll have to suck my dick.' He pushed the arrogant member towards her, willing her to take him in her mouth.

'That is so rude,' she murmured. The barest flutter of her tongue on the tender area under his scrotum made his backside contract. Carefully she bent his legs at the knee and pushed them apart, exposing him further. Moments later he felt the vibe press against his rectum. Instinctively he resisted.

'What the fuck are you doing?'

'Just relax,' she said soothingly. 'It'll hurt a lot less.'

He could not concentrate. Her hair tickled the insides of his thighs and her tongue flickered around his balls again.

'Do you apologise?' she whispered. Finally he caught on.

'Yes,' he hurriedly. 'I'm sorry. Now get that thing away from me.' He winced as she increased the pressure.

'That didn't sound very sincere. Try again.'

Her words whispered against his painfully tight flesh. His buttocks clenched, fighting off the alien presence. Her tongue wrapped around his shaft like a wet snake, tracing each purple vein and ridge. His head was spinning with conflicting sensations.

'I'm really sorry,' he said through gritted teeth. 'It'll never happen again but I swear to God if you go any further with this ...'

She tickled the underside of his glans with a saucy tongue before sucking the swollen head between her lips. Caught by surprise, his rectal muscles loosened, allowing the solid metal into his body. He tried to twist away but his upper body was in too much pain to move. Gently but inexorably she pushed further as he writhed to escape her.

'Oh Jesus ... God ... stop it ... get that thing out of me ... fucking bitch ... you'll pay ... by Christ you'll pay ...' His voice became gravelled with fury and indignation, ending on a hissed drawing of breath as her mouth closed over him again, squeezing, pulling, sucking him in up to the root. His pelvis undulated, trying to escape the persistent invasion but he was truly trapped, every movement either impaling him or bringing him closer to ecstasy.

'If you want me, you're going to do exactly what I say,' she said imperiously.

'Anything,' he moaned.

'You can start by compensating the Roscoes. They paid about ten thousand pounds for that wedding only to see it go down the pan. Then the hotel, for the damage. And the owner of the boat that was blown up. I've got it all written down waiting for you.'

'And after that?'

'The church needs a new roof. I pledged fifty thousand pounds on your behalf to the local diocese in exchange for Reverend Watson's unfortunate bowel problem last Saturday.'

'What?' He looked bewildered, struggling to take it all in.

'And you're going to buy me a house somewhere on the coast so that when you get too much to bear I can be on my own.'

'Anywhere but Cape May,' he said immediately.

'Fair enough. How about Santa Barbara?' She applied gentle pressure with the vibrator, feeling him tense.

'You've thought this all out, haven't you?' He was beginning to sound resentful but she licked along his eyelids, soothing his anger away. 'Anything else?' he asked weakly.

She tickled his nose with her hair. 'Just one more thing. Michael and I have successfully managed to stifle the interest in you by the gutter press. For now. However it only takes a word in the right ear and you will be on the front page of every tabloid newspaper from here to San Francisco. I know you were calling Greg's bluff when you said you don't give a fuck, but you do, don't you? So remember this. The moment you start treating me with Neanderthal insensitivity I'm gone and you will be in the public domain. I'm not your possession or your whore. You, on the other hand, are mine and I can do what I like with you. Have you got that?' She continued to bugger him with a gentle cork-screw motion as he tried not to shift position.

'Give me your cunt,' he whispered hoarsely.

'Have you got that?' she repeated.

'Just give me that pussy. I'm a sick man, remember?'

'Tell me about it. The magic word is . . .?' She intensified her movements, making him squirm even more. His offended ribs were protesting wildly.

'Give it to me, you cocksucking bitch,' he snarled back at her.

'That'll do.' She removed the vibe and straddled him, minding his sore spots. 'One more thing,' she added, hovering over his very tip. She slipped her hand into her panties and produced his Celtic wedding band with a magician's flourish.

His jaw dropped in shock. 'How the hell did you get that?'

'It's a long story,' she smiled. 'I'll tell you later.' She eased the ring onto the third finger of his left hand, timing it exquisitely with the easing of his cock into her receptive opening, smoother than molten chocolate. He delicately pulled at each ribbon on her panties and finally pulled them free. They fluttered to the floor as he drew her into his arms. She buried her face in the hollow of his neck and breathed his familiar musky scent, overcome by the rush of feeling brought on by him filling her so deeply. They were one, belonging only to the other. She knew him more intimately in a few weeks than she ever had in two years with Greg, even though he had been a stranger for so long. They began to move in a sensual, horizontal dance, kissing so deeply they seemed locked for all time. This was real lovemaking, the electricity of understanding between two people not afraid to look into each other's souls.

'I love you,' he whispered, over and over as he speeded down that ever-quickening path towards oblivion. At the very peak of his pleasure she whispered the words he had waited fifteen years to hear.

'I love you too, you bastard.'

Visit the Black Lace website at
www.blacklace-books.co.uk

FIND OUT THE LATEST INFORMATION AND TAKE
ADVANTAGE OF OUR FANTASTIC FREE BOOK OFFER!
ALSO VISIT THE SITE FOR . . .

- All Black Lace titles currently available
  and how to order online
- Great new offers
- Writers' guidelines
- Author interviews
- An erotica newsletter
- Features
- Cool links

BLACK LACE — THE LEADING IMPRINT
OF WOMEN'S SEXY FICTION

TAKING YOUR EROTIC READING
PLEASURE TO NEW HORIZONS

BLACK LACE

LOOK OUT FOR THE ALL-NEW BLACK LACE BOOKS – AVAILABLE NOW!

All books priced £6.99 in the UK. Please note publication dates apply to the UK only. For other territories, please contact your retailer.

CABIN FEVER
Emma Donaldson
ISBN 0 352 33692 7

Young beautician Laura works in the exclusive Shangri-La beauty salon aboard the cruise ship *Jannina*. Although she has a super-sensual time with her boyfriend, Steve – who works the ship's bar – there are plenty of nice young men in uniform who want a piece of her action. Laura's cabin mate is the shy, eighteen-year-old Fiona, whose sexuality is a mystery, especially as there are rumours that the stern Elinor Brookes, the matriarch of the beauty salon, has been seen doing some very curious things with the young Fiona. **Saucy story of clandestine goings-on aboard a luxury liner.**

THE CAPTIVE FLESH
Cleo Cordell
ISBN 0 352 32872 X

Eighteenth-century French covent girls Marietta and Claudine learn that their stay at the opulent Algerian home of their handsome and powerful host, Kasim, requires something in return: their complete surrender to the ecstasy of pleasure in pain. Kasim's decadent orgies also require the services of Gabriel, whose exquisite longing for Marietta's awakened lust cannot be contained – not even by the shackles that bind his tortured flesh. **This is a reprint of one of the first Black Lace books ever published. A classic piece of blockbusting historical erotica.**

Coming in August

DIVINE TORMENT
Janine Ashbless
ISBN O 352 33719 2

In the ancient temple city of Mulhanabin, the voluptuous Malia Shai awaits her destiny. Millions of people worship her, believing her to be a goddess incarnate. However, she is very human, consumed by erotic passions that have no outlet. Into this sacred city comes General Verlaine – the rugged and horny gladiatorial leader of the occupying army. Intimate contact between Verlaine and Malia Shai is forbidden by every law of their hostile peoples. But she is the one thing he wants – and he will risk everything to have her. **A beautifully written story of opulent palaces, extreme rituals and sexy conquerors. Like *Gladiator* set in a mythical realm.**

THE BEST OF BLACK LACE 2
Edited by Kerri Sharp
ISBN O 352 33718 4

The Black Lace series has continued to be *the* market leader in erotic fiction, publishing genuine female writers of erotica from all over the English-speaking world. The series has changed and developed considerably since it was launched in 1993. The past decade has seen an explosion of interest in the subject of female sexuality, and Black Lace has always been at the forefront of debate around this issue. Editorial policy is constantly evolving to keep the writing up-to-date and fresh, and now the books have undergone a design makeover that completes the transformation, taking the series into a new era of prominence and popularity. *The Best of Black Lace 2* will include extracts of the sexiest, most sizzling titles from the past three years.

SHADOWPLAY
Portia Da Costa
ISBN O 352 33313 8

Photographer Christabel is drawn to psychic phenomena and dark liaisons. When she is persuaded by her husband to take a holiday at a mysterious mansion house in the country, unexpected events begin to unravel. Her husband has enlisted the help of his young male PA to ensure that Christabel's holiday is eventful and erotic. Within the web of an unusual and kinky threesome, Christabel learns some lessons the jaded city could never teach. **Full of dark, erotic games, this is a special reprint of one of our most popular titles.**

Coming in September

SATAN'S ANGEL
Melissa MacNeal
ISBN O 352 33726 5

Feisty young Miss Rosie is lured north during the first wave of the Klondike gold rush. Ending up in a town called Satan, she auditions for the position of the town's most illustrious madam. Her creative ways with chocolate win her a place as the mysterious Devlin's mistress. As his favourite, she becomes the queen of a town where the wildest fantasies become everyday life, but where her devious rival, Venus, rules an underworld of sexual slavery. Caught in this dark vixen's web of deceit, Rosie is then kidnapped by the pistol-packing all-female gang, the KlonDykes and ultimately played as a pawn in a dangerous game of revenge. **Another whip-cracking historical adventure from Ms MacNeal.**

I KNOW YOU, JOANNA
Ruth Fox
ISBN O 352 33727 3

Joanna writes stories for a top-shelf magazine. When her dominant and attractive boss Adam wants her to meet and 'play' with the readers she finds out just how many strange sexual deviations there are. However many kinky playmates she encounters, nothing prepares her for what Adam has in mind. Complicating her progress, also, are the insistent anonymous invitations from someone who professes to know her innermost fantasies. **Based on the real experiences of scene players, this is shockingly adult material!**

THE INTIMATE EYE
Georgia Angelis
ISBN O 352 33004 X

In eighteenth-century Gloucestershire, Lady Catherine Balfour is struggling to quell the passions that are surfacing in her at the sight of so many handsome labourers working her land. Then, aspiring artist, Joshua Fox, arrives to paint a portrait of the Balfour family. Fox is about to turn her world upside down. This man, whom she assumes is a mincing fop, is about to seduce every woman in the village – Catherine included. But she has a rival: her wilful daughter Sophie is determined to claim Fox as her own. **This earthy story of rustic passion is a Black Lace special reprint of one of our bestselling historical titles.**

Black Lace Booklist

Information is correct at time of printing. To avoid disappointment check availability before ordering. Go to www.blacklace-books.co.uk. All books are priced £6.99 unless another price is given.

BLACK LACE BOOKS WITH A CONTEMPORARY SETTING

☐ PLAYING HARD Tina Troy	ISBN 0 352 33617 X
☐ SYMPHONY X Jasmine Stone	ISBN 0 352 33629 3
☐ STRICTLY CONFIDENTIAL Alison Tyler	ISBN 0 352 33624 2
☐ SUMMER FEVER Anna Ricci	ISBN 0 352 33625 0
☐ CONTINUUM Portia Da Costa	ISBN 0 352 33120 8
☐ OPENING ACTS Suki Cunningham	ISBN 0 352 33630 7
☐ FULL STEAM AHEAD Tabitha Flyte	ISBN 0 352 33637 4
☐ A SECRET PLACE Ella Broussard	ISBN 0 352 33307 3
☐ GAME FOR ANYTHING Lyn Wood	ISBN 0 352 33639 0
☐ FORBIDDEN FRUIT Susie Raymond	ISBN 0 352 33306 5
☐ CHEAP TRICK Astrid Fox	ISBN 0 352 33640 4
☐ THE ORDER Dee Kelly	ISBN 0 352 33652 8
☐ ALL THE TRIMMINGS Tesni Morgan	ISBN 0 352 33641 3
☐ PLAYING WITH STARS Jan Hunter	ISBN 0 352 33653 6
☐ THE GIFT OF SHAME Sara Hope-Walker	ISBN 0 352 32935 1
☐ COMING UP ROSES Crystalle Valentino	ISBN 0 352 33658 7
☐ GOING TOO FAR Laura Hamilton	ISBN 0 352 33657 9
☐ THE STALLION Georgina Brown	ISBN 0 352 33005 8
☐ DOWN UNDER Juliet Hastings	ISBN 0 352 33663 3
☐ THE BITCH AND THE BASTARD Wendy Harris	ISBN 0 352 33664 1
☐ ODALISQUE Fleur Reynolds	ISBN 0 352 32887 8
☐ GONE WILD Maria Eppie	ISBN 0 352 33670 6
☐ SWEET THING Alison Tyler	ISBN 0 352 33682 X
☐ TIGER LILY Kimberley Dean	ISBN 0 352 33685 4
☐ COOKING UP A STORM Emma Holly	ISBN 0 352 33686 2
☐ RELEASE ME Suki Cunningham	ISBN 0 352 33671 4
☐ KING'S PAWN Ruth Fox	ISBN 0 352 33684 6
☐ FULL EXPOSURE Robyn Russell	ISBN 0 352 33688 9
☐ SLAVE TO SUCCESS Kimberley Raines	ISBN 0 352 33687 0
☐ STRIPPED TO THE BONE Jasmine Stone	ISBN 0 352 33463 0
☐ CABIN FEVER Emma Donaldson	ISBN 0 352 33692 7

BLACK LACE BOOKS WITH AN HISTORICAL SETTING

☐ PRIMAL SKIN Leona Benkt Rhys	ISBN 0 352 33500 9	£5.99
☐ DEVIL'S FIRE Melissa MacNeal	ISBN 0 352 33527 0	£5.99
☐ WILD KINGDOM Deanna Ashford	ISBN 0 352 33549 1	£5.99

☐ DARKER THAN LOVE Kristina Lloyd	ISBN O 352 33279 4	
☐ STAND AND DELIVER Helena Ravenscroft	ISBN O 352 33340 5	£5.99
☐ THE CAPTIVATION Natasha Rostova	ISBN O 352 33234 4	
☐ CIRCO EROTICA Mercedes Kelley	ISBN O 352 33257 3	
☐ MINX Megan Blythe	ISBN O 352 33638 2	
☐ PLEASURE'S DAUGHTER Sedalia Johnson	ISBN O 352 33237 9	
☐ JULIET RISING Cleo Cordell	ISBN O 352 32938 6	
☐ DEMON'S DARE Melissa MacNeal	ISBN O 352 33683 8	
☐ ELENA'S CONQUEST Lisette Allen	ISBN O 352 32950 5	
☐ DIVINE TORMENT Janine Ashbless	ISBN O 352 33719 2	
☐ THE CAPTIVE FLESH Cleo Cordell	ISBN O 352 32872 X	

BLACK LACE ANTHOLOGIES

☐ CRUEL ENCHANTMENT Erotic Fairy Stories Janine Ashbless	ISBN O 352 33483 5	£5.99
☐ MORE WICKED WORDS Various	ISBN O 352 33487 8	£5.99
☐ WICKED WORDS 4 Various	ISBN O 352 33603 X	
☐ WICKED WORDS 5 Various	ISBN O 352 33642 0	
☐ WICKED WORDS 6 Various	ISBN O 352 33590 0	
☐ THE BEST OF BLACK LACE 2 Various	ISBN O 352 33718 4	

BLACK LACE NON-FICTION

| ☐ THE BLACK LACE BOOK OF WOMEN'S SEXUAL FANTASIES Ed. Kerri Sharp | ISBN O 352 33346 4 | £5.99 |

To find out the latest information about Black Lace titles, check out the website: www.blacklace-books.co.uk or send for a booklist with complete synopses by writing to:

Black Lace Booklist, Virgin Books Ltd
Thames Wharf Studios
Rainville Road
London W6 9HA

Please include an SAE of decent size. Please note only British stamps are valid.

Our privacy policy
We will not disclose information you supply us to any other parties. We will not disclose any information which identifies you personally to any person without your express consent.

From time to time we may send out information about Black Lace books and special offers. Please tick here if you do <u>not</u> wish to receive Black Lace information. ❏

Please send me the books I have ticked above.

Name ....

Address ....

....

....

....

Post Code ....

Send to: Cash Sales, Black Lace Books, Thames Wharf Studios, Rainville Road, London W6 9HA.

US customers: for prices and details of how to order books for delivery by mail, call 1-800-343-4499.

Please enclose a cheque or postal order, made payable to Virgin Books Ltd, to the value of the books you have ordered plus postage and packing costs as follows:

UK and BFPO – £1.00 for the first book, 50p for each subsequent book.

Overseas (including Republic of Ireland) – £2.00 for the first book, £1.00 for each subsequent book.

If you would prefer to pay by VISA, ACCESS/MASTERCARD, DINERS CLUB, AMEX or SWITCH, please write your card number and expiry date here:

....

Signature ....

Please allow up to 28 days for delivery.